ROSIE ARCHER

The *Bluebird Girls*

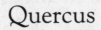

Quercus

First published in Great Britain in 2019 by Quercus
This paperback edition published in 2019 by

Quercus Editions Ltd
Carmelite House
50 Victoria Embankment
London EC4Y 0DZ

An Hachette UK company

A CIP catalogue record for this book is available
from the British Library

PB ISBN 978 1 78747 396 6

10 9 8 7 6 5 4 3 2 1

Typeset by CC Book Production

Printed and bound in Great Britain by Clays Ltd, Elcograf S.p.A.

The Bluebird Girls

Rosie Archer was born in Gosport, Hampshire, where she still lives. She has had a variety of jobs including waitress, fruit picker, barmaid, shop assistant and market trader selling second-hand books. Rosie is the author of several Second World War sagas set on and around the south coast of England as well as a series of gangster sagas under the name June Hampson. *The Bluebird Girls* is the first book in a trilogy.

Also by Rosie Archer

The Munitions Girls
The Canary Girls
The Factory Girls
The Gunpowder and Glory Girls
The Ferry Girls
The Girls From the Local
The Narrowboat Girls

This one is for the St Vincent singers.
For the laughter and the tears we've shared.

Chapter One

'Would you call this a moonlight flit?' Josie Bird's sixteen-year-old daughter Lorraine had stopped singing long enough to ask her the question.

The answer came easily. 'We've got moonlight, our personal possessions are piled high around us and our gas masks are stowed beneath the seats. Hopefully not one nosy neighbour watched us leave.' Jo stole a glance and smiled fondly at Rainey. 'Yes, we're doing a flit.'

'Not before time.'

Jo's heart constricted at the bitterness in her voice. No mother should have to listen to her daughter speak like that.

The late October wind was trying to iron out Rainey's auburn curls so she used her hands to clamp her hair from blowing into her eyes. Jo had urged her to tie on a headscarf as she had done but Rainey had raised her eyes heavenwards and muttered, 'Aw, Mum!' The open-top MG PA Midget gave no protection from the elements as Jo was unable to raise the hood due to their overflowing belongings.

'Oh!' Turning the steering wheel briskly to round the corner onto the Gosport road caused Jo to cry out. Her shoulder reminded her it hadn't yet properly healed. She bit her lip in an effort to ignore the sudden pain.

'You all right, Mum?'

Her husband Alfie had wrenched her arm almost to the back of her neck and she'd been unable to use it for some time. 'Yes, I'm fine. It won't be long and we'll soon be in our new home.' She was changing the subject, as usual. She didn't want to think about the final beating she'd been sub-jected to. It had made her decide to visit estate agents to investigate cheap housing to let.

She'd struck lucky because people who could afford to leave Gosport had gone to escape the inevitable bombing from Hitler's aircraft after the recent declaration of war against Germany. She would have preferred somewhere a bit further from Portsmouth, in case Alfie came looking for her, but beggars couldn't be choosers.

The unfurnished house she had taken was in Albert Street. Her meagre savings had been practically used up on the deposit and the first week's rent. Jo had returned to London

Road in Portsmouth, excited at what might be her and her daughter's new start away from her bully of a husband.

The car spluttered.

'Oh, no!' Jo's heart plummeted.

'Is it out of petrol?'

'Probably,' replied Jo. The fuel tank's needle pointed to full, but it had been in that position since the day Alfie had driven the carmine-red vehicle home from the barracks after winning it in a poker game.

'Present for you,' he'd said, lifting her off her feet and swinging her around. It was 1936 and he'd wanted her to believe he loved her then. Perhaps he'd thought the gift of the car would soften her feelings towards him after she'd discovered his affair with Janice Woolbetter. Every so often she pumped petrol into the car's tank, but the needle never moved.

Jo had remembered her own and Rainey's ration books and identity cards, but in her haste to get away she'd forgotten the petrol coupons that controlled fuel rationing. When bought from Morris Garages in 1935 the car had cost somewhere in the region of two hundred pounds, so she'd been told. Jo intended the two-seater should be stored in the shed at the side of the new rented house as security for the future.

'It seems all right now,' Rainey said. The engine sounded fine once more. She grinned as Jo stole a look at her, then began singing again.

Jo breathed a sigh of relief when she saw the Criterion Cinema ahead: they were almost at their destination. By the light of the moon she could just make out the film advertised on the billboards. It was *Dead End* with Humphrey Bogart and Sylvia Sidney. She wouldn't mind seeing that, if she could afford it.

A job for herself was first on the agenda, and Rainey needed to return to a school as soon as possible. She'd been doing well at Portsmouth Academy where she'd excelled at typing and shorthand, but leaving Portsmouth meant that she hadn't completed the course.

'Not much further,' Jo said, but she might as well not have bothered because Rainey couldn't possibly hear her. She was giving full voice to 'The Biggest Aspidistra in the World', her rendition just as hearty as Gracie Fields's version. Jo smiled. It made her heart happy to hear her daughter singing.

And then ahead, off Forton Road, was Albert Street. Jo gave a hand signal and turned right into the terraced street.

'Which one is it?'

'Number fourteen, the one with the wide shed. Thank God we're here.' Jo pulled up outside the front door that would open straight onto the pavement. Within moments she had the key in the lock but allowed Rainey to enter first. 'Don't put any lights on,' she warned. 'Remember the blackout. I don't think there are curtains at the windows. Let's just take everything inside the house so I can put the car away from prying eyes.'

'Mum, stop worrying. There's nobody about. It's as quiet as the grave.'

Rainey was right. The little street that led down to the railway footbridge and goods yard was deserted, but Jo knew she wouldn't begin to feel safe until the car was locked away and she and her daughter were inside the house with the door shut.

'It smells a bit funny in here,' Rainey said, dumping the brown carrier bag that had been on her lap the entire journey.

'It's only a bit of damp. Don't worry about it.' Jo put down an armful of rolled-up blankets on a broken chair. She fished out a torch from her coat pocket and gave a quick flick of light around the place. It was even more dismal than she'd remembered. She tried to imagine the small dank room with bright rugs covering the second-hand furniture she would buy when she could. 'We'll soon make it nice and homely,' she said, trying to reassure herself as well as Rainey.

Rainey gave a big yawn, then shivered.

Jo said, 'I'm tired and cold as well. C'mon, the sooner we get the stuff indoors the sooner we can have some cocoa from the flask and set about making up a bed for the night.'

She hadn't told Rainey they'd have to sleep on the floor. She didn't want to think about mice or creepy-crawlies.

Soon everything they'd brought with them was piled in the living room and Jo had cleared a space in the shed for the car. When she got back into the house she discovered Rainey had hooked a blanket over the front window, found the candles, lit one and was making a nest of bedding on the bare boards.

'I had a look upstairs, Mum. There's a mattress on the floor in the back bedroom but I didn't want to risk it. It might be full of fleas.' Rainey made a face. 'I'm so cold even the candle seems to give out heat,' she said. 'I'm not getting undressed – it's freezing.'

Jo put her arms around her daughter. Tears burned the backs of her eyes. 'I'm sorry I've taken you away from a nice home and brought you here.'

She didn't get any further as Rainey cuddled into her. 'I wanted to leave as well, don't you ever forget that. If we hadn't got away tonight, sooner or later he'd have killed you, and I need my mum.'

Chapter Two

Corporal Alfie Bird didn't want to leave the Royal Army Ordnance Corps Barracks at Hilsea to fight in France. He hadn't wanted to return home on a forty-eight-hour pass to find his wife and daughter gone, either.

All he'd done was push Jo around a bit for shooting her mouth off about him and Janice. Jo knew how upset he got when she tried to best him in an argument. It was her own fault. He sniffed and wiped a hand across his red moustache, remembering.

'I saw you this afternoon walking arm in arm with Janice Woolbetter in Elm Grove.'

She'd come straight out with it, no messing about.

'Oh, yeah? Would that be while I was overseeing weapon repairs in the stores all day in barracks?'

She'd ignored his lie. 'I was on the bus. She was laughing up at you in the rain.'

'You're mistaken. It wasn't me.'

'You promised me it was over between you and her.'

He'd begun to lose his temper but he'd kept it in check long enough to say, 'If it was raining I doubt you could tell who was with the bloody woman.'

'I recognized you,' Jo insisted.

He'd tried to sweet-talk her then. 'When I broke it off with her, I promised you that was the end of it.' Then he wheedled, 'I told you, you're the only woman for me.' He tried to put his hand on her shoulder. A little bit of comfort never hurt anyone, he thought. Jo had flinched, stepping away, standing where she'd thought he couldn't reach her and staring into his eyes, all defiant like.

'It was you, with … her,' Jo insisted, hissing 'her' like she'd found shit on the sole of her shoe.

He'd lashed out then.

Had her pinned against the wall, her face pressed into the wallpaper, her arm behind her back. 'You didn't see me,' he yelled. He pulled her arm higher.

But the bitch wouldn't give in. 'I did.'

Her voice was so small he barely heard her. Still holding her arm he twisted her away from the wall and threw her into the centre of the living room. Stupid woman lost her footing and fell. She hit the corner of a wooden chair, it toppled and she fell on the floor. She cried for a bit, then didn't make any more sounds, just lay there. She was obviously messing about, pretending, so he kicked her a couple of times, then slammed out of the house before he really lost his temper.

He'd walked up to Hilsea Lido and sat on a bench in the park. It was growing dark. He looked at his watch. As usual, Rainey would be round her friend Ellen's house but she'd be going home soon. She'd see to her mother, if Jo needed seeing to, that was. She was probably up off the floor by now, a cuppa in her hands. Why had she been so determined to rile him?

Of course he'd been with Janice. What bloke wouldn't prefer to spend the morning in bed with a plump warm blonde, then take her out to a café for something to eat? It beat going home to a stringy wife, who never believed a word he said, and looked as though she'd rather be anywhere than with him.

What if he had gone back on his word never to see Janice again? Didn't a man have the right to do what he wanted? After all, he'd spent ten years as an enlisted soldier. He provided a home for his wife and daughter and saw they were clothed and fed. Jo had known he had a quick temper when she first went with him. Fifteen she'd been, younger than Rainey was now. He'd knocked that silly young bloke for six after he'd caught her dancing with him at the Savoy Ballroom. Told her then if he took her to a dance she stayed with him all evening. She didn't dance with the first bloke who asked her just because he'd left her on her own while he went to the bar.

A few months later he'd got her in the family way. She was sixteen and looked like an angel at the register office.

A lot of water had run under the bridge since then. Oh, it was fine at first, lots of loving and laughs, but that changed after Rainey was born. Jo started moaning about feeling tired. Said it was the baby crying all the time. Well, he couldn't do nothing about that when he was in barracks, could he? When he was on leave she only expected him to get up at nights and see to Rainey! He'd told her it was woman's work. What did Jo expect? She'd have him in an apron next.

He was able to play the field a bit when he was sent away on military training. What Jo didn't know couldn't hurt her, could it?

At the RAOC barracks at Hilsea he couldn't carry on like before but Janice was special. Until a 'friend' told Jo. He hadn't laid a finger on Jo until then, well, not really. All that rubbish about her being afraid to trust him got on his nerves. Time and time again he'd warned her to stop but she wouldn't, so it was her own fault when he lost his temper. Everyone knows it ain't easy to keep a temper in check when a wife nags.

At the hospital she said she'd fallen down the stairs. After she came home she seemed to have lost her spark. She was no fun any more. Janice made him laugh, though.

Of course, Janice wasn't the only one. The years and the women came and went, but Janice was always up for it.

Money wasn't a problem. He had a crafty bit of trickery going on in the stores so Rainey didn't need to leave school to find work. She could stay on and make something of her life, become a typist, perhaps, or a private secretary.

Why, oh, why had he suggested he and Janice walk along Elm Grove in the rain to the café?

By what quirk of Fate had Jo been nosing out of the window of the bus at that exact moment?

And now had come the bombshell that he was to be shipped to France.

The British Expeditionary Force had already left, and more men were to follow. The *Royal Oak* had been torpedoed in her home base at Scapa Flow. Eight hundred men had gone down and all because of that clown Hitler.

He'd come home today to tell Jo, only to discover the bitch had left him, taking his daughter with her. Just wait until he got his hands on her, he thought. Then she'd know what pain was.

Chapter Three

Rainey pulled the corner of the blanket over her nose. It wasn't the damp, or the strange noises that sounded like small creatures going about their business in the darkness of the little house, that was keeping her awake. Even the hardness of the floor didn't matter. It was the smell of dirt. Filth left by other people. And it was her fault they were there, lying in it.

Her mother, curled up beside her, was breathing softly. Rainey wondered if she was asleep. She hoped so. She would have liked to touch her, for comfort, but didn't want to disturb her.

She thought back to the day she'd arrived home to discover her mother lying on the floor. She'd looked as if she was asleep, but she couldn't possibly sleep with her foot at that strange angle near the upturned kitchen chair – and why would she want to?

'Mum! Mum!' Rainey had fallen on her knees beside her mother. Her shrill voice must have disturbed something behind those serene features because her mother had opened her green eyes and immediately tried to rise. Pain had crossed her face. Rainey saw how she'd tried to use her right hand to push herself up from the floor, but her arm had buckled and she'd pitched forward on it.

'Is it broken?' Rainey put her arms around her mother and propped her into a sitting position. Jo had managed to make a loose fist. Rainey could see it took a painful effort.

'I don't think so. But my arm doesn't seem to do what I want it to.' Her mother used her other hand to massage her right shoulder. 'Put the kettle on, love,' she said wearily. 'I need a cup of tea.'

Rainey stood up and stared down at her mother. 'He did this, didn't he?' Without waiting for an answer she added, 'I should get you to the hospital.'

'No! The last time they asked so many questions . . .'

Rainey looked at her in disgust.

In the scullery, Rainey shook the kettle and, satisfied there was enough water in it, lit the gas. Anger was consuming her. She thought of Ellen. Her friend and her younger brother had been playing Cowboys and Indians with their father while their mother was at the market. When she'd closed their front door to come home, she was still smiling at the sight of Ellen's dad lying on the floor tied up with bits of string as the 'hostage' caught by seven-year-old Tommy.

She could neither remember nor imagine her own father making a happy spectacle of himself like that. But, then, her father wasn't home a great deal and she hated it when he was. Immediately he set foot inside the house a big black fog seemed to settle over everyone. She even thought twice about singing when he was around and she loved to sing.

'I'm not stupid, you know.' Rainey pushed open the kitchen door and looked at her mother, who'd managed somehow to settle herself in the armchair. 'This is just the latest of the many times he's taken his temper out on you. We have to leave.'

She saw the tears spring to her mother's eyes and waited for the usual protestations, but instead she heard her say quietly, 'I know. But I shouldn't have goaded him.'

Rainey didn't ask questions. Ellen had confessed to overhearing her parents whisper about Alfie Bird and 'that blonde' being spotted in a pub. Her mother must have discovered he was once again entangled with that Janice he couldn't seem to let go of.

The sad thing was her mother still loved him. She had since she was a girl and now, after taking all Rainey's father had dished out over the years, she hadn't the confidence to leave him. But if she didn't . . . Rainey didn't want to think about the consequences and, even, life without her beloved mother.

At sixteen, Rainey was old enough to leave school and get a job but her parents wanted more for her. If she left Portsmouth she could return to school in another place, couldn't she? Her mother wouldn't like her to throw away her education. But Rainey could perhaps get a part-time job and her mother would be able to go out to work, like she'd always wanted. Her father had decided early on that Jo's place was in the home. But they'd need to earn money if they left this house. If only she could persuade her mother to leave.

She watched her mother splay her fingers, saw the agony on her face as she moved her arm. Rainey sighed. Jo might have lost confidence in herself but Rainey had enough for the two of them. The kettle began to whistle. Rainey went back into the scullery and began making tea.

'I should get the doctor to see you,' she called. As the words left her mouth she knew if her mother could stand upright she would sweep away all Rainey's suggestions. She'd certainly never tell anyone that Alfie Bird knocked her about. Rainey remembered the time her mother had been taken to hospital. She'd not disclosed the truth: she'd lied to save Alfie's reputation.

'But nothing's broken. It'll soon get better. I really should watch where I'm going. Fell over that damn chair . . .'

There she goes again, thought Rainey. Already she's forgotten she's admitted Dad hit her. Now she's pretending it never happened.

Rainey slammed the teapot down on the table, causing the lid to jiggle and hot tea to spurt from the spout. With the cups in her hands she went into the living room.

Her mother obviously hadn't expected her to enter so had her jumper pulled up and was examining dark red marks blooming over her ribs. Rainey almost dropped the cups at the sight of the bruising. After putting them on the table she fell on her knees in front of her mother. 'Oh, Mum, we have to get away.' She eased Jo's jumper down, then pushed back the fair hair that had fallen across her mother's face, tucking it behind her ear. She looked into her eyes. 'If we tell no one where we're going, we can build a new, happier life.'

'But what about your friends, school?'

Rainey clutched her mother's left hand. She wanted to say, 'I'd miss them but sooner or later I have to escape into the big wide world and I'd rather do it with you beside me,' but instead she said, 'I can go somewhere else to carry on studying, if that's what you want for me.' She paused. 'We could both get jobs . . .' She'd stared into her mother's tear-stained face. 'Please?'

And that had been the start of it.

She'd urged her mother to find them a place to live. That hadn't happened straight away because her mother's shoulder had taken a while to mend sufficiently for her to gain control of her arm and hand.

Now Rainey shivered again. It was so cold in the stinking room. She looked across at the big black range. Tomorrow after they'd cleaned it they could see if it worked. That should warm the place. Light from the torch and later a dim candle had shown up bits of broken furniture they could burn.

It was a pity they'd had to leave so much nice stuff behind but the small car had been loaded to the gills as it was.

Her father would never find them here.

Into her head came the words of 'With a Smile and a Song'. She'd gone to see the picture *Snow White* with Ellen and they'd sung that tune as they'd walked home together, arm in arm. In her mind, the music played. At the pictures all the films ended happily. Her life and her mum's might not be like a film but she'd try her hardest to make sure there was happiness ahead.

One thing she was sure of: she'd never let any man treat her the way her mother had been treated.

Chapter Four

'Thanks, Mrs Perry. That's you paid up until the end of November.' Jo ticked off the money owed and wrote down in the ledger the final amount with the day's date. She took the cash, slid out the drawer and put the money into the till, then exchanged smiles with the woman in the fur coat, who walked out of Alverstoke's village newsagency carrying the latest issue of *Woman's Weekly*.

She turned to the next customer.

'Packet of Woodbines, Jo?'

'You're in luck, Tom. We've still got some left.'

The young man stepping impatiently from one foot to the other was dressed in paint-spattered overalls. He handed the exact money across the counter. Jo passed him his packet of cigarettes and he grabbed it, already turning to disappear out of the door and shouting, 'Thanks, Jo. They'll have my guts for garters if I'm missed!' The door slammed behind him and Jo was alone once more. She knew he was supposed to be painting the shopfront of the baker's opposite.

She perched on the stool in the corner and carried on marking up the copies of the *Portsmouth Evening News* in readiness for the paper-boys when they arrived. Six lads who came straight from school: she had to keep her eyes on them to make sure nothing went missing from the sweets counter.

Jo smiled to herself. She liked working in the paper-shop with the wide counter between her and the customers. It made her feel safe.

It wasn't big, just a single largish room, but it housed a lending library, shelves of magazines and comics, daily newspapers on a rack, cards for all occasions – some had been there a very long time, judging by the state they were in. Cigarettes and cigars sat on the back shelf.

Jo had been advised by her boss, Mr Harrington, to try to keep her regular customers happy by putting aside their favourite smokes beneath the counter whenever she could because it was likely, due to the war, tobacco would soon be in short supply.

The shop also sold shoelaces, matches – ordinary and red Swan Vestas – cotton reels and a myriad of odds and ends that customers rarely wanted. Outside, on a rack attached to the wall, there were more daily papers.

Jo liked the smell of the newsprint and was happy that Mr Harrington trusted her on her own in the shop. Mostly she was busy serving and answering the telephone to irate customers when the lads were late with the deliveries. When it was quiet, she got ahead of herself, checking the payment ledger, dusting shelves, leaving notes for Mr Harrington to re-order goods, and looking through glossy magazines that she could never hope to buy.

The bell tinkled again. 'I don't suppose you've got any of those leather bootlaces hidden away somewhere, Jo, the long ones?'

Jo looked up to see a tall red-haired man in greasy overalls. He didn't look happy.

She knew who he was: Syd Kennedy, the owner of the small garage on the corner of Coward Road. Earlier he'd picked up his usual *Daily Mirror* but he didn't often come back to the shop.

Leaving the pencil she'd been using to mark up the papers near the till, she smiled at him, apparently taking him by surprise. 'Actually we have,' she said, and balancing on the stool, she reached high up on the top shelf and pulled down a battered cardboard box. She set it on the counter and slid off the lid. As the contents were revealed, his hand sprang forward, brushing accidentally against her fingers. It was well shaped and looked as if he had recently washed it, but lines of grease lay in his fingernails.

'Oh.' Jo pulled back her hand as if she had been burned.

'I'm sorry. I didn't mean to startle you.' He was contrite. 'I was just trying to see if the laces were the right sort.' His face had reddened.

Jo's heart was beating fast. She stared at him. Since moving to Gosport she couldn't erase the fear that Alfie would suddenly pop up and hurt her again. Sooner or later she knew he would come looking for her. Her fear of him had made her wary of all men. While she was inside the house she kept the front and back doors locked and only left her home alone to go to work. When Rainey wasn't at school they went into town to discover cheap treasures in second-hand shops to make the small house more homely. Week by week it was becoming more of a place of safety.

'No harm done.' She forced herself to smile at Syd, who seemed almost as embarrassed as herself. She shuffled the assorted laces, pulling out a sturdy pair of black leather strings. 'Will these do?'

A smile broke across his face. 'Oh, well done,' he said. 'I can sort out my work boots now.' He looked down at his feet. Jo couldn't see what he was wearing because the counter was in the way. 'Damned lace broke this morning,' he said. 'How much?'

'There are no prices on the box.' Jo picked up the lid and looked at it, then wrinkled her nose – no price there either. She thought for a moment. 'Why don't you take them and pay Mr Harrington when you come in next?'

'If you're sure? I only live above the garage.'

'I'm sure it'll be all right.'

'Well, thanks,' he said. 'It's not very comfortable walking about with one bootlace. I thought I'd have to make a quick repair with a bit of string and that wouldn't impress my customers, would it?'

'No,' Jo said, putting the lid back on the box and watching him walk out of the shop. The bell clanged behind him. After returning the box to the top shelf and resolving to ask Mr Harrington for missing prices, then write them on the articles to which they applied, she felt ashamed that she'd nearly jumped out of her skin when Syd Kennedy had touched her.

She rubbed her shoulder. When she had reached up high for the laces, it had twinged. She wondered how long it would take her arm to recover completely and stop reminding her of her suffering.

'All right, Jo?'

Mr Harrington had emerged from the passage door that led from the living quarters he shared with his wife, Bella. He was a small round man in his sixties with twinkling eyes, practically a carbon copy of his wife. Jo had liked him as soon as she'd met him for the first time when the Labour Exchange had sent her to apply for the job. 'I am,' she replied. 'The papers are all marked up and the magazines and comics are slipped inside.'

'Well done. I suppose it's time you were on your way.'

She was allowed to leave early each afternoon so she could be home for Rainey when she got in from St John's School.

The newsagency didn't pay as much as the factories and armament yards that needed women workers now that the men were leaving to fight in the forces, but Jo knew she wasn't ready to work with a crowd of people after being at home for so long. Rainey had a Saturday job in the green-grocer's at the end of Albert Street and, with careful planning, their combined wages enabled them to live frugally.

Mr and Mrs Harrington were kind people but not blessed with children. Bella Harrington didn't enjoy good health so she rarely served in the shop, but each morning at eleven o'clock she went over the road to the bakery and came back with a freshly baked confection that she would present to Jo with a cup of milky Camp coffee.

Mr Harrington rose early in readiness for the delivery of the morning papers. He often went back to bed after the paper-boys had returned from their rounds. Jo arrived at nine just as he was about to walk their beloved elderly Dalmatian, Freckles. The timing suited her because she was able to see Rainey off to school before she left the house.

Now she said, 'I've left a note. Syd Kennedy owes for a pair of leather bootlaces. I didn't know how much they were.'

'I shan't worry too much about asking him for a few pence, not when he does all sorts of favours for me. You ready for home, Jo?'

Jo nodded.

'Off you go, then. See you tomorrow.'

Jo collected her handbag and headscarf, then lifted the counter flap. She went through the Harringtons' living accommodation into their hallway, where her coat hung on a hook opposite the long mirror. Jo stared at her reflection. In the short time since they had left Portsmouth she thought she had changed. She looked quite different. There was a glow about her face, which no longer had a haunted expression. She realized that, for the first time in years, she was happy. When she was dressed against the cold outside and had tied her headscarf over her hair, she shouted her

24

goodbyes. She left by the Harringtons' rear door to collect her bike from their garage.

The bike, with its wicker basket, was a godsend. She'd discovered it hidden at the rear of the shed at Albert Street. After a clean and with the tyres pumped up, she could ride it to the shop, then home again – she pedalled down Green Lane and along Queens Road to cross the railway bridge to Albert Street – and into town for shopping, saving on bus fares.

Each time she put the bicycle into the shed she looked longingly at the MG. She had the registration book but needed to apply to the local issuing clerk for coupons. Alfie might discover her whereabouts from the Divisional Petroleum Office. However, she often gave it a quick polish with a rag, wishing she could take Rainey out somewhere for a treat but she didn't dare risk running out of petrol.

It took about twenty minutes to cycle home in the November cold. The trees were leafless and frost was already making white patches on the pavements and roads. By the time Jo reached number fourteen she was shivering.

Her heart lifted as she opened the front door to a blast of warm air from the range and the sound of her daughter singing along with the wireless. She could smell cooking and sniffed appreciatively.

Rainey stopped singing long enough to yell, "'Lo, Mum. I got home a bit earlier this afternoon so I've made some potato cakes. I've got the kettle on.' She sounded so happy, Jo thought, and in that moment she knew that more happiness would follow.

Chapter Five

'Don't forget you're coming up the school with me tonight to see the teachers, Mum. It's parents' evening.' Rainey's words broke through the cut-glass voice of the wireless announcer's.

'Hang on, Rainey! I can't listen to two people at the same time. Can you hear what he's saying? The Germans have dropped bombs on the Shetland Islands!'

Jo threw down the tea-towel she was using to dry the dishes at the stone sink. 'That's the first on British soil!'

'It's a long way from here—'

Jo rounded on her. 'But don't you see, love? It's started. All this talk of war, the rationing, the handing out of gas masks, it's really happening, my girl!'

Glenn Miller music was now pouring from the set.

'Does it mean you're not coming to the school?'

Jo shook the end of the tea-towel at her daughter. 'Of course I'm coming, although what the teachers will have to say when you've only been there five minutes I don't know. Is there any tea left in that pot?'

Rainey took off the lid and peered into it. 'Yes.'

'Pour it for me, love. I need a sit-down and a cuppa. You finish drying up.'

Jo took the willow-patterned cup and saucer from the scullery into the kitchen and sat down at the table where earlier she and Rainey had eaten their evening meal. Idly she stirred her tea. She had been a young girl when the last war had ended and that was supposed to have been the war to end all wars. Her father had never returned from the fighting and her mother had succumbed to the influenza that had swept the country shortly after. An elderly aunt, her father's sister, had brought her up.

Jo was sixteen and eager to be married to Alfie before their child was born. Her aunt had given her permission to wed but had passed away before Rainey arrived.

Alfie used to say he'd like to put her in a matchbox and carry her around in his pocket so he could see her whenever he wanted. That had been in the early days before he'd hit her. He hated to see her reading. He'd snatch the book from her, tearing it. He liked her to stay in the house and questioned her long into the night if he suspected she'd disobeyed him. It got so it was easier to do his bidding than to bear the aftermath of his silences.

She shivered. Alfie wasn't in this little house, this sanctuary. She was free. As free as she could be with the war news hanging over everyone. Alfie would be sent to fight for his country. While she hoped for his safety, the prospect of him being far away from her and Rainey was comforting.

She sipped the stewed tea. She could hear Rainey clattering about in the scullery. A smile broke over her face. Rainey was a credit to her, a lovely girl. Look how she'd knuckled down and helped scrub the house from top to bottom, starting that first morning she'd woken up on the floor in a nest of blankets.

Jo gazed around the bright kitchen, remembering.

That first morning the shed had proved a treasure chest. They'd discovered all sorts of materials they could use to renovate the small rooms. Their greatest find had been the tins of apple-green distemper. She and Rainey had set to and covered the downstairs walls and the stairwell. A further hoard of white paint had come to light in the back garden's coal cellar.

Jo had blackleaded the range after Rainey had cleared out all the grey ash. When it was lit and giving out a satisfying heat the kitchen had begun to feel cosy.

Jo had discovered a second-hand shop in Queens Road and she and Rainey had come to an agreement with Ted, the owner. He would transport their goods free of charge with his horse and cart if they bought two nearly new beds, a sofa and an armchair, a table, two kitchen chairs and a quantity of damp orange boxes that Jo intended to dry out and paint to make cupboards. He had also promised to remove from the house the furniture left by the previous tenants, including the stained mattress.

With the security of the newsagency job, Jo had felt confident in spending the last of her savings. Now 14 Albert Street wasn't a palace but it was a cosy home.

Jo finished her tea and stood up, glancing in the big oval mirror hanging over the range. She caught the smile on her face and a fleeting resemblance to her daughter. How on earth she'd managed to produce a green-eyed, red-haired beauty like Rainey she had no idea. It was a miracle. Only their eyes were similar, eyes that Jo's school-friends had raved about. Where Rainey's singing voice had come from was a mystery.

And Rainey was singing again now. That Bob Hope number, 'Thanks for the Memory'. The words came easily and clearly. Jo's heart swelled with pride.

'I don't know how you can remember the tunes let alone

the right words,' she said, as her daughter emerged from the scullery to hang the wet tea-towel on the string line they'd made above the range.

'Our music teacher at school goes on at me because I can't read music. You'll meet her tonight.' She pulled a face. 'All them dots and lines get jumbled up, but I only have to hear the tune once and I can remember it. She'll be wanting you to buy a recorder.'

'A recorder?' The word exploded from Jo's mouth.

'For music class, Mum. I've been borrowing one of the school's. Please don't give in to her and get one. I don't want to play the stupid recorder.'

'It'll be easy to say no. We haven't the money for anything that isn't essential. You wait until I see her.'

'I warn you, Mrs Wilkes is pretty persuasive . . .'

'You just leave her to me,' Jo said. She might feel at bit apprehensive in the company of men but aggressive women didn't worry her at all. If something needed to be said then Jo had to say it. It would be similar to the chores she'd thought of as men's work. Like the house painting: all right, she knew it wasn't perfect, but it suited her and Rainey, and the sense of relief and happiness they'd felt when it was finished was worth every bit of the hard work involved, especially now her shoulder was healing.

Rainey came from the passage where they'd screwed hooks in the wall near the front door for scarves and coats. She passed Jo her green gabardine, and after Jo had put on her boots, mother and daughter left arm in arm to venture into the cold November night.

'Good thing the school's not far away. This wind is biting cold,' said Rainey. 'You won't go on at me if some of my teachers find fault, will you?'

'Considering I uprooted you from one place to another and was lucky to get you into St John's at short notice I'll be glad whatever you're up to. I'm well aware you had it in mind to go out to work full time.'

'Don't start, Mum. I'm in school and still banging away at the typewriter like you wanted . . .'

Jo squeezed Rainey's arm. 'I know, love, and for that I'm thankful. I only want you to get a decent job.'

'A decent job is surely one you're happy to work at.'

Jo sighed. 'Rainey, if you'd asked me six months ago if I would like working in a paper-shop I'd have thought you were barmy. But it's one of the best things I could have done to put food on the table and take my mind off what's happened to us. They're good people, the Harringtons, but you deserve better than toiling in a shop or factory.'

Jo's words caused Rainey to fall silent.

A car passed them, its headlights dimmed because of the blackout. White lines had been painted at strategic points on the kerbs to stop people tripping. The moon was not completely hidden behind clouds so it helped light their path, but Jo was glad when they met up with other parents and children going to St John's School. She held tight to Rainey – it was already icy underfoot.

The teachers Jo needed to see were located in various rooms around the school. Luckily Rainey knew exactly where to go. Jo noticed many of them looked harassed. Most were kind and said they were pleased with how Rainey had adapted to the change of schools.

Mrs Belcher, the typing mistress, wasn't so enthusiastic. 'The girls in my class are quite advanced. Rainey has trouble keeping up.' Jo noticed her bun had become unpinned and her red lipstick looked like a slash across her thin mouth.

'She probably needs time to settle in. She was doing well at her previous school.'

'Perhaps she shouldn't have been moved then, Mrs Bird.'

Jo took a dislike to the woman and her condescending tone. No wonder Rainey had slipped behind in her work with this Gorgon. Nevertheless, Jo was worried. An office job was a good way for Rainey to make something of herself.

'You never told me that Mrs Belcher was a cow,' she

said, as they left her classroom to mingle with other parents looking for their children's class tutors. 'Do you really find it so hard to keep up with the others?'

Rainey sighed. 'Mrs Belcher has favourites and I'm not one of them. I do try, Mum, but it's hard when she keeps on at me all the time.'

Jo stared at her pretty daughter. It had started then, the petty jealousies. Rainey was a sweet girl and eager to please. She was also unaware of her good looks. Women and girls could be hateful, poisonous even, when they felt threatened by beauty.

Suddenly Rainey stopped walking and pulled Jo round to face her. 'Look, Mum, I know you want what's best for me so I'll try harder, all right?'

Jo smiled at her. Why did her daughter always manage to make her feel better?

At the end of the corridor they came to the music room. Jo knocked on the open door. A small square woman over-flowing from a chair behind a littered desk smiled broadly. A little white dog appeared from nowhere to greet Rainey and she started to make a fuss of it.

'Welcome, welcome.' The woman struggled to her feet and came towards Jo with her hand outstretched. 'I'm Alice Wilkes and this is Toto, after Dorothy's little dog in *The*

Wizard of Oz.' She motioned to a single chair in front of the desk and Jo sat down. Rainey stood at her side, Toto at her feet, gazing up at her adoringly.

'Isn't he lovely?' Rainey said.

If Rainey thinks we can support a pet as well as ourselves she's got another think coming, Jo thought, but she said nothing, just nodded and looked around the room. Bright posters of musicals adorned the walls.

'I'll come straight to the point,' Alice Wilkes said. She shoved her fingers through her crisp grey hair that stood to attention around her face, like a bottle brush. 'How do you feel about providing a recorder for your very talented daughter?'

Jo mumbled, 'I have to be honest, we need every penny we can get hold of at the moment.'

She got no further for Mrs Wilkes said, 'Good, good, never mind about that. I may have a more suitable proposition for you anyway. I run a choir that meets on Wednesday evenings. Though I say so myself, we're a talented bunch. A few girls of all ages with good voices – some have exceptional voices.' She nodded towards Rainey. 'And there's a few parents too, with aspirations.' She chuckled and the scent of lavender wafted towards Jo from the woman's tweed suit. 'What I intend to do is visit hospitals, school halls, and show them what we're capable of. A few songs, perhaps, some carols, as Christmas is fast approaching. I've had a long chat with Rainey here.' At Jo's side Rainey fidgeted. 'All in the strictest confidence, of course, but she tells me that, apart from work and maybe the cinema, you rarely leave the house.'

Jo opened her mouth to protest but Mrs Wilkes was on a mission and quickly spoke again. 'I'd like it if you'd allow Rainey to join our happy band of warblers, and I think you should come along yourself.'

Jo gasped, then protested, 'I can't sing!'

'Pish! That's what everyone says. I'm not looking for perfection, just commitment and enthusiasm. It's for charity. With this damned war looming, we need to entertain people. We'll sing everything from Gilbert and Sullivan to "Knees Up Mother Brown". We'll make all our own costumes, arrive at local venues under our own steam . . .' Mrs Wilkes paused. 'One or two arrive here by bus or bicycle and the others walk. No excuse for you, though, you live practically next door to St John's. Now, how about it?'

Jo sat looking at the woman whose enthusiasm practically flowed in her veins. Then she glanced at Rainey's face. The glow that emanated from her daughter's smile was brighter than the lights in the classroom.

'Please?' Rainey mouthed. 'It's something we can do together.' The hope in her eyes was unmistakable.

Swept along by the pair, Jo opened her mouth and asked, 'If I agree will I still have to buy a recorder?' Jo wanted to make sure Mrs Wilkes hadn't forgotten she'd said there was no need for her to pay out money she didn't have.

'Bugger the recorder,' declared Mrs Wilkes. 'That was simply a ruse to get you here. I guessed that if I asked you to provide one you'd be more likely to come and see me. Then I could hustle the pair of you to join my choir.'

Jo stood up from the chair and held out her hand to seal the deal. She ignored the twinge as Mrs Wilkes grasped her fingers. She was smiling as she walked towards the door. What an extraordinary woman, she thought. 'Excuse me,' she said, to a slim woman with a fox fur slung over one shoulder and wearing incredibly high heels. The woman, whose face was caked with Pan Stik, moved to one side, allowing Jo and Rainey to pass. A wave of Californian Poppy enveloped Jo. Without looking at either of them, the woman said, 'I hope she gets this over with quick. I'm meeting Jim down the Fox in half an hour.'

It was then Jo noticed a small dark-haired girl practically hidden behind her.

''Lo, Ivy,' muttered Rainey. Jo saw her raise her head and stare at Rainey, a smile lighting her face. She had the most incredible dark eyes peering out from an untidy fringe. Her thick dark hair dropped to her shoulders, reminding Jo of an Egyptian princess. The girl raised her eyes to Heaven, as if showing Rainey she'd rather be anywhere else than there with her mother.

When they were outside in the cold once more and heading homewards, Rainey said, 'It's going to be good for both of us to mix with people. We'll enjoy the choir, Mum.'

Jo said, 'I hope so, love.' Then she added, 'She's a pretty girl, that Ivy.'

'Aw, come on, Mum. What you mean is why does Ivy's mum look like a tart?'

'Rainey Bird! I never brought you up to know words like that, or use them about other people!' Jo was quiet for a while, concentrating on stepping on bits of pavement that seemed mostly frost-free. She was also thinking over Rainey's words. When she herself was fifteen, what had she known about tarts? Not a lot, she thought. But she'd already sampled the delights of the flesh with Alfie Bird. Did that make her a tart?

Rainey squeezed her mother's arm. 'It's all right, Mum. Everyone knows what Ivy's mum does to earn a living. Ivy Sparrow is a good friend of mine but don't ever let her hear you say a word against her mother because, small as she is, she'll knock your block off.'

Chapter Six

Twenty-four-year-old Blackie Wilson had grown up in the theatre. He might even have been born in a trunk, but he'd never thought to ask either of his parents before the car in which they were travelling to Paris had hit a wall. Dandi and William Wilson were no more the darlings of the Portsmouth stage, and Blackie was an orphan. His hair was the colour of a blackbird's wing and his curls bounced across his forehead, no matter how many times he pushed them back. His father had called him his little Blackie Bird Boy and the name Blackie had stuck.

His paternal grandfather, who had lived in a damp basement flat in Southsea, had taken him in so he might run errands to the Rocking Horse public house to purchase the old man's daily ale. Ol' Sam fed and clothed him and, in his own way, loved him. It could have been worse. At least Ol'

Sam had chased off the young kids who ridiculed Blackie, because he had one blue eye and one brown, until he'd thought his grandson old enough to fight his own battles. A gypsy friend of Sam's said Blackie had ghost eyes, but he'd been drunk at the time and didn't comment further. One of the few bright sparks in his life was Madame Nelly Walker, his late parents' manager. Wonderfully kind, she allowed him to pester her at the Academy Buildings in Portland Road, Southsea, where her many stage acts rehearsed. She'd married Herbert Peters in 1911, and later Herbert had taught Blackie all he knew about business management. Blackie had practically lived at the South Parade Pier Theatre in the early thirties, daily watching three hours of the non-stop variety entertainment Madame Walker provided.

Madame had tried to make a juvenile star of him. After all, his curly dark hair and infectious smile added up to the film-star looks Madame convinced herself would raise her bank balance After all, Dandi and William Wilson had been song-and-dance headliners.

Blackie smiled to himself. His mother and father might have been stage naturals but he certainly wasn't! He made a mess of tap-dancing. His voice was like a tomcat's yowl, and he couldn't act. Good-looking, yes. Gift of the gab, without a doubt, and he could persuade a monkey to hand him the last banana from a bunch, but people would never part with a penny to watch him onstage, not even to see his odd-coloured eyes. Madame, worried about the onset of early blindness in Blackie, had paid a doctor to tell them that heterochromia was caused by the pigment melanin acting differently in his irises, and would pose no future problems.

Of course, his eyes were the first thing anyone noticed about him. He was used to strangers staring – in fact, he waited for people to do a double-take. It gave him immense confidence, knowing exactly how people would behave when they first met him.

When his granddad died, kind-hearted Madame and Herbert took him in. He followed Herbert around like a little dog. He was better dressed now, for Nelly Walker made sure all her many acts had the best of stage clothes, including Blackie, whom she and Herbert treated like their son. He soon became the darling of the tap-dancing girls and female singers. He had an early initiation into sex and became quite adept at wriggling out of embarrassing situations well before he was twenty-one.

It was his quick thinking and sharp attitude that Herbert liked. Instinctively Blackie knew which fledgling singer, dance duo or comedy act would make it to the top. Herbert began to rely on him in the day-to-day running of the theatre.

Blackie felt that at last he was beginning to repay the kindly pair for all they'd done for him.

Then Herbert suggested Blackie should join the Territorial Army. 'Make a man of you, son. Get you away from stage make-up, feather boas, silk stockings . . .'

Even now Blackie could hear Herbert saying those very words to Madame and she had protested and cried – real tears, too – to no avail.

He cursed Herbert for his advice. He cursed him for the snow and the cold and his hunger. If he hadn't listened to the man he admired more than anyone else in the world he wouldn't now be sitting, waiting to get killed, in this bleeding listening post in France, which was no more than an icy foxhole, with freezing snow falling thick and fast.

Even worse was the pig of a corporal he was sharing it with, who wouldn't shut up about his wife. Apparently she'd scarpered, taking his daughter who, he was convinced, had a better voice than Vera Lynn.

'My Rainey sings "We'll Meet Again" so sweetly you'll want to cry. Makes Vera sound as if she's got a cold.'

'Keep your voice down, Corporal. We don't want to broadcast to the enemy that we're here.' Blackie thought for a moment. 'I suppose she's prettier than our Vera, is she?'

'Prettier? My Rainey's sixteen. You're looking at a dainty

filly against a carthorse!' The corporal foraged in his top pocket and took out a photograph that had obviously been shown around a great deal. He stuck it in front of Blackie's eyes.

Blackie had seen a few beauties in his time but he was struck dumb by just how lovely the girl was. He could only whistle softly in response. Eventually he managed, 'Your daughter?'

'My Rainey,' said the corporal, replacing the photo in his top pocket. 'She should be on the halls in Portsmouth.' He sniffed and wiped his hand across his orange moustache.

'She's certainly got the looks,' muttered Blackie. He didn't add that he, too, came from Portsmouth and was involved with Madame Walker, whose most talented men and women not only played the local halls but appeared all over Britain and on the Continent. He hadn't rowed up the Solent in a bucket: one whiff of what he might be able to do for wannabe singers, and half the men in his regiment would be showing him pictures of their kids. He had to admit the girl was a looker, though.

'How long you been in France?' Blackie asked.

'How the hell should I know?' The corporal snorted. 'You might as well ask me where the rest of my blokes are. We all got scattered – well, the ones that didn't cop it after we'd bedded down in a barn for the night. Bloody Jerries caught us napping, that they did!' He gave a sudden laugh as if it was a funny story he was telling.

'We left Southampton for France full of good cheer with a bloody band playing "Run Rabbit Run" an' I've been running ever since. We drove through Le Mans, then Lille and other little towns, where the girls handed us wine and bread and blew kisses at us. You'd have thought we was on holiday. It seems months ago now. This is a bloody long winter.' He sighed, and Blackie saw how tired he was beneath the grime that covered his face.

'I always thought the first men to be sent to France would be experienced soldiers, not the Territorials like me,' said Blackie.

'What the fuck do you think I am?' The corporal glared at him. 'I'm experienced.'

The war was making strange bedfellows, thought Blackie. Regulars and TAs in the same foxhole. Who'd have thought it? One thing he was certain of: he wouldn't trust this bastard any further than he could throw him. The things he was saying made sense in a disjointed way but something wasn't quite right. Maybe the fighting had got to him and turned his brain. That happened to a lot of men. Had he really got cut off from his unit behind enemy lines to end up back here?

'Our boys were horribly sick on the crossing to Cherbourg,' Blackie said. 'The Channel was heaving and so were we. The bloody crossing took fourteen hours. Talk about dehydrated and stinking of vomit. Our first stop was Château de Varennes. I can't tell you how bloody excited I was a few days later when we stopped near the racing circuit at Le Mans, at the army's big supply depot.'

'I know it well,' said the corporal.

Of course you do, thought Blackie. The man was one of those who knew everything.

'Did you know it's left over from the first war?'

Now what was the corporal on about?

'Bully-beef. That's why it's practically inedible.'

Blackie sighed. Still, he could be right, the food was bloody awful. But the intense cold was even worse.

He wasn't allowed to leave the observation post until a patrol returned to relieve him, though he had been surprised to find the corporal already there after he'd crawled along a short tunnel covered with icy bushes. The bloke he'd relieved didn't seem to find it strange that there were two men in the foxhole, so why should he?

Every sector of the front had similar positions to conceal men for several hours so they could observe and report enemy movements. Blackie had a field telephone that connected him to company headquarters. Usually it was a lonely job being in the foxhole and at first he'd been glad of the corporal's company. But now the man was getting on his nerves and he was wondering where he had come from. He wasn't from Blackie's regiment. Was he a deserter? There was one way to find out. He opened his mouth to ask.

'Ssh!'

Blackie heard a terrible rumbling noise, growing ever louder, so heavy the earth shook. Then it stopped.

A jolt of fear ran through him.

There were voices, movement. Not the usual night sounds of animals or branches cracking with the cold.

A slit in the ice showed a German tank had come to a halt not far from where he and the corporal were lying. For the first time that night Blackie thanked God for the falling snow that must have obscured the listening post. Now he could see men climbing from the tank and lighting cigarettes.

He looked into the narrowed eyes of the corporal and was certain he saw his own fear reflected there.

His hand hovered above the field telephone. He should send a warning back to headquarters. But to move would mean certain discovery, and after discovery would come a bullet. He could hardly breathe for fear, and all the time he was praying the corporal would not move a muscle.

Waiting was nerve-racking. The seconds seemed like hours. Just as Blackie was sure they would be found and killed, the three men began passing a metal flask among themselves. A burst of laughter pealed forth.

German activity had increased in the area recently – wasn't there heavy artillery fire across the border daily? The bastards were everywhere.

He thought then of the sanitizing tactics the enemy used. A barrage of shells fired across a small area followed by Germans marching across the already decimated ground firing at anything or anybody remaining alive. Please, God, he prayed, don't let that happen here.

The corporal was watching him, unmoving and silent. Blackie could barely hear the man's breath. Outside in the snowy waste the men were talking. Blackie reached for the field telephone but the corporal stilled his hand and shook his head.

'Let me,' the man mouthed, and wriggled closer to Blackie. 'Let my Rainey know I did one thing really good.' He pushed the photograph and some letters at Blackie, and before Blackie could stop him he slithered out of the fox-hole and stood up. From his belt he'd snatched a grenade and was now running towards the tank. One of the men dropped the flask he was holding.

A stab of gunfire erupted. The corporal had reached the Germans.

The flash almost blinded Blackie. Snow and metal were tossed into the air. He fell back against the wall of earth, stunned, his ears ringing from the force of the grenade blast.

Blackie could now see the body of one German lying twisted some small distance away. Nearer were the mangled body parts of other men. Of the corporal there was nothing.

The tank was untouched.

Despite the darkness the snow gave off an eerie whiteness that was now splattered with red.

Blackie could see the German's eyes were open wide. There was no surprise on his face, just a ragged hole in his head.

He willed himself to keep still, his mind and body in turmoil.

Was anyone else in the tank, waiting? Would they come for retribution? Looking to make sure no one else was in the foxhole?

His hand stayed on the telephone until his fingers grew numb and were covered with ice.

He wondered if the shock had dulled his senses because

he couldn't fathom the time lapse between the blast that had killed the men, and the present. He thought of the corporal and his last words. What had they meant? That he had wanted to die was obvious. Was it to save him, Blackie, or to rid himself of some other torment? If so, that would explain his strange behaviour.

There was still no movement from the tank.

If he didn't stretch himself he would freeze to death. His fingers moved stiffly over the telephone and, with great difficulty, he picked up the receiver and listened.

It was dead.

Now he had a choice. Either crawl from the hole in the snow and risk getting shot by the enemy or stay and allow the Germans to discover him. Then he would be shot for sure.

Blackie stared again at the dead men and the snow beginning to hide them.

He knew he must survive not only for his own sake but for the corporal, whose family deserved to know how brave he had been. His fingers, despite the freezing cold, felt for the letters and the photograph now in his pocket.

Blackie took a deep breath and began to crawl from the look-out post.

Chapter Seven

'Want a sandwich, Ivy?'

'That'd be nice, Bert.' She looked up from the exercise book in which she was writing and smiled at the café proprietor. 'Bacon?'

'You want bacon, bacon it is. I had a delivery from a friend of a friend today.' A piece of cigarette paper clung to Bert's chin where he had nicked himself shaving.

It was warm in the Central Café on the corner of North Cross Street. Outside the streets were white with frost. Condensation ran down inside the windows and was soaked up by the grubby nets. Soon Bert would pull the blackout curtains across and eliminate the night.

Ivy heard the sizzle of fat in the pan and the enticing smell of bacon began drifting across to her, chasing away the stink of fags. She knew Bert sometimes bought goods from dubious sources, and he said those people would look after him when rationing came. Most people in Gosport were glad to get whatever they could find to feed their families. Bert's family was his customers.

From the wireless on the shelf came band music.

'How did your mum get on with your teachers?'

'How does she get on with anyone? They either love her or get put off by how she pays the rent.'

'You shouldn't say things like that, love. She worships the ground you walks on.' Bert slapped two doorsteps of bread onto a board and spread them with margarine.

'If I can't be honest with you, who can I be honest with? We both know because of her lack of learning she wants better for me. Della's my mum and I love her . . .' Ivy was almost sixteen but the things that came out of her mouth often made her sound much older.

Bert, his grubby apron stretched over his ample gut, stood in front of the Formica table and set down her sandwich. Ivy looked at it happily. 'Smells delicious.'

'Get it down you. It tastes as good as it smells.'

Ivy used both hands and lifted the bread. She bit off a mouthful and chewed. 'You must have known I had to get Mum out of bed when I got home from school so there wasn't time for tea.'

Bert nodded. 'I told you not to go hungry,' he said. A frown replaced his gap-toothed grin.

Ivy reached out and patted his hand. 'Mrs Wilkes went on and on about me being in the choir she's got going.'

'That's good—' Bert never got to finish his sentence.

'Anyone servin' in this place? A cuppa would be nice.'

Bert rolled his eyes. 'No peace for the wicked,' he said, and shuffled off to serve the customer.

Ivy watched him return behind the counter. The tables needed clearing. Used crockery and overflowing ashtrays showed he never lacked for customers. To Ivy it was familiar and comforting. When she'd finished eating she'd give Bert a hand. She watched him pour thick dark tea into a large white mug.

The thickset man said loudly, 'That's all you 'ad to do, mate, give us a cuppa.' He banged his fist containing the tea money forcefully on the counter.

Ivy's heart missed a beat. She didn't want the man to cause trouble. Not that Bert couldn't handle himself – he'd fought in the Great War and come out intact – but he had a little extra something up his sleeve, did Bert. Bert scooped up the money and she saw his eyes dart beneath the counter to where his walking stick stood propped ready if needed.

The shiny black stick held a secret. Bert could whip out

the handle in the blink of an eye to wave a sharpened sword that glinted like silver in the electric light of the café. Ivy knew there was more to the story but she had yet to be told.

It usually did the trick of calming down unruly customers.

Bert didn't need to use it this time. There was no bother: the man, satisfied now, took his tea and shuffled off, sitting down heavily at a table near the window.

'Thanks, mate,' called Bert, amiably. He looked towards Ivy and winked. She grinned back. Bert was like the father she'd never known. She trusted him. She knew he would always be there for her as long as they lived at the Central Café.

He said he was a rabologist, a collector of walking sticks. The swordstick had been his first acquisition. 'You should never just look at a walking stick someone's holding and ignore it,' he'd told her. 'Each stick tells a story.'

In his living accommodation on the first floor he kept his collection of more than a hundred. Each was similar, but with differences. Bert had told Ivy that canes and sticks turned up everywhere, especially in second-hand shops after house clearances. Her dearest wish was to present him with a type of stick he didn't already possess.

'Look at the carving on that,' he'd said, the first time he'd shown her his collection. He'd held a lacquered stick with a fine bone handle. 'Someone somewhere in China took trouble with that. I bet it could tell a few tales if it could talk.'

Ivy liked the sticks with carved animal heads best. She could imagine someone spending hours shaping the handles, perhaps to resemble pets they'd loved. Bert had offered a stick to Della that had spikes that folded into the handle. He'd told her it might even save her life if a client attacked her.

'What do I need with that when I got Jim to protect me?' She'd laughed, tossing her fox fur around her neck and allowing it to hang down over her ample breasts so it could stare at everyone with its sharp glass eyes.

Bert told Ivy that the earliest mention of a walking stick was in the Bible.

'In the Book of Genesis, chapter thirty-two, Jacob said he'd crossed the Jordan with only his staff, which was a fancy name for a walking stick.' Ivy liked listening to Bert: he knew a lot about all sorts of things.

She also liked living in the top flat above the Central Café. Flat? It was two rooms that looked down over Murphy's, the ironmongers, and out towards Gosport ferry, where the boats, like squat beetles, crossed the harbour to Portsmouth. Those two rooms were home. Bert wouldn't allow any 'guests' upstairs so Jim, her mother's so-called friend, provided a room above the Crown near the bus station.

When Ivy was small and asked her mother where she went every night, Della had said, 'I'm a sort of nurse. I look after patients and make them feel better.'

'Can't you do it at home?' Ivy had asked. She didn't like her mother leaving her.

'Bless you, Ivy, Bert wouldn't like that. Anyway, Jim's my boss and when I tend my patients, Jim looks after me.'

Ivy disliked Jim because he looked at her funny, like he could see into the very core of her. Still, she didn't have much to do with him, so it was all right. Every night her mother met Jim in the Fox next door to the Central Café. After a quick drink he took Della out to do 'a bit of business', as Della called it.

Ivy knew her mother's business put food on the table and paid the rent.

When Ivy reached the grand age of fourteen she'd asked Della if she could leave school and go to work. If she was bringing home a wage her mother might stay at home more often.

'You'll leave school when I say you will and not before.' She'd never seen her mother so angry. 'Without an education you'll end up like me. Is that what you want?' Then she'd grabbed Ivy's shoulders and shaken her until her head rattled – at least, that was what it had felt like. Then, just as suddenly, she'd stopped, pulled her daughter close and cried.

Much later, after Ivy had joined Mrs Wilkes's choir she was immensely grateful that she had stayed on at school. She was put next to Bea, who was a year or so older than her, a girl full of life, though sometimes she could be withdrawn. Bea's voice showed her fluctuating emotions.

Bea used to urge Ivy to join her and her much older friends for a drink in the Fox, but the thought of bumping into her mother and Jim put Ivy off. Besides, she wasn't used to visiting pubs and much preferred the café.

Now she thought back to earlier in the evening when she'd seen Rainey Bird and her mother at St John's. She liked Rainey. Her voice was clear, and all her words came out as if she'd had proper singing lessons. Rainey told her she hadn't and couldn't even read music. But she got all the words and tunes exactly right first time.

Mrs Wilkes said their voices complemented each other. How, Ivy wasn't sure, because she thought she sounded like a foghorn. Mrs Wilkes told her that her voice was 'smoky' like Billie Holiday's. Billie Holiday sang on the wireless and when Ivy heard her sing 'Can't Help Lovin' Dat Man' she thought Mrs Wilkes must have a screw loose in her head somewhere. If Ivy could sing like that she knew she'd have the world at her feet.

The café had emptied now. With the blackout curtains

shutting out the weather and the night, the place looked homely. Her sandwich was eaten and Ivy yawned. She slapped her geography book shut and closed her wooden pencil box. She went round the tables collecting the used crockery and piled it on the counter ready for washing up. Bert called, 'You should get upstairs, love.'

'Want a hand with anything?' she asked.

'No. It'll be quiet until the pubs turn out. Give me time to clear up.'

Ivy said goodnight as she left through the side door that led up the uncarpeted stairs.

Chapter Eight

'The government announces bigger family allowances for servicemen . . .'

Jo turned off the wireless. More money for service families meant nothing to her. She'd waived her right to any money from Alfie by running away from the house he'd provided for her and Rainey. She was sure there was no way she could collect anything without the army authorities becoming aware of her new address, and if that happened, Alfie would also find out where they were. It was not a risk she wanted to take.

'Ready, Mum?'

'Almost,' answered Jo. She was using her fingernail to hook the last of the lipstick from its cylinder. She had another, Bright Cherry, but that one wasn't her favourite.

'We don't want to be late.' Rainey sounded peevish.

'Not likely to be. The school's only five minutes away.' She caught Rainey looking at her in the mirror's reflection and smiled.

Jo knew how important her first appearance at choir night was for Rainey. But Rainey wasn't aware of how scared she was of meeting people. Yes, she saw new faces at the newsagent's but that was different. She didn't need to become friendly with them, only interact, and, besides, the large wooden counter was between them and her.

Today Syd Kennedy had come in, his teeth shining white in his oil-splodged face, and had stood discussing the weather with her. He'd made her laugh. He said the wind whistled through his garage workshop like a fart in a colander. Naturally she couldn't help giggling. Then he'd gone red, blushing with awkwardness at his choice of words. Mrs Harrington had come in then with a cup of coffee and a bun for her so Syd had paid Jo for his paper and left hurriedly.

Mrs Harrington had told her Syd was a nice man whose wife had died some years ago in childbirth. 'That man is as straight as a die. He wouldn't have it when my husband told him not to bother with the few coppers for the laces. He put the money on the counter, shook his head and laughed as he walked out!'

She'd watched Jo bite into her bun. 'Anyway, there's not

a thing in this shop that's not got a price on it now.' Jo had looked up to the top shelf and saw the scribbled pencil marks on the box of odds and ends.

'Oh, Mum!'

Jo heard Rainey's long-drawn-out sigh: it was meant to hurry her. 'Get my coat then.' She smiled as Rainey practically ran down the hallway.

Huddled together, they walked, mindful of the icy pavements, towards St John's School.

Jo could feel the excitement mounting in her daughter as, eagerly, she pushed open the door to the music room. Jo stopped, took a deep breath – and froze. The half-glass door slid shut behind Rainey, leaving Jo in the corridor, her heart beating fast and her neck prickling with fear. Through the glass, she could see a semi-circle of chairs containing women and girls of various ages. All were laughing, talking loudly and totally unaware of her. It was but seconds that she stood outside alone but to her it seemed hours.

Suddenly the door was pulled open, and in front of her stood a rounded woman with fair hair and a beaming face. Rainey had made a beeline for Ivy, the girl she'd met at the teacher's evening, and was totally unaware that Jo hadn't followed her into the room.

'Welcome, I'm Maud Herron.' Her hand snaked towards

Jo's arm and pulled her gently into the warmth and noise. 'There's nothing to worry about, we're all mates here. But I do know exactly how you feel.'

Jo allowed herself to be drawn towards two empty chairs. Maud sat down and said, 'Mrs Wilkes has just answered a call of nature. Be back in a minute. That your girl you come with? Rainey?'

Jo, her head spinning, tried to answer her, but Maud interrupted, 'What's your name, love?'

'Jo,' she managed, looking around once more for her daughter.

As though reading her mind, Maud said, 'Don't you worry about your girl. She's sitting with the young ones. My Bea's with her – she's the blonde – and Ivy. She'll be all right.'

Jo was about to say something but stopped as the door clattered open and Mrs Wilkes swept in with the little dog. 'That's better,' she said, and promptly sat down at the upright piano with its back to the class. Toto curled up beside it, having turned around three times to make himself comfortable.

'Never goes nowhere without that dog, she don't,' whispered Maud. 'It's like a bleedin' shadow.'

Jo looked at Maud's broad-smiling face and immediately felt her fears recede. She grinned back.

'Welcome to our new girls,' said Mrs Wilkes, staring straight at Jo. The position of the piano allowed her to see the class. 'Their names are Jo –' Jo tried to slither down in her seat, '– and Rainey Bird, and I'm sure you lot will make them welcome.' Mrs Wilkes started clapping and the others in the room followed suit.

The welcome over, she sorted through the briefcase of music at her feet, rose from the piano stool and handed out a sheaf of foolscap papers to a woman at the end of the line. 'Pass these along, Meg, if you wouldn't mind.'

'I can't read music,' whispered Jo to Maud. The fear that had been slowly subsiding had come back with a vengeance.

'Anyone can read words,' hissed Maud. And when Jo took a page and passed the rest along she saw the single sheet contained the words to popular carols and well-known winter songs. Her eyes were drawn to 'Jingle Bells'.

'I never knew there was a second verse,' she whispered to Maud.

'Just make sure you get the words right, then,' came Mrs Wilkes's voice. 'We're going to make a start on learning the right words and tunes to these carols.'

'What about the stuff we've been practising?' asked a large woman with spectacles.

'We're going to learn these as well,' Mrs Wilkes said, and

immediately struck a chord on the piano to show who was in charge. Then she looked at her audience, and said, 'I know St John's Choir hasn't been going long but I thought, with Christmas just around the corner, we could sing and make some money for charity.'

Other people would see and hear them sing! Jo's gasp was lost among the cheering that erupted.

Mrs Wilkes silenced everyone with a glare and began to play.

At first Jo was scared to open her mouth so she listened to the voices about her. Some were small, some were loud. Maud nudged her arm. Still unsure, Jo looked at the words on the paper and began hesitantly to join in.

It wasn't very long before she was listening to herself and marvelling at the sound that was coming from deep within her. After a while she began to feel a little more confident. Her singing seemed to be releasing a tension that had been building inside her. She glanced at Maud, who gave her a wink.

After they'd gone through the sheet, with Mrs Wilkes stopping them every so often to explain how the notes should be interpreted and making them all repeat the verses until she was satisfied, Jo saw the hour and a half had passed very quickly.

Maud said, 'You've got a good alto voice.'

Jo looked confused.

'Contralto. This side of the room is the altos, that side the sopranos.' She made a chopping movement in the air with her hand, demonstrating the two halves of the class. 'Don't worry, Mrs Wilkes won't let you strain your voice to sing in a key that's not suitable for you.'

'Oh!' said Jo, thinking she'd ask Rainey what exactly Maud had meant when she got home. She looked behind her for her daughter and saw her putting on her coat while chatting animatedly with Ivy and the blonde girl, who had a voluptuous figure.

'That's my Bea,' said Maud, proudly. 'She's a bit older than your girl and Ivy but Mrs Wilkes likes them to sit together. Bea joined this group when it first started, then talked me into coming along. Your girl goes to St John's with Ivy, doesn't she?' Before Jo could answer, Maud added, 'I believe we both live in the same direction so we might as well walk home together.'

Jo nodded. She'd enjoy that. She was just about to say something when Mrs Wilkes planted herself in front of her. 'How do you feel, Jo? Coming back next week?'

Toto was chasing his tail, not realizing it was the other end of himself. His paws were making clicking noises on the parquet flooring.

'Oh, yes. I really enjoyed it,' she said. In fact, she couldn't remember when she'd last felt so much at ease with herself. It was as if the singing had lifted her and her worries had faded.

'Well done,' said Mrs Wilkes. Then she put out her foot and stopped Toto in mid-whirl. 'Oh, you silly dog,' she said, and followed it up with a loud warning to all the class: 'Learn your words by next week!'

Chapter Nine

'Did Mrs Wilkes get you to sing that stupid song you've been learning?'

Rainey stared at the broad-shouldered young man with the mop of blond hair falling over his forehead. Blue eyes twinkled in a tanned face. He was sitting in the threadbare armchair beneath the window, his long legs draped over one arm. On the other lay a book, cover uppermost: Graham Greene's *Brighton Rock*.

'Mind your own business,' snapped Bea. 'Don't take any notice – he's got a screw loose!' She twirled a finger against her temple and laughed at Rainey. 'Simple, is my brother Eddie.'

Maud didn't pause on her way to the scullery. 'Stop it, you two. I get fed up with your bickering!'

'I'll make the tea, Mum.' The young man, Eddie, rose

fluidly. 'Just don't let her pinch my chair.' Rainey saw Eddie was tall and athletic. He disappeared into the scullery. The smell of dinner still hung in the air.

Bea nipped quickly around the table and sat in the chair her brother had vacated.

He poked his head back around the door. 'I bet you wouldn't jump in my grave as quick as that!'

'Act your age, lad,' came the throaty voice of an elderly man sitting at the table reading a newspaper. 'You wouldn't think two grown kids would squabble so much, would you?' He pushed his spectacles further up his nose. Rainey saw one arm was fixed with sticking plaster. He was obviously talking to her so she shook her head.

'Well, sit yourselves down,' said Maud. She pointed to several chairs around the table and an armchair nearer the fire. 'Eddie!' The young man looked into the kitchen. He had a kettle in his hand. 'Let me introduce you to my son. He's a builder, and I wish he'd find some nice young girl and settle down to get him out from under my feet.' She waved towards Rainey and her mother. 'Rainey, Jo,' she said. 'They started at the choir tonight.' He smiled, nodded in greeting and disappeared again. Rainey heard the clink of cups and saucers.

Maud put her hand on the old man's shoulder. 'This is

my late husband's father, Solomon,' she said, 'We all call him Granddad.' Solomon made a mumbling sound. Rainey saw that his hands were shaking as he fiddled with the pages of the newspaper. 'Sit by the fire and get warm, you two.' Maud gestured Rainey and Jo to chairs, then explained to Solomon, 'They live in the next street so I brought them home for a cuppa.'

Rainey watched as her mother squeezed past the table to sit in the armchair. Jo nodded at everyone but Rainey sensed she was out of her depth and patted her hand. Maud had suggested on the way home that the two of them come in and meet her family, and Rainey knew Jo hadn't had it in her to refuse.

The old man was breathing heavily as he hauled himself to his feet. He turned towards the scullery.

Rainey heard Eddie say, 'You want me to come down to the privy with you, Granddad? It's slippery out.'

Maud's lavatory, like Jo and Rainey's, was at the bottom of the garden.

'I can walk there. What am I – a baby?'

The back-door latch clicked and a blast of cold air found its way into the warm kitchen before the door banged shut again.

'You'll have to excuse Granddad. We love him dearly but

he went through the Great War and the gas got him.' Maud paused. 'Not only that, but his nerves are shot to pieces. His nightmares are terrible.' She raised her hands, warming them by the fire. 'He came to live with us when his wife died but there's not room for us all in this place. Squashed in like sardines we are. Eddie has to share the front room with him. There's no way Granddad can manage the stairs. Me and Bea got the bedrooms.'

Rainey heard her mother making sympathetic noises as Maud continued, 'The council are building new homes in Gosport and we've got our name on the list but now with this damn war the men are going in the services and all the building's slowed down. Even materials are getting scarce. My Eddie knows all about that – he's had to let men go.'

As if on cue Eddie appeared in the doorway, carrying a tray containing a brown teapot, crockery, milk and sugar. He set it on the table. 'Can someone else see to this? I'd best go down and make sure the daft ol' bugger hasn't fallen on the ice.' Rainey could tell by the gentle way he spoke about his grandfather that he cared deeply for him. Eddie stared at her, as if noticing her for the first time. 'Sorry I didn't greet you properly before.'

'It's all right,' Rainey said. 'If I hadn't come here you'd still be sitting reading in your favourite chair.'

Bea cut in: 'After you've drunk your tea do you want to come up to my bedroom?'

Rainey wasn't sure how to answer that, but as Eddie turned to leave he said, 'Don't let her start singing up there!' And then he was gone. Maud was setting out the cups and saucers.

Bea grabbed hold of Rainey. 'We'll have our tea later.'

Rainey heard Maud ask Jo, 'You didn't say how you washed up here in Gosport? Unmarried mum, are you?'

'Something like that.' Jo's reply was quick.

As Rainey trudged up the steep stairs after Bea, she decided if that was what Maud thought, she'd go along with the story. After all, neither she nor her mother could tell the exact truth in case her father came looking for them. And Jo had had Rainey very young, so what other answer could there be? Her wedding ring was no protection against rumour.

At the top of the stairs, Bea said, 'I haven't closed the blackout curtains.' Rainey waited outside the back bedroom until the light went on, then followed Bea inside.

It was of a similar size to her own but there the resemblance ended. A double bed covered with a candlewick bedspread was unmade. Dresses hung from the dado rail. Underwear was piled on a chair near the bed. A mirror was propped on the top of a chest of drawers and face powder spilled from a compact onto the wooden surface, mingling with glass earrings and necklaces. Used to austerity as she was, Bea's room reminded Rainey of Aladdin's cave. The air was heavy with perfume. Rainey thought it was the loveliest bedroom she'd ever seen – and gasped when she spotted the portable gramophone perched on a kitchen chair by the side of the bed.

She pounced on the pile of records beneath the chair. Decca, Victor, Parlophone, Columbia, most were foxtrots and swing. The record on the turntable of the red HMV 102 was Count Basie's 'Swing, Swing, Swing'.

'I'd love one of these,' said Rainey. 'Can't afford it, though.'

'I didn't buy it,' said Bea. 'I get good money at Woolies but it doesn't last long. It was my birthday present from Eddie.' Bea picked up the little tin of gramophone needles and shook it.

Rainey ran her fingers over the handle that wound the machine. 'But I thought you and your brother hated each other.'

'Don't be daft!' Bea was laughing at her. 'We're the best of friends. We just like teasing each other. I'll really miss him when he leaves home.'

'And is he going soon?'

'Probably not. Just when I think he's serious about some girl, it all blows up in his face.'

Rainey laughed. They were a lovely family, she thought. 'Can you play a record?'

Bea looked towards the alarm clock, then shook her head. 'Best not. It's getting late and I'm supposed to be on my best behaviour. Don't want the neighbours banging on the wall because of the noise.'

Rainey glanced at the clock, too. It was almost ten. 'Me and Mum ought to go,' she said.

Bea shrugged her shoulders. 'Before you do, take a look at this.' From a top drawer she pulled out some papers. 'Mrs Wilkes has had me and Ivy learning this one. It's originally an old English folk song. She said it might even be Russian. She's been wanting another voice to harmonize with us. She'll pick you, I know she will.' She tossed her long curls away from her face. Rainey wondered if Bea knew how pretty she was. Betty Grable! Yes, that was who Bea reminded her of.

'I can't start learning anything until Mrs Wilkes asks me . . . if she does.'

'Shall I sing it through for you?' Once more Bea didn't wait for an answer. She sat down on the bed beside Rainey, and although she held the paper in her hand, she didn't look at it.

'Where the bluebird goes, I will follow
Out in the rain
No one knows . . .'

Bea sang softly and with such feeling the words brought tears to Rainey's eyes. Bea's were closed, as if she'd been transported somewhere she had always wanted to be.

When she stopped singing, she opened her eyes and said, 'With Ivy's husky voice in my ear I feel like I'm far away and so happy and sad at the same time I could burst.' She gazed at Rainey. 'I expect you think I'm silly for saying that.'

Rainey found her voice. 'No, no. Oh, the words say exactly how I sometimes feel.' She knew the tune would haunt her. 'I hope I'll be asked to sing with you.'

'Of course you will! Why d'you think she wanted you to join the choir?'

For a moment there was silence.

'You really think so?' Rainey loved to sing. Her mother said she'd been born singing. And for the first time in her life someone, Mrs Wilkes, actually believed she *could* sing!

Bea pushed the words at her. 'Take this and learn them. I already know them.'

Rainey held the paper. 'It's a bit different from the stuff

we sang tonight, isn't it? Could even be sort of swingy, jazzed up a little.'

'Mrs Wilkes is a surprising woman. What we sang tonight is only a little of what she's had us learning. Like she said, now it's coming up to Christmas she wants us to sing in front of people, and any money we make will go to good causes.'

'Rainey, we have to go now. Good thing we never poured out your teas, they would have been wasted!' Her mother's voice came up the stairs.

Rainey turned to Bea. 'Oh, I have enjoyed myself tonight, and with you, Bea. Thank you. I think you and I are going to be good friends, and Ivy, of course.' Impulsively she threw her arms around the older girl, hugging her tightly.

Bea said, 'I'd like that. Ivy's great but she's always got her nose in a book, studying, and you can't prise her away from the café, only if it's for something very special.'

Rainey ran down the stairs, the song sheet folded in her pocket, happier than she'd felt in a long time.

Chapter Ten

'I wish we had presents to give everyone.'

'Mum, the crackers are for everybody and so is the mock apricot flan.' Rainey paused. 'Those carrots, mixed with the last of the jam and some almond essence, really do taste like apricots. And don't forget the potato shortbread.' Rainey's boss had presented her with a box of vegetables as a Christmas bonus.

'I suppose so,' Jo said. 'But it's not like giving everyone a proper present.' Jo hated being unable to afford gifts. 'I was lucky to find that market trader selling crackers so cheaply – there were only a few boxes left. People are stockpiling everything for when rationing comes in. This Christmas is only an imitation of the one we had last year when there was more money . . .' She shivered. The sun was shining but it was very cold on Christmas morning.

'Are you saying you're not happy, Mum?'

'Oh, Rainey, I'm happier than I've been in years.' Her eyes misted. 'I'm sorry to be such a misery. It's lovely of Maud to ask us round to share their Christmas dinner. I've got a card for her – well, for the whole family, really.' Normally Jo liked to send cards but that was another expense she'd had to forgo. She thought of the Christmas card at home in the sideboard drawer. Syd Kennedy had given it to her last night just before she'd left the shop, but of course she'd not sent him one.

Syd had left it on the counter and had been practically out of the shop before he called, 'Christmas card for you, Jo, and have a good couple of days off.'

As the door banged behind him Jo had opened the envelope to find a card with a snow scene and the words, 'Happy Christmas from Syd'. It had made her feel all fluttery inside. Then she chastised herself: he was only being friendly. It meant nothing more than that.

She knew the Harringtons wouldn't expect her to buy them presents: during her and Mrs Harrington's daily coffee chats Jo had let slip she was finding it difficult to manage. Their Christmas box to her was a card with a pound note inside and a thank-you note for being a willing worker. She was also to expect a small pay rise when she returned after the holiday. There were no newspapers published on Christmas Day and Boxing Day so Jo was looking forward to spending her time at home with Rainey.

'Are you enjoying being in the choir, Mum?' Rainey's question surprised Jo.

'Do you need to ask?' To Jo it was the highlight of her week. An hour and a half on a Wednesday evening when she and Maud met on the corner near Forton Road and walked arm in arm to St John's.

She was glad that Bea and Rainey were such firm friends, though she sometimes wondered if the difference in their ages was a good thing. Maud often told Jo of the lads who called for Bea to take her dancing at the Sloane Stanley Hall. As far as Jo knew, Rainey wasn't bothered about boys, or dressing up and dancing. She was pleased that Rainey also spent time with Ivy. With both girls attending St John's and singing in the choir, it was natural for them to be friends, but Jo was relieved that Ivy wasn't as flamboyant as Della, her mother, who was hardly ever at home.

Jo's heart swelled with pride when the three girls sang together. Each had an individual style but their voices complemented each other. All were of a similar build and height but each had individual appeal. Bea was always smiling, her blonde hair a frame for her natural prettiness, while Rainey was a bright Titian chrysanthemum next to Ivy's Cleopatra-like sultriness.

Jo had fallen in love with the soulful words of 'The Bluebird Song'. It was certainly nothing like the popular Christmas songs she and the other women had practised.

The Saturday before Christmas Mrs Wilkes had announced that she'd like as many as possible to turn up near the ticket office at six in the evening to sing for the customers taking ferries to Portsmouth. 'Dress warmly,' she had said. 'It's bound to be blowy near the sea. We'll sing for about forty minutes and I'd like a couple of volunteers to take round baskets for contributions.'

Jo thought she could never ask people for money. Maud had put her hand up, as had another woman, Jean.

Yes, it had been cold, it had even begun to drizzle, but at the end of the singalong Mrs Wilkes had counted the money, thanked them for turning up and said, 'We did well. Nearly ten pounds. I shall make it up to a nice round figure and we'll present it to the Children's Ward at the War Memorial Hospital when we visit them a few days before Christmas. All agreed?' The resounding cheer that followed showed everyone was in agreement.

At first Jo hadn't wanted to sing in a public place. Suppose someone recognized her singing her heart out? Suppose they told Alfie and he came after her?

She'd worn a headsquare and a woollen scarf that hid most of her face, and had tried to hide behind Maggie, a large lady. But Maggie had pushed her forward: 'Get in the front, you're smaller than me.' Luckily Mrs Wilkes had a very dim lantern, and they had to obey the blackout, so even at the front she couldn't easily be seen. Those who had learned their words were fine and able to sing out loudly, but those who hadn't struggled to read in the near darkness. Due to the extreme cold passers-by didn't stand and watch, but they dug in their purses and trouser pockets and put money in the baskets.

Jo now banged on Maud's door.

'Use the key!' Maud's voice came loud and clear so Rainey slipped her fingers through the letterbox, pulled out the key on the string and they went into the warm.

'Welcome,' shouted Maud, from the scullery. She poked her head around the door, her cheeks rosy with heat from the stove. 'I'm seeing to the dinner. Make yourselves comfortable.'

Jo and Rainey had already shed their coats and scarves on the hooks at the front door. Bea called downstairs, 'Come up here, Rainey. Merry Christmas, Jo.' Then she disappeared back into her bedroom where music spilled from the gramophone.

The two men were sitting at either side of the fire, Solomon with his eyes closed but wearing a home-made paper hat that had slipped rakishly over one ear. Eddie put down his book, got up and welcomed them, a big smile on his handsome face. Jo set down her Christmas offerings on the shiny wooden sideboard with a crocheted runner on the top. A pudding dish full of assorted nuts with a nutcracker sat in the middle between a box of dates and a bowl of shiny red apples. She removed the cardboard lid from the crackers but left her clean tea-towel covering the food.

Rainey wished everyone a happy Christmas, then escaped upstairs. Jo saw the wooden kitchen table had had its leaves extended and was set for six, with four kitchen chairs and two wooden orange boxes with cushions. The room was decorated with paper chains that must have taken ages to lick and stick together. Bits of holly peeped from behind the frames of *The Laughing Cavalier* and *The Blue Boy* hanging on the walls. Eddie gave Jo a peck on the cheek, which made him blush. 'Happy Christmas, Jo,' he said. The smell of cooking made her feel hungry.

Eddie was wearing a faded pair of corduroy trousers and a warm grey flannel collarless shirt. Jo saw he had new slippers. 'A present?' she asked softly, not wanting to disturb the old man.

Eddie nodded. Again Jo felt agitated that she'd not been able to bring gifts for everyone.

'There's a cuppa out here with your name on it,' called Maud. Jo stepped down into the whitewashed scullery, where a stone sink was full of dirty pots and pans. Shelves filled with crockery lined the walls, a gas copper sat in the corner and Maud was stirring a saucepan on the gas stove. 'We've got a chicken,' Maud said. 'Eddie always brings home the Christmas dinner. A customer of his has a farm and sets aside something for him as a way of showing his appreciation.'

'I'm only sorry I haven't brought much, but I left crackers on the sideboard along with some potato shortbread and a flan. I hope that's all right?'

'All right? That's wonderful. They'll be lovely at teatime.' Maud went on with her stirring. 'Dinner's nearly ready. Drink your tea, and then if you'd call them two girls we can sit down and eat.'

The dinner was a pleasant affair with everyone chatting and laughing, except Solomon, who was finding it difficult to stay awake.

With the fire glowing, the meal cooked to perfection and the large bottle of sherry that Maud produced from the cupboard, Jo didn't know when she had last felt so content. She had spotted Maud frowning at the level before pouring the drink into glasses.

When she'd filled them for the second time, she stood up and said, 'A toast to all who can't be with us.'

They clinked glasses. Jo thought of Alfie and was glad he wasn't there. She looked nervously at Rainey who had cleared her plate, drunk her first small sherry and was about to start on the second. Her eyes were bright and her cheeks glowing. Jo didn't think Rainey had tasted sherry before. It was sweet, flavoursome and sticky.

'Now, Mum,' said Bea, 'don't get maudlin about Dad.'

'Our father never really recovered from the Great War,' supplied Eddie. He was sitting next to Maud and put his arm around her shoulders. 'His injuries shortened his life. But he was a brave man.'

'You're right, son,' said Maud, smiling at him. She pushed her plate away and stood up. 'Christmas pudding, anyone?'

'Maybe later for me,' said Bea. 'I'm full.' She looked at Rainey, then at Eddie, and said, 'If everyone else is, why don't we three clear the table and wash up while the rest of you have a sit-down? Then we can all play a game. What about whist?'

'Too many for whist,' said Eddie, 'and I can't see Granddad doing anything except looking at the insides of his shut eyes!'

'Don't be horrible,' snapped Bea.

'I wasn't. Anyway, you only need four for whist, and if Granddad sleeps and I read my book, which, by the way, everyone, my lovely sister bought me . . .' He nodded towards the armchair where Agatha Christie's *And Then There Were None* lay face down '. . . that'll take us up to teatime when we can eat cake and try some of Jo's flan and shortbread.'

'Agreed! Everyone?' Bea was obviously pleased by his idea. She'd already started picking up the condiments and sherry bottle ready to take into the scullery. Rainey jumped up and helped.

'Sounds good,' said Jo, 'but I ought to help with the washing-up and clearing away.'

'No, you sit an' talk to me,' said Maud.

Jo looked at Maud in her floral wraparound pinafore. She still had a headscarf tied turban-wise around her hair with three curlers poking out at the front. She had been so intent on preparing dinner for them she'd not thought about prettying herself. Jo thought how lucky she was to have such a good friend.

'It's not Christmas every day,' Maud added. Then she frowned. 'I heard on the wireless that men are being called up left, right and centre.'

Jo was watching Eddie, who was stacking dirty plates on

top of each other. 'You'll miss Eddie when he goes,' she said, as he carried the plates into the scullery.

'Don't upset him,' Maud said, as though Eddie was still in earshot. 'He wanted to go into the air force but he failed the medical. Rheumatic fever as a kid left him with a heart murmur. Fair cut up about it he was and still is.'

'That's a shame,' said Jo, softly. She could imagine the tall, good-looking young man in an air-force-blue uniform. She could almost feel his distress at not being able to fight for his country.

Maud was foraging in a drawer and pulled out a pack of well-used playing cards. Then she stepped over Solomon's outstretched legs. 'Why don't you sit back near the fire,' she said kindly, helping him up and settling him in the comfortable armchair. 'He'll soon doze off again,' she said to Jo. She then plumped up the cushion on the other armchair ready for Eddie. She busied herself setting the four kitchen chairs around the table and putting the orange boxes in the corner. From the scullery came the sounds of great hilarity, followed by Eddie saying sharply, 'No!'

Maud listened, shrugged, then continued tidying.

The three voices were high, the girls giggling every so often and clattering dishes.

Jo smiled at Maud. 'That was a lovely dinner,' she said.

'My pleasure. After a good game of cards we'll start on the tea,' Maud said. She was now at the sideboard and picking out six crackers, which she set to one side. 'Thanks for these. We'll pull them at teatime, when everyone's slept off the meal.' She nodded towards Solomon. 'There's a few left in the box still.' Suddenly she frowned. 'Where's that bottle of sherry?' Then she answered her own question: 'The little blighters! They've taken it into the scullery. No wonder they all sound so happy doing the washing-up.'

Jo didn't know what to say so she kept quiet. She'd never known Rainey touch strong drink before. She'd been the first to turn up her nose at the smell of it on Alfie when he'd come home from the pub. But hadn't she seen Rainey drink the small glass at the dinner table, then accept a second?

Just then Eddie stepped back into the kitchen. 'All done,' he said brightly. He made his way around the table to the armchair and sat down opposite his sleeping grandfather. He picked up his book and began to read. Maud was staring intently at her son.

He must have felt her gaze for he looked up. 'All right, Mum?' Jo decided he hadn't touched any of the missing sherry. Or, if he had, he was hiding it well.

Next to come into the kitchen was Rainey, who still carried a tea-towel and looked as if she had no idea where to put it. She gave a giggle and left the damp cloth on the polished wooden surface of the sideboard near the box of crackers.

Jo's heart fell. She knew immediately that Rainey had been drinking the sherry. Her coordination was shot to pieces as she retrieved the tea-towel and dropped it again, saying, with another giggle, 'Whoops!'

Jo's eyes flew to Maud, who was staring at Rainey as if she had never seen her before in her life. Another giggle and a push from Bea made Rainey stumble. She held on to the sideboard for support.

Bea said, moving past her, 'Oh, goody, crackers.'

Jo saw Eddie shake his head as he mouthed, 'I'm sorry, Mum,' at Maud, shrugging as he added, 'I couldn't stop Bea. You know what she's like.'

Bea, in a heightened mood of joy, grabbed two crackers and, with one in each fist, turned to Rainey. 'Come on,' she said. 'A double pull, one in each hand.'

Rainey's fingers tightened round the ends and Jo watched as the girls pulled the crackers that exploded with two sharp bangs, one after the other. Rainey squealed and fell to her knees, looking for the cracker's contents, but Jo's attention was quickly drawn to Granddad Solomon who, eyes open wide with fear, had slid down onto the mat and tried to crawl beneath the table. Fat tears fell from his eyes as he began shaking and putting his hands over his ears while he rocked backwards and forwards, keening.

'Stop it, you two, this instant!' Maud yelled at Rainey and Bea. Then she dropped to her knees, put her arms around Solomon and tried to soothe him.

Eddie was also on the floor, his arms around Solomon. He looked up at Jo. 'Those loud bangs have reminded him of the exploding shells from the trenches during the war. He can't get over it.' He glared at Bea. 'I told you two simpletons to leave the damn drink alone.' Rainey and Bea were looking sorry for themselves.

'What can I do?' Jo asked. 'I'm so sorry – I don't know what's got into Rainey.' She glared at her daughter. 'Shall we go home, Maud?'

'Make a fresh pot of tea,' said Eddie. 'Me and Mum'll get Granddad to bed in the front room.'

Jo knew she must have looked worried, for Maud said, 'Kids take a drop of drink and don't think about the consequences. There was a good half a bottle left. They should never have been so thoughtless. Maybe it's my own fault for not putting that sherry away sooner. Bea's been getting quite a taste for the hard stuff lately. It's not your Rainey's fault. You just make a nice pot of tea, love.' To Bea, in a very sharp voice, she said, 'You go to your room, take Rainey with you, and I don't want to hear a peep out of either of you. If you dare to play that blasted gramophone I'll come up there and break every record you've got.'

The two girls shuffled off upstairs.

Granddad was sobbing as Eddie and Maud managed to haul him along to the front room.

Jo busied herself making tea. After a little while Eddie came back and stood in the scullery doorway. 'Sorry you had to witness that,' he said. 'He can't escape the horrors of war and, as a rule, Bea knows better.'

'It wasn't only Bea. Rainey must share the blame,' she said. 'When I get her home, I'll talk to her. I don't keep drink indoors – it's too expensive for one thing, and both she and I have seen what it can do . . .' She paused. She didn't want to tell him about Alfie and how he grew nastier the more he had to drink.

Eddie pulled out a tray and set it on the wooden draining-board. 'Bea quite often goes out with her mates from work and doesn't know or want to know when to stop swilling it back.'

Jo didn't want to hear him blaming his sister so she changed the subject. 'Solomon must have had a hard time of it during the Great War.'

'He won't talk about it,' said Eddie, putting cups and saucers on the tray. 'Never has. Some days you wouldn't think there's anything wrong.' He began pouring milk into a jug. 'Granddad can be chatty and he plays a good game of draughts, but the next day the tiniest thing, a noise, a newspaper picture, a song, can set him off. It's like living with two different people.'

'Surely the doctors have an opinion.'

'They know exactly what's wrong with him. Shell shock, it's called. They kept him in a special hospital for a long time, and when he came home they said he needed care and a stable environment. He used to sit alone for hours in a shed in the garden, Mum said. Apparently it was a leaky old thing but he wouldn't budge from it.

'You see, he'd been gassed in Ypres. He wouldn't talk about what had happened . . .'

'Telling my friend all the family secrets, Eddie?' Maud had returned from the front room. 'He's asleep now. I gave him one of his tablets.' She sighed. 'I'll be happier when Solomon can move into Lavinia House.' Jo must have looked confused. Maud continued, 'It's a big old house at Bridgemary. A fully trained nurse owns it. She lives there on call twenty-four hours a day. There's a cook and a cleaner. The lodgers are all elderly. It will be warmer for him than this draughty house and I could do with a rest.' Maud drew a hand across her forehead. 'I don't want him to leave us but I can visit practically every day.'

Eddie took up the tale. 'It wouldn't be so bad if we could move to a bigger house but the council give priority to families with young children, as they should.'

Maud poured the boiling water into the teapot. 'Look, it's Christmas afternoon. What say we three relax in front of the fire and make a start on Jo's apricot flan?'

Chapter Eleven

May 1940

Blackie had no idea of how much time had elapsed. It came to him one morning that the shock of what had happened with the corporal and the tank was passing; it would never entirely leave him but he must go on living. He no longer broke out in a sweat at every burst of gunfire. He had no map, no compass or rations. He had prised a water container from one of the dead Germans' belts. He had a haversack containing his gas mask and his own canteen of water. He also had a rifle and rounds of ammunition. The incessant enemy machine-gun fire made the nights long, and the air stank of cordite and death.

It seemed to him that it would be only a matter of time before he was taken prisoner or killed, or perhaps so badly wounded that he would wish he were dead. Arras: the name was familiar. Was that where he was? Or had he dreamed it in one of the snatches of sleep he allowed himself?

For some time now he had existed by living rough in the countryside, stealing from deserted derelict farms that had already been ransacked. Wherever he went he was conscious of the smell of rotting flesh – farm animals and human. The snow and ice that must have disguised the stench had long been replaced by a thawing sun and he noticed green shoots pushing through the earth; the chill in the air had been replaced with blessed warmth that only reminded him of how strongly the stench of his own stale sweat clung to him.

When he came upon human habitation in a wrecked village he thought at first his imagination was playing tricks on him. He discovered two British men cowering in the cellar of a house.

'You were lucky we didn't kill you,' one of them, Pete, said. He was a weedy man, tall and thin, like a tree that had outgrown its strength.

The sky showed through the ceilings. They'd found the makings for coffee. Water boiled courtesy of a Primus stove. Blackie had been so long without living company that his confidence was knocked sideways.

Malc, Pete's mate, said they were part of the rear-guard of the British Expeditionary Force. 'We were blowing up bridges until we got cut off from our unit.'

Blackie took an instant liking to him. He was a family man who insisted on showing photographs of his wife and kids. It made Blackie think of the picture of the girl he kept in his top pocket, the corporal's daughter.

While they were waiting for the little stove to heat the large pot of water the shelling began again. Sitting there, Blackie could almost believe they were like three youngsters camping out, until the nerve-racking shriek of incoming shells and explosions got nearer.

Malc stirred in the coffee. 'Might not be like yer mother makes it but it'll taste just fine.'

Blackie was thankful he wasn't alone any more. His mouth watered at the thought of the hot drink. 'The bloody mortar bombs are close,' he said, automatically ducking as noise rent the air.

A volley of shells made the three men dive for cover.

Shrapnel scored a hit in the big saucepan. The hot coffee spurted everywhere.

Blackie cursed, but the word was lost in the swearing coming from Malc and Pete! A hasty retreat across fields and into woodland saved their lives. Blackie was fagged out

– his legs felt like lead – but he knew that to rest would be his undoing.

'I can smell the sea,' said Pete. Blackie thought he was off his head.

Soon they met up with two more British soldiers, who were trying to get to the coast. Dunkirk, Blackie was told. Their orders were to get to Dunkirk.

'We're well and truly scuppered,' said a wounded man with a stick. 'If we can get to the beaches we've been told we can be taken home across the Channel, evacuated, by our own people. It's our only chance. The Germans have taken over the Frenchies' territory and are picking us off like bleedin' fish in a barrel.'

The five men ploughed onwards.

Approaching Dunkirk was like going into Hell. More soldiers joined them. Constant aerial attacks by the Germans meant men fell like flies.

'The town's on fire!' shouted Pete, then copped it with a stray bullet. The hole in his neck was gurgling blood. Malc dropped to his knees. Blackie could see Pete was already out of it. 'Leave him!' he screamed, tackling Malc into a ditch as a plane roared overhead, strafing the ground with gunfire.

'My fuckin' knee!' Malc groaned. 'I've been shot.' His face was running with sweat and dirt.

'Could have been worse,' said Blackie. 'At least we're still alive.' He knew then that he wouldn't leave Malc until they were safe . . . or dead.

Oil tanks blazed. Huge cranes that normally slid along the dockside rails were crumpled and smashed, like broken spiders. Thick smoke covered everything, making it difficult to breathe, but at least it gave them cover from the marauding planes.

Not so the beaches, where live mines awaited them.

'For fuck's sake, would you look at that!' blurted Malc.

Boats of all sizes, warships and small craft, seemed to be running a ferry service.

'The beaches are our best bet,' said Blackie. 'Look! The harbour's packed with sinking and burning ships.'

'No!' gasped Malc. Blackie felt the older man sag against him. He was out for the count but Blackie knew he would somehow find the strength to haul him across the dunes. If only he had something to give the poor bugger. The pain must be excruciating. Blackie had used his shirt as a kind of tourniquet above Malc's knee. 'Go on without me,' Malc mumbled, and his head lolled back again.

'Shut up,' said Blackie. 'I hate Southampton Scummers but I'm buggered if a Pompey bloke would leave one behind.' Malc had let it be known he lived in Southampton.

Portsmouth and Southampton football fans hated each other and their fights were legendary.

Blackie dragged Malc across the dunes, the blackened marram grass cutting every spare bit of flesh it could reach. Masses of men were doing the same, all with one idea: to reach the ships in the sea. Another air raid had the men screaming and cowering. Hundreds of men were in the water queuing to be rescued, and the constant firing from the planes was turning the water red as the bullets hit them. There were corpses floating in the sea. Some still had their tin helmets on. So many bodies, some still alive, but it looked like they were drowning in their own blood.

Blackie waded into the sea, breathing in the stink of cordite. It burned the back of his throat.

He saw a piece of billowing blue material and moved towards it but the nurse who had come to help the dying was dead. He felt as if the carnage about him was not real but a passage in a book or a scene in an uncensored film and wished he could close the book or leave the picture-house.

Malc, buoyed by the water, seemed lighter now.

Blackie pushed him into an over-full rowing boat that wasn't going to stop. He too managed to climb aboard. Something caught at his upper leg, like the bite of sharp shrapnel, perhaps a bullet? The boat was heading towards a destroyer. Shells whistled above his head.

Suddenly the destroyer was hit and began listing. The deck was so close that Blackie could see injured men sliding into the water. They were dragged down by their heavy uniforms. All around him men were dying and Blackie feared for the pull of water that would be the end of him. He'd got this far but death was everywhere. Still he wouldn't let go of Malc.

And then the miracle occurred. A motor torpedo boat threw out rescue ropes. Amazingly, Blackie was able to grab one. The thirty-foot vessel was low in the water and Blackie managed to shove Malc onto the webbing, then strong hands pulled them both aboard.

Blackie was soaking wet and packed like a sardine with the other men. Shivering with cold, and the fear that the small boat would be attacked, he didn't let go his hold on Malc.

'Aw right, mate?' A gaunt man nudged up against him. Blackie could only nod. He was aware only of the pain in his leg.

'With God's will and a few more hours, we'll be out of this carnage,' the man said. 'We're hoping to follow the French coast, then sail west to the North Goodwin Lightship.'

Blackie stared at him. The route meant nothing to him. He felt Malc's body twist beneath his tightly curled fingers.

'Poor buggers,' Blackie heard the man say. He wasn't sure who he was referring to, him and Malc or the poor sods in the water.

'Let's pull him out of the wet.' The man grabbed at Malc, lifting him clearer of the sludge swirling in the bottom of the boat.

Blackie looked about him. There were fishing boats, pleasure craft, yachts and men shoulder high in the sea still waiting and scrabbling to board one. And all the while planes screamed overhead, bombs fell, ships hit mines and bodies disintegrated.

There was still enough feeling in Blackie's hands for him to know that Malc was hanging on to life and that comforted him. He thanked God for the clement weather but the slight wind encouraged the stench from the burning gasometers, the flaming town and the wrecked ships to linger in the air, like mist.

Blackie watched the chaos receding as the thirty-foot vessel chugged further into open water. The gaunt man was staring at him.

'When, if, we reach the Goodwin Sands, Dover'll be our next stop,' he said.

Blackie could only nod.

*

When the boat docked at Dover, Blackie was handed a mug of tea and a paste sandwich that he thought was manna from Heaven. It was the first food he'd eaten in three days. He watched as Malc was loaded into the back of an ambulance, then he was helped in beside him. Blackie, unable to believe he was home, fell asleep.

His dreams were unreal, lurid, of the corporal and how he had come to be in the foxhole.

Chapter Twelve

'Goodbye! Goodbye!!'

The voices in the charabanc rang out loud and clear, perhaps not in tune, definitely not with the right words, but enthusiastically.

'Wasn't it lovely?' Ivy turned to Rainey, sitting next to her. 'I know I'll always remember tonight.'

Rainey stopped singing long enough to squeeze Ivy's hand. 'We could do that,' she said. 'Us three. Our voices are good enough to sing on a stage.'

Ivy thought of the lavish production of *White Horse Inn* at the London Coliseum that Mrs Wilkes had arranged for the choir to see. 'I'd never have enough courage to sing in front of a proper audience like that.'

'Audiences are just people and we've been singing to people.'

'I hardly think singing in the drizzle to passers-by down at the ferry counts as an audience. Nor does warbling away to bedbound people in hospital,' Ivy said. Rainey had more courage than Ivy. It was she who suggested they sway in time to 'The Bluebird Song'. Mrs Wilkes had liked that.

'If you can grab just one person's attention, you have them in the palm of your hand. The rest of the audience will follow suit,' Rainey had said.

Ivy smiled at Rainey. 'I wish I was more like you.'

Rainey said, 'You're an individual. We three complement each other. Our voices are different but we blend well. Otherwise Mrs Wilkes wouldn't bother with us.'

Just then, Mrs Wilkes heaved herself up from her seat at the front, leaving Toto to jump onto it. She motioned for silence. Toto, of course, was not allowed in the theatre so the driver had been in charge of him while the choir watched the production. The man had not been happy about that. He'd mumbled, as the charabanc had emptied, 'I'm a driver not a bloody dog minder.' Nevertheless, when everyone had boarded the vehicle at Charing Cross for the return journey, he'd had the little dog nestled safely in his arms.

'I hope you all enjoyed that treat.' She was interrupted by cheers. 'Pish! Calm down. Now, as you know, St John's School kindly financed our trip for educational purposes and I hope this won't be the last show they'll pay for. I feel it's important for you to see how paid singers, dancers and actors behave on the stage – though, of course, there's only a few of you who can trip the light fantastic.'

'We go dancing, Mrs Wilkes,' shouted Bea. 'At the Sloane Stanley Hall!'

'Is that what you call it, Bea? Dancing?' Mrs Wilkes smiled at her. Everyone laughed, including Bea.

'If my mum had had to pay for this I wouldn't be here,' Rainey said quietly, to Ivy. 'There's no spare money in our house.'

Waving her hands for silence, Mrs Wilkes continued, 'Because we've been collecting money for charity it seems St John's have made us ambassadors for the school. Though, sadly, some of our singers couldn't be here.' Maud hadn't been able to leave Granddad, so Ivy had been told, and Jo had had to work, but most of the choir had taken advantage of the trip. 'I hope you were aware of the strong, harmonious singing during the many crowd scenes. There can only ever be a few outstanding voices but the background singers, the villagers, I shall call them, are every bit as important as the stars. You are a choir.' She waved her hand expansively. 'Not one of you is any more important than the next singer.'

The charabanc lurched and Mrs Wilkes stumbled but, gripping the back of the seat, managed to stay upright.

Bea called, 'I thought it was lovely. I especially loved Gretl with her lisp.'

Another voice shouted above Bea's: 'Josepha was the star!'

'Well, I'm glad you all enjoyed *White Horse Inn*.' Mrs Wilkes had waved her hand again for silence, but the choir's high spirits had taken over and once more the charabanc was filled with songs from the show. Ivy heard her say, 'I think they all liked it,' as she gathered up Toto and placed him on her lap. Ivy also saw the smile of contentment on her face before she sat down.

She said, 'My mum's agreed I can go to the dance on Friday night as long as I come home when you do.'

Rainey grinned. 'Well, my mum said it's all right for me to go as long as I walk back with you.'

They beamed at each other, then joined in with the singing.

Through the open doorway of the Sloane Stanley Hall's Spring Dance Rainey could see Bea in the garden. The young soldier had his arms around her and was kissing her fiercely. When Rainey had first spotted the dark-haired man in khaki he had been pulling Bea across the dance-floor, but she'd seemed eager enough to follow him outside.

Rainey hated herself for watching, like some Peeping Tom, but she had the feeling something was wrong, especially in the way the soldier had tipped the small bottle to Bea's lips. Bea had thrown back her head afterwards and laughed, then stumbled against him but had, nevertheless, taken another drink.

The couple were partially hidden behind an elm tree and Rainey felt guilty. After all, Bea was older than herself and Ivy. Maybe that was normal behaviour for eighteen-year-olds.

A shiver went down her back as she remembered the scenes she'd stumbled into when her father, drunk, was mauling her mother. Intervening had resulted in her getting in the way of a fist but she'd seen the sorrow and gratitude in her mother's eyes.

'Are you a wallflower?' Ivy sat down heavily beside her. She was breathless after a foxtrot. Rainey never expected to be asked to dance. She knew she was pretty – someone had told her she looked like Rita Hayworth – but she thought that somehow she exuded the sort of unscented perfume from her pores that told the opposite sex to stay away from her. Even at school, where almost every girl had a boyfriend, or at least someone who fancied her, she couldn't stand in the cloakroom swapping tales: there was nothing to tell.

'Thank you,' said the tall, skinny lad, who had brought

Ivy back to her seat. He melted into the crowded dance hall that smelled of cheap perfume, sweat and cigarette smoke.

Rainey said, 'Yes, and I thought there was no drink allowed here.'

'You know there isn't. It's just tea and lemonade.'

'If Bea has any more she'll fall over.' Rainey hadn't meant to sound so scathing, but since the sherry episode at Christmas, she'd been wary of Bea's motives.

'What d'you mean?'

'Just look out of that door and you'll see.'

Ivy stared into the garden. Then she leaped from her chair and battled her way through the dancers.

Within moments Rainey saw Eddie moving swiftly along the seated people at the edge of the dance-floor. A girl with long dark hair and a face like thunder was staring after him. Ivy tagged behind him, trying to keep up with him.

As Eddie and Ivy charged into the garden, the back door slammed.

Rainey wanted to follow them, but thought Eddie and Ivy could cope quite well. Bea wouldn't be happy that too many people should witness what was about to happen or, indeed, had already taken place.

The five-piece band was still playing and couples were smooching to a waltz when the back door snapped open.

The young soldier staggered through, blood streaming from his nose that his red handkerchief wasn't capable of staunching. He didn't speak or look around, simply hurried out of the big front doors. Drops of blood made small shiny circles on the parquet flooring.

Rainey drank some of her flat lemonade.

A few surprised dancers watched the soldier's exit but the band continued playing and the couples didn't falter in their steps.

With the soldier gone Rainey could imagine Eddie and Ivy attending to Bea. She wanted to go out to them but her imagination had taken over. Supposing the soldier had hurt Bea. It would be like seeing her mother after her father had attacked her. She'd rather not have to look at the damage.

Her mind drifted back to before the dance when she and Ivy had called for Bea at her house. They'd lounged in her bedroom, while Bea put finishing touches to her make-up, and admired her discarded dresses. Rainey had even picked up a couple and put them on hangers, hooking them up on the picture rail. One, a soft green wool, was featherlike to the touch and Rainey wanted so much to try it on, knowing its colour would enhance the orange lights in her hair. 'This is gorgeous,' she'd said.

'Have it, if you want,' said Bea.

Rainey had shaken her head. The dress was cut low. Her mother would have a fit if she saw Rainey in it. Besides, Bea was bigger up top than Rainey was and she knew the dress would hang dejectedly on her. It made Bea look glamorous, like a gangster's moll she'd seen in a film.

'You have lovely clothes,' said Rainey.

'I've been working since I left school at fourteen,' answered Bea.

Eventually Bea chose a deep red dress that clung to her like a second skin and flared out about her knees.

'You'll show your suspenders if you twirl fast in that,' Ivy warned. She had her black school skirt on and a fluffy pink jumper with a pretty marcasite brooch in the shape of a star her mother had lent her. Knowing Ivy was going to wear her black skirt, Rainey had decided to do the same.

'So what if I show my stocking-tops? They're bought and paid for!' said Bea, with a shake of her blonde hair.

Arm in arm they'd walked to the Crossways, Bea chattering about some of her friends from Woolworths who were going to be at the dance. Rainey remembered that even then Bea had scoffed at the beverages to be on sale. 'Some of my friends will bring little bottles of refreshments,' she'd said, with a wink. 'That gets people in the mood.'

'I'm excited enough,' said Ivy, then, 'I thought Eddie might be coming?'

'He'll be there. He's gone to pick up Dolores, some new girl he fancies.'

Ivy had gone quiet. Eddie was very good-looking, thought Rainey, but much too old for Ivy to think about. That was if she ever thought about him at all. Usually Ivy prattled on about Leslie Howard, who had played Ashley Wilkes in *Gone With the Wind*. Too much of a milk-sop, thought Rainey. From what she'd seen of men, they said they cared, then ended up knocking ten bales out of the woman they were supposed to love. Even Rhett Butler had left Scarlett in the end.

The door opened. Ivy and Eddie emerged with Bea clamped firmly between them. She had on fresh lipstick but her eyes were swollen, like she'd been crying. She was smiling but Rainey knew she was pretending.

Most of the dancers were totally involved in the music and only one or two people stared at the trio walking towards Rainey.

When they reached the table, Eddie said, sounding impatient, 'I've got the van outside. I'll give you a lift home. Better not walk back alone in the dark. These two are coming with me.' He looked tired. There was a red mark down the side of his cheek.

'And Dolores?' Rainey asked. It seemed only polite to ask after the girl he'd brought to the dance.

'She's going home with her friends. Thanks for looking out for Bea,' he said, as though his sister wasn't standing next to him.

It was then Rainey noticed Ivy's brooch was holding together a tear at the front of Bea's red dress.

Chapter Thirteen

'Toto, come in, you silly dog.' Alice Wilkes pulled her long cardigan about her ample figure. The nights in May could be chilly and standing at the back door, waiting for her pet to complete his business in her large, leafy rear garden, had its disadvantages. Her little darling loved to disappear among the trees and bushes that separated her house from the beach at Stokes Bay. 'Toto,' she called again, and was relieved to hear scuffling as he emerged from the undergrowth.

Alice bent down and the small white dog jumped into her arms. Her heart leaped with joy as his wet, warm tongue licked her cheek.

After pulling the blackout curtains closed, she set down the dog. Immediately he made for the kitchen and his water bowl, his paws slithering over the lino. Alice smiled at the small footprints. She turned on the two electric lamps either side of the fireplace in the sitting room and picked up the *Evening News*, positioning herself on the comfy sofa.

'Would you believe the German troops are being issued with English phrase books for when they invade our shores?' Toto jumped up on the sofa and nuzzled her hand, making the newspaper crackle. 'Pish! They'll find it difficult with all the barbed wire on the shoreline, won't they? The submerged mines will soon put a halt to their nonsense.' She sniffed and pushed her reading glasses further up the bridge of her nose. 'They'll never get to us. Our boys will make sure of that, don't you worry.' Toto wagged his tail.

Alice was tired. Her choir had been lively tonight. She'd introduced the idea of doing a pantomime: *Snow White*. If they began practising again now it should be ready before Christmas. Bea, Rainey and Ivy could perform 'The Bluebird Song' to break it up a bit.

She yawned. After she'd cycled home with Toto in the wicker basket on the front of her bike, all she'd wanted was a cup of tea and a sit-down. Sometimes she wished she was nearer St John's, but she'd lived in this house nursing her parents during the influenza outbreak that had scoured the country after the Great War. Her mother had died first. She'd thought she'd never have to face the horror again.

Daddy had been blue in the face, trying to catch his

breath, and she'd cried because she couldn't make him as clean as she wanted because clots of blood kept pouring from his mouth.

He'd died, like so many others. She'd inherited this house and a little money. She'd given up her dream of playing the piano professionally. Deep in her heart she knew she wasn't good enough to become a concert pianist, even though music was her passion. When Alice sat at the piano she could allow whatever mood she was in to pour through her fingers onto the keys. The music released her anger, her frustration, even her occasional happiness. She could hold a tune, too, not singing brilliantly but enough to accompany herself as she played the popular songs of the moment. Later, her job as a music teacher had given her something to focus on while she waited for news of Graham. She was still waiting now, if the truth be known.

Graham wasn't hers. She'd wanted him to be but he couldn't leave a wife and two little boys, could he? And Alice wasn't a home-breaker.

It was enough that they met for walks along the beach and sometimes a picnic in Stanley Park. They'd first met just after the Great War had begun. Gosport's Silver Band was in fine fettle and she'd been sitting in a deckchair in the sun, enjoying the music, when she'd dropped her programme. Bending to the grass to retrieve it she'd bumped heads with the man next to her, who was trying to pick it up for her. They'd begun chatting, and afterwards walked along the front.

Then she'd looked forward to seeing him on the occasional Sunday to listen to the band. His wife didn't share his love of music. He could play the piano, the violin, compose, and he taught music at a private school in Southsea.

Alice lived for those few stolen hours with Graham, the delight of tea and custard creams in the sea-front café where they discussed music. There was never anything improper. The most she'd ever asked him was his first name.

He loved shows and films too, again something she was interested in, though she had little time to spare for them.

He'd been genuinely upset that fateful afternoon when he'd told her he had to go and fight. She wondered, distressed, how the children would fare without their father and how his wife would cope. She wanted to tell him she would miss the Sunday walks that had become the highlight of her week but she didn't. After all, what right had she to say such things to a married man?

She wasn't gregarious and, besides, her parents didn't like her to bring friends home. Or for her to visit others. 'Don't impose on people,' her father said.

The children at St John's sometimes called her Mrs Wilkes.

She never said she wasn't or hadn't been married. It suited her to let everyone think she was a war widow.

Alice put down the paper. There was hardly ever anything but bad news in it, except that John Steinbeck, her favourite author, had won the Pulitzer Prize for *The Grapes of Wrath*, which Alice had thought superb.

She rose, trying not to wake Toto, but he opened his eyes anyway, then jumped down to follow her into the kitchen.

'A cup of tea and a biscuit?' Alice had had dogs all her life but Toto was special, her shadow, her friend. 'The choir was in fine voice tonight, wasn't it?' She often asked questions but was well aware her dog wouldn't reply, though sometimes he looked at her and she could have sworn he'd understood every word.

She began making a pot of tea, all the while thinking how hard the women had worked tonight. She hadn't told them yet, but she intended to enter them in the Fareham Music Festival. Two classes: one as a choir; the other, Ivy, Bea and Rainey singing 'The Bluebird Song'. She'd never attempted anything like that before. And, of course, it wouldn't do to tell them just yet. Why worry her singers unnecessarily?

'It would certainly be a feather in the cap of St John's if they win, wouldn't it, Toto? And it'll give them something else to think about instead of this blasted war with Germany.'

Chapter Fourteen

Summer 1940

'Guess what I've been doing!' Jo rushed into the kitchen, setting down two brown carrier bags with string handles on the table, then throwing her cardigan onto a chair, not that she'd needed it today as the weather had been sweltering. She could smell something cooking and hear Rainey singing in the scullery.

'Well, I hope you've been to work.' Rainey poked her head around the door. 'The kettle's on. I've got sausages in the oven and I was given some veg that have gone a bit floppy but they'll cook up all right.' Her eyes fell on the bags. 'What have you got?'

'Let me start at the beginning.' Jo felt like a young girl. She had a grin a mile wide. 'When I got to Alverstoke today there was bunting hanging everywhere and people were putting up stalls beneath the trees and through the streets. Mrs Harrington told me it was the August Fayre.' Jo eased off one shoe, flexing her toes. 'Ah, that's better. Well, I must have looked daft because Mrs Harrington said they hold the fayre every year. All the shops stay open late because the village gets filled with people coming to buy stuff, and she said the Silver Band marches through playing . . .'

'Slow down, Mum.' Rainey was laughing at her.

Jo took a deep breath. 'I served in the shop until twelve, then Mr Kennedy – you know, Syd from the garage – came in to get his paper. I've never seen him without his overalls. He had a suit on, very smart he looked, but it was boiling hot outside. I was warm in the shop, even in this.' She smoothed down her blue summer dress with the sweetheart neckline.

'"Surely you're not keeping Jo in here all day when there's all sorts going on outside," he said, and guess what?' She looked at Rainey.

'I couldn't possibly,' said Rainey.

'Mr Harrington told me to get out among the stalls and take my purse with me to pick up a few bargains. He said to Syd, "Go with her to keep an eye on her!"' Jo kicked off her other shoe. 'Well, you could have knocked me down with a feather. So there I am, wandering along the village streets in the sunshine, and look!' From one of the bags a green lampshade with a fringe appeared. 'Threepence!' She thrust it into Rainey's hands. 'Go lovely in your bedroom that will, and it's hardly got a mark on it.' Then she dived into the brown bag again and this time brought out a cream silk blouse. 'If you don't want this I'll have it.' She shook it, releasing the smell of lavender. 'Go nice with my grey slacks.' Then she tipped books onto the table. 'We've got enough to read here until next summer.'

She picked up the second bag, which was heavier, and took out a large sponge cake wrapped in greaseproof paper. 'It's an eggless sponge. Got it off the WI stall with some home-made jam and chutney. They sell stuff ever so cheap, and because it's from the Women's Institute you know it's good.'

Jo stood back and admired her purchases. 'I think I did very well,' she said. Then, 'Oh, I got you this.' She foraged in the bag again and came out with a little velvet pouch bag.

'What's that?'

'Open it and see.'

Jo watched as her daughter released the strings of the pouch and onto the table fell a silver cross and chain. 'Mum, it's beautiful.' Rainey turned it over in her fingers.

Jo could see she really liked it. 'All the stuff on the stalls comes from the people of the village. The woman who sold it to me said it had belonged to her daughter. She looked very sad. I didn't ask any questions but I knew you'd love it.'

Rainey was turning the necklace over in her hands. 'Perhaps she lost her daughter.' She lifted her head. 'It's beautiful, thank you.'

In the silence that followed Jo saw tears in Rainey's eyes. 'Thought you were making me a cup of tea,' she said. 'I'm parched.'

A while later, sitting at the table, Jo was listening to the singing coming from the scullery and drinking her tea. Then Rainey stopped in the middle of a song and called to her. 'So who's this Syd, then?'

'I've told you about him before,' said Jo, though in truth she wasn't sure whether she had or not. 'He comes in for his paper every day. He owns a small garage.' She laughed, remembering that after they'd been to the fayre he'd taken her on a tour of his empire, as he called it. The garage was in Coward Road. He didn't sell petrol, it was more a workshop with living accommodation above. With the shutters raised, he showed her the large bay where he mended cars. It was very oily in there and she'd had to walk carefully to keep her dress from brushing against greasy fixtures. He didn't show her his living quarters, which was fine because she wasn't sure about being alone with him, or any man for that matter.

'Would you like a quick drink in the Village Home?' he'd asked. 'They stay open longer today.' The pub had been heaving with customers.

She'd felt quite guilty sitting there when she knew she should have been at work in the paper-shop. But Mr Harrington had insisted she go and enjoy herself.

In the pub the talk had been all about the air raid on Gosport.

'Imagine the vicarage at Spring Garden Lane being the first place to cop old Hitler's bombs,' said a woman.

'Our Anderson shelter's been delivered but it's not up yet,' confessed Jo. 'We hid under the stairs during the raid. My daughter and I were terrified by the noise. The searchlights showed through the blackout curtains.'

Syd came back from the bar with a port-and-lemon and a pint. Obviously he'd caught the end of the conversation: 'I'll pop round and dig the shelter in for you,' he said.

Jo was too embarrassed to answer him so she smiled instead. While she sat there sipping her drink she saw through the pub's windows that the stallholders were packing up. She thought how Syd had waited patiently by her side as she sifted through clothes and bric-à-brac. She'd glanced at him, fearful he was bored. Alfie had refused to go shopping with her, said it was woman's work. On the odd occasion it was necessary he had moaned constantly. But Syd carried her bags and chatted, seeming happy to be in her company. Sitting in a pub with him had felt very strange, but nice.

Rainey brought her back to the present. 'I think you like Syd, and I bet Mr Harrington engineered your afternoon so you could be together.'

'Don't be so daft!' Jo felt herself colour. 'And where's them sausages, I'm starving!'

But she wondered if there was any truth in what Rainey had said.

Chapter Fifteen

Bert gave a final polish to the maple tippling stick. In its handle, hidden from view, was a small flask that had once contained whisky. It amazed him, the many dual personalities sticks and canes had. He set it down beside another favourite, the one with a compass in the handle.

He'd started collecting walking sticks when he'd come across one beside the body of a German soldier in a trench during the Great War. The dead man had been pretty high-ranking and the stick, despite the mud, had glittered in the pale sun. Bert saw why: it was a swordstick and the blade had been half drawn from its sheath. And so began his obsession with sticks.

To most people they were simply an aid to walking, but to Bert every stick told a story, and he was proud of the collection he'd built up over the years from rummage sales

and second-hand shops. He put them into three catego-
ries: professional, which contained the tools of an owner's
trade; novelty, which held opera glasses, spectacles, cameras,
snuffboxes, pillboxes, or had carved animal heads and more;
and weapons, the older, the better. He'd read of a con-
cealed blade found in a stick in Tutankhamun's tomb. He
didn't have one as old as that but he was the proud owner
of a stiletto-hatchet cane, found at a school bring-and-buy
sale. He also had a life-preserver, a cane with spikes folded
into the handle, a past favourite of ladies of the night as
they walked the streets touting for business. The swordstick
was his particular favourite. It hung beneath the counter in
case any of his customers turned nasty. It was intended to
frighten, certainly not to maim. Bert was too soft-hearted
for that.

He rose from the armchair and gathered the sticks
together, putting them safely in the cupboard with his
cleaning materials.

He walked to the window high above North Street and
peered across at the harbour. It was in darkness now but
who could fail to be moved by the sight of it in daylight?
Ships and tankers, ferry boats – even Nelson's *Victory* was
there for everyone to feast their eyes upon, and he had a
bird's eye view.

He was tired but knew he wouldn't sleep yet on such a warm night. Maybe a drop of whisky might help. He looked around his room, which contained a double bed, a table and chair, a chest of drawers, a wardrobe and a shelf of books, mostly classics, that he dipped into occasionally.

All the rooms in the three-storey lodging-house-cum-café were simple but clean. Some had their own sinks and gas stoves. He had a few regular tenants, but everyone had to share the lavatory at the bottom of the garden with his café customers. He kept that clean by swilling it out every day and frequently lime-washing the walls and floor.

Bert lifted the sash window and let in the stuffy night air. He breathed deeply. He could smell cordite and brick dust from the last raid that had played havoc in Portsmouth. The dockyard was the prime target, along with the ships moored in the harbour.

He thanked God he wasn't expected to fight again. The Great War had been bad enough. His lungs were scarred with the gas, so bad he'd had to stop fighting in the boxing ring. The fear of the gas had never gone away. Nightmares left him shaking with terror, and damp cold weater often left him short of breath. He'd left the services and the hospital in his thirties, with money enough to buy this café on the corner. He'd been there ever since. He could still handle himself against drunken customers, if the need arose, but now he was in his fifties he wasn't as nippy on his feet as he used to be. Mind you, he still had his hair and all his own teeth.

He closed the blackout curtains and put the light on. This room was his sanctuary. He went to the chest of drawers and pulled out the bottle of whisky, pouring himself a nip. He wouldn't let himself wonder what Della was up to.

It was enough that she trusted him to keep an eye on Ivy.

Della. When she'd first turned up in the café one wet, windy night, with the baby in her arms, she'd said her name was Doris. It had changed to Della after she'd met that greasy git Jim in the Fox. Bert had let her live rent-free in return for helping out in the café and mopping down the stairs. He'd felt sorry for the scrap of a child with the big dark eyes. Later, when her hair had grown straight and lustrous, he'd thought Ivy looked like an Egyptian princess.

Della had tried picking up blokes in the café but Bert wasn't having that. He didn't want any trouble with the police and told her so. 'Don't do it on my doorstep,' he'd said. Then she'd met Jim, and overnight she'd become a masseuse. She couldn't even pronounce the word properly! She'd told Bert, 'I'm a sort of nurse and help people to feel better.' Della had told that to Ivy as well. Of course Ivy believed her, until she grew older and discovered the truth.

Ivy was well aware of the relief her mother gave to gentleman callers in the flat opposite the bus station at the ferry, but she wouldn't let anyone say a bad word against her. Ivy knew she couldn't read or write, but Della was determined that Ivy would have the chances she'd never had when she was young and for that she needed money. Ivy loved her mother with a passion unusual in a girl of that age.

Della was proud of Ivy's sultry singing voice, and thrilled when Mrs Wilkes had asked her to join St John's Choir. Bert, too, was proud. He didn't have any kids of his own and to him Ivy was like a daughter.

The woman he'd left behind during the war had gone off with a sailor, and Bert had long since given up on women, except Della, who had wriggled into his heart, like a rainbow after a downpour. Often he'd close up early so he could go along and meet Ivy from St John's when she went to choir practice. Then she wouldn't need to walk home alone in the dark.

'Who is my real dad?' Ivy had asked him once.

'I believe he was a music-hall star with a wonderful voice,' Bert had answered. Then he'd looked at her sadly.

She had started to laugh. 'Pull the other one,' she'd replied. Truth was, he didn't think Della remembered.

He was sipping his whisky, the bottle a present from a customer, when there was a knock on his door.

'Can I go down and get some milk, Bert?' Ivy stood there, small in a long nightdress covered with a silk kimono Della had passed on to her.

Honest as the day was long, was Ivy. Some of the tenants never asked, simply stole stuff from the kitchen downstairs, but not Ivy.

'I've got some here, pet,' he answered. He took a half-full bottle from the pan of cold water standing on the window-sill. Bert didn't need a gas stove in his room but he liked to keep a Primus in case he needed to boil a kettle for tea. Ivy had followed him inside and he could smell Amami shampoo. She must have washed her hair.

'Mum's forgotten to get milk today.'

He handed her the bottle. 'Keep it. I don't need it.'

He could sense her excitement and the words tumbled from her lips. 'Mrs Wilkes is entering us for a music festival at Fareham before Christmas,' she said. 'The judges are influential people and we might even get a certificate if we're good enough.' She paused, then burst out, 'And we're to do the panto this year. She's hired the David Bogue Hall! People will have to pay to see us!'

He looked at her excited face. 'She must think you have a chance of winning a certificate or she wouldn't do that. Is it the whole choir or just a few chosen singers?'

'Bea, Rainey and I are singing "The Bluebird Song" – it's an old folk song – and the choir are going to do a short medley.'

Bert drained his glass and stared at her. 'And do many people enter contests like this?'

'Up and down the country, so Mrs Wilkes said. There'll be choirs from all over competing. If we score enough marks we get a certificate. Mrs Wilkes said we must take advantage of this now before the bombing puts an end to all unnecessary travelling and stops people using public transport up and down the country.'

'And has she got more dates for you lot to sing before Christmas?'

'She has, and more to follow next year, in 1941. The panto is *Snow White and the Seven Dwarfs*.'

'And you are?'

'I'm to be Sneezy!'

Bert chuckled. 'Well, you can put me down for a ticket.'

Chapter Sixteen

'Are you crying?' Syd removed his arm from the back of the cinema seat and Jo felt a handkerchief dancing in front of her face. She took it gratefully.

'It's not real life,' he said softly, 'only Bette Davis working her acting magic up there on the screen.'

'But she thinks she's cured and she's not, and she's going to die.' Jo gave a sniff, trying to hold back more tears.

'Sssh!' came a voice from a seat behind them.

Jo looked at Syd through the swirling cigarette smoke dancing in the beam of light from the film projector in the Criterion Cinema. He was a kind man.

When the film ended, people began shuffling from their seats.

'You ready?' asked Syd, 'This is where we came in.'

Jo sniffed again, tucked his handkerchief up her cardigan

sleeve and began fumbling for her jacket that had slipped to the floor among the empty ice-cream tubs and sweet wrappers.

'So,' asked Syd, standing up, 'did you like *Dark Victory*?'

'I did,' Jo said. 'Bette Davis made me believe in her character and I couldn't help crying for her.'

She'd refused the first time Syd had asked her out, then felt mean because she remembered how shy and tongue-tied he'd been. When he'd scraped together the confidence to ask her again that day in the newsagent's she knew she would agree. When she'd mentioned to Rainey she had doubts, her daughter had told her she was being silly. 'He's on his own, you're on your own. He hasn't asked you to marry him, he just wants to take you to the pictures.'

'But I'm a married woman,' said Jo.

'Not to our new friends in Gosport,' said Rainey. 'They think you're a fallen woman.'

'I still think I'm going to meet your father around every corner.' Jo shivered.

'Now that's stupid, because he doesn't know where we are and more than likely he's now serving abroad. What are you going to do? Stay indoors for ever, only going out one evening a week to choir?'

When Rainey put it like that, Jo realized it made sense.

'Do you miss him, Rainey, your dad?'

Rainey had put her hands on her mother's shoulders and stared into her eyes. Her voice was sarcastic. 'I miss looking at his face as he steps through the door to see what kind of a mood he's in. I miss him hurting you . . .' She'd gathered Jo to her and her voice was softer as she continued, 'That Syd sounds a nice bloke. You liked walking through the fayre with him, didn't you?'

Jo had nodded.

'Go to the pictures with him then, if you want.'

Buoyed with new confidence, when Syd asked again, Jo had agreed. Perversely she thought it was worth the wait to see the delight on his face.

She'd enjoyed his company and the film, and now as he pushed the brass-handled door of the cinema and held it open for her to step onto the pavement, she said, 'Do you want to come to my house for a cup of tea?'

Syd stopped battling through the crush of people leaving the Criterion. 'I don't want to compromise you, a woman on her own with a daughter. If neighbours see a man entering your house they might put two and two together and come up with five.'

'Actually, I've got something I want to show you—'

Jo didn't get any further for a man shouted, 'Don't stand in the doorway. We want to get home, mate!'

Syd took Jo's arm and they melted out into the drizzle.

By the time Syd's van stopped outside Jo's house, the rain was bucketing down and Syd held a newspaper over her hair while she unlocked the front door.

'Phew,' he said. He took off his jacket, shook it, then hung it on a hook inside the door.

'Come on through and sit down. I'll put the kettle on.' Jo put a poker to the range, teased the fire into life, then went into the scullery.

'Nice place you've got here,' she heard Syd say.

'It wasn't when we moved in,' she answered. 'My Rainey did wonders with a scrubbing brush and paint.'

'Where is she tonight?'

'She's round her mate's house. They're practising some music.'

Jo paused, a cup in her hand that she was about to put on a tray. She was alone in the house with a man. Her heart began to beat fast. Don't be silly, she told herself. Don't spoil things. This is Syd and he's a good man. He's not about to hurt you.

But what if . . . ?

The cup slid from her fingers and crashed to the floor.

In an instant Syd was in the doorway, bending down and picking up the shards of broken china. Jo stood, silent, shaking. Then she blurted, 'I've become wary of being alone with a man.'

Syd held the remains of the cup in one large hand. He stared at her, then said, 'I won't stay, Jo. I wouldn't like you to think I might do anything that would upset you.' Carefully he put the broken pieces on the wooden draining-board. His voice was soft as he said, 'I think in the past you've not been treated well.'

Tears sprang to her eyes. 'I feel terrible now,' she gabbled. She was trying to make amends for her strange behaviour.

She remembered her earlier panic in the Criterion when they'd sat down in their seats in the dark. Whatever would she do if he wanted to hold her hand? she'd wondered. Or, even worse, tried to kiss her? Syd had done nothing except put his arm on the seat behind her head, not even touching her. And there it had stayed until the usherette had brought round the tray of ice creams. Then he had risen, moved past her and walked towards the searchlight, returning with two tubs.

'I do like you,' Jo said. 'But I . . .'

'It's all right,' he said kindly. 'I understand how you feel.'

'No,' she said. 'You can't possibly.' Jo hated not being in control of herself. 'I wanted to show you something . . .'

'Another time perhaps,' he said quietly, moving towards the passage.

'But it's the main reason I brought you here.' Jo realized what she'd said, how it must have sounded, and felt the blush start from her neck and cover her face.

A sudden smile lit his face. 'Jo. It's all right, honestly, it's all right.' She had the sudden feeling he wanted to hold her, give her a cuddle, to make sure she understood she hadn't offended him. She let out a big sigh. Her heart was still hammering. He would leave without her showing him . . .

Jo took a deep breath, went to the sideboard and took a key from a drawer.

She walked down the passage, took his coat from the hook and passed it to him. She opened the front door. It was still raining, the drops hard and straight, like stair rods, hitting the pavement and bouncing back up.

'Wait till I open the shed door, then come,' she said, pulling a coat over her head.

The lock was cold and slippery but opened easily. She slid inside the musty-smelling shed and called, 'Syd! In here!'

Within moments he was beside her, breathing heavily and cursing the rain. Then: 'Oh, my! She's a beauty.' He ran a hand lovingly over the shiny red surface of the car. He squeezed himself along the side of the wooden building. 'Can I get in?'

'Course,' said Jo. The rain was pelting on the tin roof. 'She doesn't go now but it's what I drove to Gosport in. She had all our worldly goods in and I remember Rainey singing all the time to keep our spirits up. The car belongs to me. I have all the documents.'

Syd was sitting in the driver's seat running his hands over the steering wheel and the dashboard. Jo saw he was in a little world of his own: his love of cars had swept everything from his thoughts. In the shed's confined space, the smell of the leather seats was heightened.

'Can't be much wrong with this little beauty. I bet I could soon get her going again—'

Jo broke in: 'I just wanted to show the car to you.' She knew she was blushing again as she added, 'We don't have anything else of value. It's my insurance for the future.'

'Jo.' Syd slid his long legs out of the car. He now stood in front of her, staring into her eyes. 'There's a war on. What happened round the corner in Spring Garden Lane, and the rest of Gosport, the bombing, isn't going to stop. Let me get this car running. Sell it. Bank the money.' For a moment he was thoughtful. 'What would you do if one of Hitler's planes dropped a bomb on her?'

'If that happened, I'd be gone as well,' she retorted.

'Maybe, but if you'd banked the money and your girl was alive at singing practice, she'd be well looked after. Think about it.'

Chapter Seventeen

Eddie looked at the piles of rubble, his mind and body numb. He knew every street in Gosport but these hillocks of brick, stones, broken roof slates, water pipes twisted into grotesque shapes, shattered glass and smashed furniture were like nothing he'd ever seen, not even on the building sites. Everything was covered with dust. More floated in the air, like some strange sandstorm.

He turned to face Harry Weldon, who was wearing the tin hat and the armband that told everyone he was an air-raid warden. 'This can't be White's Place?' A row of terraced houses had stood there, with white and red polished doorsteps. Children played in the street and women gossiped in their curlers.

Harry Weldon put his hand on Eddie's shoulder. 'It was,' he said. 'It got a direct hit. No one else is coming out of that alive.'

'No one?'

Harry dropped his hand and shook his head. Eddie thought he looked worn out. The man's eyes were dull and his face was streaked with dust. Gosport had been bombarded all summer long and now, into autumn, there seemed to be no let-up.

'Daisy Elkins at number four crawled from the wreckage but she died on the way to the hospital. Bloody Hitler. Your street's all right, though.' Harry took off his helmet and scratched at his sparse hair. 'The Hun are after our airfields,' he said. 'Bloody pilots must be blind – they missed Lee-on-the-Solent and Rowner.' He replaced his hat, 'Still, that means our planes can get them back.'

A voice called Harry's name. Eddie watched him walk wearily away.

Eddie set off towards home but paused at the corner of the street near the pub. In the large backyard near the wooden casks he could see the bodies laid out in rows on the stone floor, covered with sheets. Some had tags because the rescuers knew their identities, but many did not.

Eddie wanted to be at home with his sister, grandfather and mother.

He'd already walked Liz home after the darts match in the Corncob. They'd had a bit of a kiss and cuddle behind the neighbour's garden gate where overhanging honeysuckle ensured they weren't seen.

Liz was one of those girls who wanted to settle down and Eddie knew he wasn't ready for marriage just yet. So when the siren had wailed and Liz said, 'Come into our Anderson,' he'd declined. The last thing he needed was her family asking him questions about this and that.

He'd watched as she'd banged on the shelter's door, then gone back to his hiding place beneath the honeysuckle.

He could hear bombs whistling down and drew his head further into the collar of his jacket every time one hit the ground. He knew they weren't that close but he could still smell the cordite in the air and see the clouds of dust as the bombs landed. The sky was orange. Searchlights swept above him and the ack-ack noise of ground fire rent the air.

He thought of his mother and hoped she'd been able to persuade Granddad to go down to the shelter. The old man had taken it into his head he'd be safer under the stairs as long as he took his gas mask with him. That put Eddie's mother at even greater risk because she had to stay with him. He'd be shaking and crying and saying over and over again, 'I don't want to die. I'm not going out in that lot.' And all the while the tears would run down his face.

Eddie had dug the garden to a depth of four feet to install

the Anderson shelter. Made of curved corrugated iron, the shelters were supposed to withstand all but a direct hit. But they were cold, damp and airless, and broken masonry sounded horrific when it fell on the earth-covered roof. His mum had made it comfortable inside with wooden bunks and a paraffin heater. She'd even brought down a kettle and the makings for tea. They'd be taking their blankets from the beds soon to stop the cold getting at them.

Eddie had no idea how long he'd stood there with the sweet scent of the late honeysuckle vying with the smell of burning. He had his back to the brick wall and he thought of how the war had practically finished him as a builder. His employees, mostly able young men, had gone off to fight, and even though the local council had granted him the job of building new houses at Bridgemary, the bricks and wood were the devil to get hold of.

There was talk of allowing some of the enemy prisoners of war to work outside the camps but as yet he thought that was only a rumour.

The all-clear had sounded. The raid was over. He'd walked through the allotments and round the back of the Criterion cinema and come across the devastation of White's Place. Now he wanted to be with his family, make sure they were safe.

He thought about the three girls and their singing. By Christ, they were good! Better than some he'd heard wailing on the wireless. He liked Ivy: she was a quiet, classy sort of girl despite the tales he'd heard about her mother. God knew she wasn't responsible for her birth. Rainey he couldn't quite fathom. She never talked about herself or where she'd come from, yet she seemed grateful to be included any time his mum invited the girls round.

Bea, his sister, was a right handful. He tried to keep an eye on her and mostly she was fine when she was with Ivy and Rainey – it was like they kept her in check, or the singing did. When she went out with her mates from Woolies, though, anything could happen and frequently did.

His mind went back to that dance at Sloane Stanley Hall. The drinking wasn't a one-off. Somehow Bea had developed a taste for it. He shuddered, thinking about her being pawed by that oaf of a soldier. In the morning when she'd finally deigned to come downstairs his mother had said, 'It was a good job Eddie was there last night to sort you out.'

The little vixen had laughed at him. 'What d'you want?' she'd said. 'Flowers, chocolates? Good doggie, a bone to chew?'

Despite everything Eddie smiled to himself. Bea was his little sister.

*

Bea looked over the sailor's shoulder and up into the wintry sky. Her head was swimming. It was like all the stars were dancing in the blackness of night. She wondered if anyone had told those glittering objects about the blackout.

His fingers were pushing away her suspenders, pulling her knickers aside and now something warm and hard was being thrust inside her.

'Can you feel me?' His voice was muffled against her neck. She remembered he was taller than her so now he must have his knees bent to make them both a similar height.

The taste of the orange juice was metallic in her mouth, more like the orange juice the government provided for children. Not that she minded: all the gin had been sharp. She wished he'd keep still so she could go on gazing at the universe above them, like diamonds lying on black velvet. The smell of the Brylcreem on his short hair was making her feel sick.

'You dozy mare! It's all down my bell bottoms. It stinks!'

Bea was sliding down the wall. 'I'm sorry,' she said. The two words were just about audible before another gush of vomit erupted from her. It splashed out and onto the stone slabs of the Fox's backyard. The sailor shoved her aside, and as her shoulders slid sideways along the bricks, she lost the will to stand. Bea slithered down and sat on the freezing slabs.

'You're disgusting!' She heard the words and wondered who the sailor was talking about. Then he left. As she closed her eyes she heard his voice again: 'Moira, your mate's in a state out here. Come and sort her out.'

Chapter Eighteen

Alice Wilkes set down the phone in the staff room at St John's. The secretary's message from the town hall at Fareham said her choir had been accepted for two classes: Classic Choir and Harmony Group. 'Now we'll let the judges see what we're made of, Toto.'

The little dog opened one eye at the sound of her voice, then went back to sleep curled beneath the desk. 'Even if we only get a place, it'll be a feather in St John's cap,' she said. Toto's ear flicked. 'But I'm willing to bet my three girls will end up with a first.'

She thought back to Wednesday night and smiled. The run-through of *Snow White* had been hilarious. But she'd never thought it would be anything except extremely funny when she had taken in the huge foam-rubber feet she had spent a long time designing in the shed at the bottom of her garden.

She'd made strings to tie around the knees so when one of her dwarfs knelt down, the feet stuck out, instantly cutting the girl's height in half. Of course she needed seven pairs of these enormous feet but now she knew they worked, and provided the choir with laughs, she was ready to cut out more and also to use a couple of red flannel petticoats to cover the foam to make them look like enormous boots.

On their knees, cushioned by the foam, the seven dwarfs would discover walking didn't hurt at all. Alice had known that the huge roll, purloined from a failing amateur dramatic club, would come in handy one day.

The whole choir had got together and put their hearts into designing costumes not only for the panto but for a choir uniform. Alice was happy everyone was so enthusiastic. There was no doubt they would make a success of their sewing. She was also pleased that most had bothered to learn their lines. After expenses had been paid the remainder of the panto's ticket money would go to charity; she'd let her choir decide which one.

Bea had been absent from practice. Maud apologized for her. 'Not well,' she'd said. It was the first choir meeting she'd missed.

'Toto, I know pride comes before a fall,' Alice said, 'but

I have a special feeling about Bea, Ivy and Rainey. They'll go far.'

'The wireless said our boys shot down a hundred and eighty enemy planes in one night,' Jo announced.

'And we drowned four thousand Germans when a navy sub torpedoed one of their ships,' Rainey chipped in. 'I heard that on the wireless as well.'

'Do you think it'll be over for Christmas?' Ivy asked.

They'd stopped on the corner of Maud's street outside the ironmonger's. All the way from St John's they'd been walking around piles of bricks and rubble shovelled nearer the pavements so the road would be clear for traffic to move freely.

No one spoke of Bea. It was as if they were scared to mention her name.

Jo shivered. 'You can feel the winter bite in the air, can't you? And I don't know what's worse, that or the stink of cordite.'

'I can't ask you in tonight,' said Maud. 'Eddie's waiting with Granddad. He needs someone with him all the time now the planes are coming over nightly.' Even in the darkness Ivy could see she was worn out. Bea's name hadn't passed Maud's lips except when she had apologized to Mrs

Wilkes for her daughter's absence. The gossipmongers had done enough, though.

Ivy watched as Jo stepped forward and gave her friend a hug. She wondered if Maud had shared anything with her.

'We understand.' Jo looked at the two girls for confirmation and they nodded. 'You know where I am if you need me,' Jo added.

The air was filled with unsaid words, thought Ivy.

On the corner of the next street the remaining trio paused. Rainey's voice was firm. 'You go on, Mum. I'm going to walk Ivy home.'

A startled look crossed Jo's face.

'I can get the bus back, don't worry.' She kissed her mother's cheek and Jo walked away.

'Try not to be too late,' she called.

Ivy slid her arm through Rainey's. 'They don't want to talk about Bea but I think we'd better, don't you?' Ivy gave a sideways glance at Rainey. 'You know there are all kinds of rumours going round about her.'

'I went to the house but she wouldn't see me. First time I've not heard her gramophone blaring out.' Rainey paused. 'Eddie came to the door, which surprised me – he does work sometimes. He said she was unwell and asleep.'

'Well, he's hardly going to tell you what really happened, is he?'

'And I suppose you know the truth?'

'I do. I was in the café with Bert. The manager of the Fox came in after taking Bea home. He said her so-called mates from Woolworths had deserted her. They aren't friends, they're leeches.' Ivy looked sad.

'So what happened?'

'Moira and the others thought it was hilarious to let this sailor fill her up with gin and orange, then take her outside.'

'If the manager saw what was happening, why didn't he put a stop to it?'

'Don't you think he blames himself? He thought the drinks were for all the girls. This sailor, all mouth and trousers, told his mate he was going to do her. His mate told him he hadn't a chance, so it was a kind of bet. Those stupid girls thought it was funny to see Bea getting drunk.'

'She can't hold her drink. Remember at the Sloane Stanley Hall when—'

'Rainey! You listening or not?' Ivy saw her friend was looking contrite.

'I bet the manager of the Fox didn't tell you any of this.'

'Of course not, but I never went up to our rooms, like Bert told me to. I hid on the stairs and listened. Bea felt sorry for the sailor because he'd told her he was sailing in the morning and might never return. You know what she's like, soft as putty sometimes. He took her outside for a bit of a kiss. By that time the gin had got to her and she puked all over him!'

Rainey smiled. 'Good!'

'He shouted to one of the Woolworths girls, then he was off on his toes. Of course, no one knew him from Adam. If they did they weren't going to say what ship he was on.'

Ivy waited for Rainey to speak but when she didn't she changed the subject and said, 'Look, Mrs Wilkes is doing us three a big favour and not just to put St John's and her choir on the map. She's giving us a little taste of what it's like on the stage. Our three voices are good together. Three,' she repeated. 'I don't know about you but I want to do something with my life, not stay working in Gosport.'

'I thought that was why we're doing typing.'

'To work in a soddin' office in Gosport!' Ivy almost exploded. 'I want more, Rainey.' She was serious. 'I want to pay my mum back for all she's done for me.'

'So?'

'Mrs Wilkes is offering us a way out. She's making a showcase of us at the David Bogue and she's put us in for the music festival, but we need Bea.'

'What are you saying?'

'It's up to us to make sure she doesn't get mixed up in any more trouble, and we can do that by sticking together, through thick and thin.'

'Like babysitters?'

'If you like. It also means we can't let her stay at home stewing about what's happened to her. She's already missed coming to practice tonight. A few more misses and she might not come back at all.'

'But she's older than us!'

'Doesn't mean she's as bright, though, does it? Tell me, what d'you want out of life, Rainey?'

'To sing. I've been singing all my life, I can't imagine not singing . . .'

'And I want money, nice clothes and respect. If singing can get me those things, I don't want Bea messing it all up.' She stared at Rainey. 'Besides, we've got to help her get over this because she's our friend. You in or out?'

'In.' And in war-torn Forton Road Ivy hugged Rainey. Her plan was starting to come together.

Chapter Nineteen

The lad took his drink to where Ivy was sitting and dumped it down. Tea sploshed over the rim, into the saucer and onto the table.

'All on yer own?'

Ivy looked up from the Pitman's office training book she was reading. The typing class was due to take tests soon and she knew how much it meant to her mother for her to gain a diploma: when she wasn't singing or learning words for the panto, she was studying. She eyed the mess on the table, swirling the orange squash in her glass. 'I'm studying for an exam.' She prayed he wouldn't sit down. The stench of beer wafted over her. She glanced up at him. Although he slouched she could see he was tall. A shock of fair hair hung over his forehead. He used the spoon to stir his tea and the liquid in the saucer slopped over towards her book. 'Watch it!' she said, as he picked up the dripping cup.

'I've seen you in 'ere before.' He leaned over her. There was spittle at the corner of his mouth; a particle flew towards Ivy. He drank noisily then set the cup unsteadily on the Formica table.

The wireless was playing loudly. The café door banged open and more lads pushed rowdily inside.

''Ere he is.'

Ivy began to panic. She hated being hemmed in. She closed her book and started to rise.

The blond youth put his hand on her shoulder, forcing her back onto the chair.

'I come in special to talk to you. I know what your mum does an' I want to know if you do it as well.'

Ivy stared at him. She knew exactly what he meant. 'Don't you talk about my mum.' Calmly she picked up her glass and threw the squash over him.

He staggered against the table, face dripping liquid. The cup and saucer jumped and tea spilled as the cup overturned. 'Ooow!' He screamed, his hands immediately going behind him as he felt a sharp jab in his back. His hair and eyebrows were wet and the front of his jumper soaked.

Bert's voice rose above the kerfuffle. 'Get out, the fuckin' lot of you, and if I ever see you in here again you'll get more and worse!'

There was an exodus to the door from the newcomers.

The fair-haired youth bent over the table using it as a one-handed prop to stand. Ivy saw tears in his eyes. Bert stood behind him, his favourite walking stick in his hand. He unsheathed the wooden cover showing the youth the shiny blade. The lad's eyes widened. 'You try anything with her again and it won't be just a bloody poke with a stick you'll get. I'll cut you to ribbons.' Bert sheathed the weapon and slammed the door on the hobbling youth as he made his painful exit. 'You all right, love?'

Ivy was trembling and her skirt was wet with tea. Wordlessly she nodded.

'Come on, get yourself upstairs and washed. You spend far too much time in this place.' Bert foraged in his pocket and produced a ten-bob note. 'Go to the pictures tomorrow night with Rainey.' He paused, the stick now hanging from a chair, and tucked the money into Ivy's hand. 'Get that Bea to go an' all. 'Bout time she come out of hiding.'

Ivy rose unsteadily and fell into Bert's arms, his smell of bacon fat and fresh sweat comforting. She remembered the conversation she'd had with Rainey and was more determined than ever that nothing like this would ever happen to her again.

'Well, I can hardly take her along with me, can I?' Della's voice was pitched high.

'She was in 'ere when she was accosted by them louts,' said Bert. 'Seems one's had his eye on her for some time.'

Della sat on a tall stool by the counter, the fur's fox eyes glinting in the light. She crossed nylon-clad legs. 'She's all right in here.'

'You're not listening to me. She's not safe anywhere. Look what happened to her mate. Much as I love the girl, she needs you, Della.'

Della shook her head. 'I can't be in two places at once and I got to make sure there's money put by for her future, as well as feeding and clothing her now.' She stared at him, then sighed. 'Thanks, Bert, for looking after my Ivy.' She slid off the stool and went around the counter. Bert was spreading marge on bread for her sandwich. He stopped what he was doing and looked at her. Della barely reached his shoulder even in her high heels. She stretched up and kissed his cheek. He shuffled his feet awkwardly. 'I don't know what I'd do without you,' she breathed.

'I'll tell you what you can do. You can give over going

down to that bloody brothel that Jim calls his "massage rooms". You're not the only tart he's got.'

Bert had never called her a tart to her face before and it stung.

Her thoughts were scattered by the strident sound of the air-raid siren.

Previous conversation forgotten, Bert said, 'Shout up the stairs for your girl and anyone else in their rooms, Della. I'll turn off the utilities. Good job we're closed up. We'll get down the cellar.'

Ivy stood in the doorway, breathing heavily after running down the stairs. 'There's no one else in the building.'

Della said, 'At the beginning of the war that wail sent us scurrying to shelters like headless chickens and what for? Nothing happened. We got used to the damn thing.' She was peeping out of the blackout curtains. 'Now those German planes mean business.' The sky was filled with bombers, too many to count. She saw Ned, one of the air-raid wardens, cycling along North Street, shouting, 'Take cover! Get in the shelters!'

'Down the cellar steps!' warned Bert. 'Got your gas masks?'

Della shrugged.

'I got yours, Mum,' Ivy shouted, above the noise of the planes.

She was a good girl, thought Della. Ivy knew she hated carting the square bag everywhere.

Just before she turned from the window Della saw an aircraft spiralling out of control. She could see bombs falling . . .

'Get a move on, girl,' Bert said, chivvying her down the stone steps, after moving a gent's bike away from the doorway.

Bert had made up a couple of beds with only inches to spare between them to save space. He kept a Primus stove down there, with an alarm clock that he never forgot to rewind. Even so the large, damp room had water running down the walls. Once upon a time Bert had kept stock there but mildew ran wild. Now there was an old armchair, a table upon which sat tin mugs, an oil lamp and a shelf of swollen books.

Della saw he had picked up a flask and the bank bag with the café takings.

Ivy was already sitting on one of the beds with the Pitman's book.

'Take the other bed, Della,' Bert said, throwing the money on the table, then putting down the flask more carefully, along with his walking stick. 'I'll be fine on the chair.' When she didn't move, he added, 'The beds ain't damp. Them's fresh coverings.' He sat down in the armchair.

An extra loud bang made the table jump. Bits of plaster fell down around them. Della made her way over to Ivy, who was now lying on the bed with her eyes closed. She was scared, Della could tell, but rather than say anything, her daughter would pretend sleep. She bent over Ivy. 'I'm sorry, love,' she said. 'I'm not a good model of a mother, am I?'

Ivy opened her eyes. 'You're the only one I've got, though.'

Della laughed. She thought suddenly of her own mother, who'd drunk herself to death a long time ago. She unclasped her fox fur and put it at the bottom of the bed, then kicked off her high heels. With a contented sigh she curled herself around her daughter. 'If we've got to go, at least we'll go together.' Her daughter smelled of school and freshly washed hair.

'If you're going to sleep there, I'll have the other bed,' said Bert.

He heaved himself up from the chair and the bed creaked as he lay down, facing away from Della.

She could hear thuds and bangs coming from outside and occasionally the walls seemed to shake, then settle again. She listened to Ivy's even breathing and guessed that her child now slept. Della carefully moved the book from Ivy's hand and set it down out of the way. She loved Ivy with a fierceness that knew no boundaries.

Della shivered, remembering the hands that had touched her while her mother was spark out on the living-room sofa, gin bottles and fag ends souring the air. She had been too young, too scared, to leave the two rooms they lived in.

She'd learned to spot the men who would come for her when they'd had enough of her mother. The trouble was, she wasn't strong enough to haul the big wardrobe in front of the door to keep them out of the bedroom. The rest of the flimsy furniture was no barrier to their advances. Oh, she'd told her mum all right, but Big Florrie could only see as far as the next drink in a bloke's hand. Della's escape would have been school, but when she was tiny her mother couldn't be bothered to send her. Then, when she did go, the taunts from the other kids about her dirty clothes and smelly hair put a stop to her learning. She'd rather roam the Gosport streets than be jeered at. Della soon found she could charge for what her mother's boyfriends had taken for free.

She remembered the time she'd approached a bakery she'd heard was hiring assistants.

'Can you write down orders, girl?' the manager had asked.

Della couldn't read the names of the cakes and bread,

even though the fragrant batches were clearly marked. She'd shaken her head and slunk away, knowing she was good for only one thing. The thing she could let men do to her while her mind soared to different places.

At thirteen she remembered crying out her mother's name when her baby was born in a flower-shop doorway. At first she'd thought the tiny scrap was dead. But when she held the little girl in her arms, she began to cry. Della thought she'd never held anything as precious as that child. There were vases of daffodils among pots of trailing ivy, its green leaves shiny and beautiful in the shop's windows, so Ivy became her name. She'd slept with the child latched to her breast and was awoken by an elderly woman, a cleaner, who took off her coat and spread it about Della. 'If you can walk, come home with me, child.'

Elizabeth Petty had been more of a mother than Big Florrie ever had.

For two years Della lived with her, cleaning and cooking and earning her keep. Mrs Petty tried to teach her to read but whenever Della looked at a line of words they jumbled themselves into nonsense. She could write her name but no more, although she was as sharp as a tack. From Mrs Petty Della learned how to care for her daughter. Della loved Ivy but she had no mothering skills except those that came naturally. Then Mrs Petty began to do and say strange things. One time the police brought her home. Della used to stay awake to make sure Mrs Petty didn't leave at nights. A son Della had never seen before came to the house and got his mother to sign a paper. It wasn't long afterwards that Mrs Petty was taken away. The son sold the house and the furniture, and Della was out on the streets again.

When Della turned up at Bert's café, she was sixteen and Ivy was clutching her skirts. Bert, feeling sorry for her and the clinging child, took her in to clean and occasionally cook. He was a perfect gentleman, a rough diamond but loved the bones of Ivy. Then, when Della was seventeen, Jim came into her life. He told her he loved her and he bought her pretty things. Of course she fell for him and his sharp suits, his expensive watch, his flash car. Bert wouldn't allow any funny stuff, as he called it, above the café so sometimes Della left Ivy with Bert and spent time at Jim's place.

When Jim asked her to sleep with a friend of his because he owed money and Della's body would clear the slate, she agreed because she loved him. One man spiralled to several, and to show his gratitude Jim gave her money and bought her and Ivy presents. To show her love and trust of Jim, Della began working nights at the premises opposite the bus station. Now she had money to put aside for Ivy. Was

Della happy? No. But she'd make sure Ivy never wanted for anything.

Now, listening to the bangs and thumps from bombs outside and the crash of falling furniture and crockery inside, Della realized both Ivy and Bert were asleep. She was cocooned between the only two people who loved her. She had long ago realized that Jim used her.

Her arm tightened about her daughter. Ivy was clever. Della wasn't sure who her father was but Ivy had a talent for learning. She had a voice to melt a snowman's icy heart and her office skills would soon land her a decent job.

Maybe Ivy would go away, leave Gosport. That was fine. Della wanted Ivy to do well and she'd move heaven and earth to help her.

The steady wail of the all-clear penetrated the walls of the cellar.

'It's five in the morning,' said Bert, looking at the clock. He yawned, scratched his head, got up from the bed and went across to the table. He poured two thick black cups of tea from the flask, came back and handed one to Della. She took it with a smile. They sat, not speaking but companionable, while Ivy slept.

'I thought, from the noise last night, the stairs had caved in,' said Della, handing him the cup when it was empty.

'We're still here,' said Bert.

After putting the crockery back on the table, Bert tried the door at the top of the steps, while Della shook brick dust from her fox fur.

The door opened a crack but would go no further. 'Bike's stuck across the passage,' Bert said, and managed to shove it out of the way. Its bell rang as it tumbled to the ground.

'Can I have some tea?' Ivy murmured.

'There's some in the flask,' answered Bert. 'Good morning, Ivy.'

'That'll be stewed,' said Ivy, wide awake now.

'Make some fresh in a minute,' said Della. 'When we get out of here.'

She stood on the stairs, looking past Bert. Glass covered the hallway. The front-door panels had shattered. Bert went straight into the café. He wasn't swearing so she guessed, despite the noise she'd heard last night, there wasn't much damage. Ivy scrambled past, moaning about the bike.

Della left the passage and stood in the street, looking about her. Red dust from Gosport bricks clung to every surface and hung in the air, like mist. People were emerging from the Fox and Murphy's the ironmonger's. They looked dazed.

The sky across the ferry was orange, and black smoke

poured into the heavens. An ARP man covered with dust was pushing his bike carefully through glass and rubble.

'What got hit?' Della called.

'Part of the Dockyard's still burning,' he shouted back. 'The shipyard near the ferry went up. Timber's still burning. Anybody hurt in there?' He motioned towards the café.

'No, thank God,' answered Della.

'Give it a few hours if you're hoping to get out of Gosport. The road to Fareham's in a hell of a state.'

Della watched him skirt around a tumbledown wall. She called to the manager of the Fox, who was standing in the rubble scratching his head and looking at the broken window in the bar: 'You all right, Sam?'

He shrugged. 'Put your shoes on, Della, before you cut your feet something terrible.'

Della looked down. Her nylons were laddered. One of her red-painted toenails poked through a hole. 'Silly cow.'

Chapter Twenty

'It's funny not hearing her gramophone, isn't it?'

'She could be out, Ivy,' Rainey said.

'I don't think so.' Ivy banged on the door of Bea's house. After a short while it opened to reveal Eddie, his shirtsleeves rolled up. Ivy couldn't help herself. 'Why aren't you at work?'

Eddie looked sheepish. 'Building work's going through a sticky patch. I got a sub-contractor doing repairs and small stuff. Someone's got to be here for Granddad because Mum's got a cleaning job to help out.' He paused. 'Regular policeman, aren't you?'

Ivy knew she was blushing. If only Eddie wasn't so good-looking, and kind. In a way he reminded her of Bert, a similar sort of solid man. 'We've come to take Bea to the Criterion to see Mickey Rooney and Judy Garland. It's *Babes in Arms* and we know she'll love the singing.'

'You'd best come in before the neighbours start earwigging.' He stood aside and allowed them to pass along the passage into the kitchen.

Granddad was asleep in his chair, a newspaper across his lap.

Eddie's blue eyes fixed on Ivy. 'She won't go with you. She's hardly been out of her bedroom since . . .' He couldn't finish the sentence.

'What about her job?' Rainey looked at Eddie.

'I telephoned to say she was quitting.' For a moment there was silence, except for Granddad's snoring. 'She can do without the girls she was with that night. Anyway, she couldn't face the gossip.'

He used his fingers to push back his blond hair. 'We decided it was for the best.' Ivy saw he was exhausted. She felt a fluttering inside her just looking at his worried, honest face.

'I can understand that,' Rainey said. 'Did you tell the police?'

'What can they do?' Eddie was angry. 'The manager of the Fox said best to leave things be. Local gossip will be bad enough. I agreed with him. That bloody sailor could be anywhere in the world by now.' His face was hard. 'If I ever meet up with him I'll kill the bastard.' He sighed. 'I'm glad you didn't let the grass grow under your feet before you came round. Bea's only missed one choir practice but already she's saying she's thinking of packing it in—'

Ivy put her hand on his arm. 'We've got to get Bea to stop hiding away. She needs to start feeling good about herself again.'

Eddie was staring at her. So was Rainey. But Ivy knew they had to bolster Bea's confidence, not only because she was their friend but because with the mood she was in now she might permanently drop out of the choir, and all the hard work they'd put into 'The Bluebird Song' would go down the drain, along with their hopes and dreams. It needed three voices. Two weren't enough.

'She couldn't stand on a stage and sing, not now.' Eddie's brow was furrowed.

'Not straight away, but she can get back into the land of the living by coming to the pictures with us.'

'She's in bed, not washed or anything.'

'Don't make excuses. Why d'you think we came round early? There's plenty of time before the second showing. Why don't you make us a cup of tea?'

Eddie looked bewildered. Ivy knew he was more used to giving orders than taking them, but he went out into the scullery and Ivy heard the pop of the gas.

'Come on,' Ivy said to Rainey, and made for the stairs.

Ivy knocked politely on Bea's bedroom door then, hearing no answer, opened it and went in, dragging Rainey with her. The room smelled of stale perfume and Ivy had to step carefully over the clothes and magazines on the floor. She went to the sash window and lifted the bottom panes, allowing fresh air in.

She heard Rainey say gently, 'Come on, love.'

Ivy turned and saw the inert bundle in the bed. Rainey's soft words had done nothing. Ivy picked up the glass of water on the chair by the bed and pulled back the candlewick bedspread. Bea's eyes were tightly shut but they opened wide when the water hit her. She sat up, bewilderment on her swollen face, her blonde hair dripping.

'What d'you think you're doing?'

'Putting fire back into you.' Ivy grinned at her.

'I'm not ready—'

'Course you are.'

Already Ivy was trying to scrub Bea's face using the bedspread. 'We're not going to let you rot in that bed.' Ivy tugged at the bedspread and blankets, pulling them off her. 'Get up, washed and dressed. We're going to the pictures.'

'I can't. I feel so ashamed.' For a single moment silence reigned.

'So you ought to, drinking yourself silly like that,' said Ivy. 'But what he did was wrong. He took advantage of you. You've got two choices. Let the damn bloke spoil the rest of your life or get on with it.' She bent down and took Bea's hand. It was damp and clammy. 'I know what it's like having people gossip about you,' she said. 'You sink or you swim.'

Bea was staring at her. 'I packed in my job.'

'Get another one. Go and work in Priddy's Hard armament factory – they're always wanting girls.' Ivy started humming 'The Bluebird Song', then looked at Rainey, who was sitting on the end of the bed holding Bea's favourite grey slacks and fluffy pink jumper, ready for her to put them on. 'Come on, Rainey, sing!'

Rainey joined in, then stopped. 'The film is Mickey Rooney and Judy Garland.' She started singing once more, and stopped again. 'C'mon, Bea, we need three voices.'

Just as Bea's feet touched the floor Eddie's voice floated up the stairs: 'I've made the tea an' I never thought I'd be glad to hear that bleedin' song again.'

Chapter Twenty-one

'I'm never going to be able to thank you enough for what you're doing for me, Syd.' Jo liked it when he was in her shed, tinkering with the car. It gave her the chance to do some of the little things for him she'd almost forgotten how to do for a man. She'd baked a Madeira cake, his favourite, intending to wrap it and send him home with it later. She'd been saving her sugar and marge rations for ages.

He finished wiping his hands on the oily cloth and said, 'I'll be here when the bloke calls tomorrow night. I've told him cash only, no cheques.' He stared hard at her. 'Look, you don't have to sell this little beauty, if you want to keep her for yourself.' He ran a hand lovingly over the MG's bonnet.

He'd probably be as tender with a woman, Jo thought. 'Syd, of course I want to keep her but half of Queens Road went up in smoke the other night and that's only across the railway lines. I'm scared stiff for myself and Rainey. Besides, I can't afford to run a car and I've got used to my bike, so I'd rather have the money for the MG in the bank for when Rainey needs it.'

'There you go again. You never think of yourself, do you? Anyway, where is Rainey?'

Jo grinned at him. 'She's gone to the pictures with her mates. Look, I need to pay you for fixing this car, especially for sorting out the petrol gauge. It's never worked properly before.'

'I don't want your money. I said I'd get her up and running in my spare time and you've more than repaid me with hot dinners.'

Jo wanted to throw her arms around his neck but she held back, as usual. She felt the blush rise to her cheeks. He stared at her, then said, 'Jo, if you really want to thank me why don't you let me into your confidence? I'm not stupid. You've not been treated right and it's made you wary of me when there's no need . . . I'd like to get to know you better. I'll keep anything you tell me a secret, I promise.'

Jo had revealed nothing of her life before coming to Gosport but now the desire to blurt it all out nearly over-whelmed her. The words burst from her lips. 'Not here, inside. I do want to tell you because sometimes I think I'll go doolally bottling everything up.'

Jo made him sit by the range, and after she'd made tea, she told him why she and Rainey had left Portsmouth.

Syd listened without interrupting. When she'd finished he said, 'It makes sense now, why you shy away whenever I come near you.' His face was inscrutable.

'I never used to be like that,' Jo said, and wiped her eyes. 'I'm on edge all the time, waiting for him to find me. Common sense tells me he must be abroad fighting, or he'd have found us before now. Every time there's a knock at the door I start shaking.'

'He sounds a right bastard!' There was disgust in Syd's eyes. After a while he said, 'You could find out where he is. After all, you're still his wife.'

'No!' Jo almost shouted. 'I don't want him to find me, ever.'

Jo could see Syd wanted to comfort her, and she wanted relief from her suffering more than anything, but she didn't have the courage to move into his arms. 'Please keep my secret,' she said.

For a moment he gazed at her. Then he said, 'Jo, I'll do anything for you, anything.' And Jo believed him. He turned to leave, and as he reached the front door, he said, 'You know where I am if you need me, but I'll be here tomorrow night to make sure you get a good deal on the car.'

On the screen Judy Garland strode purposefully along, arm in arm with Mickey Rooney. A crowd of young people marched behind them, singing.

For a single moment Bea was unashamedly happy. She stole a look at Ivy's rapt expression in the dull light of the auditorium and sighed. Never in her wildest dreams had she imagined she would spend this afternoon with Ivy and Rainey. As if she had read her mind, Rainey squeezed her hand and Bea smiled at her.

If they hadn't come to the house today she'd still be in bed, her mind going over and over what she had allowed to happen to her. If she hadn't been falling-down drunk she would never have contemplated stepping outside with that sailor. While it was true he shouldn't have taken advantage of her, she hadn't resisted his advances. It was like she'd needed someone to care about her, and when he'd wanted her body it was like he'd wanted all of her. Self-loathing swamped her. Bea forced herself to stare again at the screen.

'Are you all right?' Ivy's whisper cut into her thoughts.

'I think so. Thank you,' Bea said, turning towards her. 'For everything.' Ivy would know exactly what she meant.

'Sssh!' came an angry female voice from behind them. It was followed by the rustling of sweet papers. The smell of lemon sherbet was added to the stifling warmth of the cinema.

Bea met Ivy's eye and simultaneously they grinned.

Why, Bea wondered, did she crave attention? Why did she always end up making a fool of herself? Or hurting others?

She thought back to last Christmas. It had taken her mother days to get Granddad settled again. Her drunken prank had spoiled the day for everyone. She'd involved Rainey in that as well, hadn't she? Poor Rainey, who'd never touched a drop of sherry in her life before then. It hadn't been a nice thing for Bea to do, had it?

Bea knew she was lucky to be living with people who loved her. Many of the girls she worked with were alone. Homes bombed out, families gone. She had a family, but it wasn't complete. She didn't have a dad, did she?

You don't miss what you've never had. That was a lie. She did miss having a father, in lots of different little ways. Ella Budgeon's came to pick up his daughter from the back entrance of Woolies every night. She'd run to him and they'd walk home together.

She remembered sports day at school. Her mum had worked full time at Sunbeam Laundry then. A neighbour had come in to sit with Granddad. There had been no one to see how fast Bea ran to win a race or jump the hurdles. She'd watched fathers give their children hugs, a hand on the shoulder, a pat on the arm. And she pretended it didn't matter that her own mother and brother, nine years older than her, never came to the school. She knew they needed to work to bring in money but she was still hurt by their absence. The awful thing she had let happen to her in the yard at the Fox had made her understand how selfish she was. She could have refused the drinks her friends offered. She hadn't, though, because she liked their attention too much.

Her mother loved her, and she'd shown that love by never once mentioning that Bea might have been at fault for going into the backyard of the Fox, drunk, with a sailor she had only just met. Her brother Eddie cared for her, and the two friends on either side of her were giving her another chance at friendship.

Eddie had held her and told her it would be all right. But Bea would never forget the helpless look in his eyes when he realized he couldn't confront the sailor. Bea had made her own brother feel less than a man.

If she had stayed at home wallowing in her own selfishness this afternoon, Ivy and Rainey might have left her alone.

If they had, she doubted she would ever have returned to the choir. She would have destroyed the opportunity she'd been given to sing in the pantomime and the festival, and Rainey and Ivy would have suffered. She didn't want to be responsible for that. Mrs Wilkes could probably find a duet for Rainey and Ivy but the three of them were good together, weren't they?

Bea knew what she had to do. She must manage without the confidence the drink gave her. It wasn't as if she liked the taste. The effect was what she needed. Too much, and she couldn't control herself. But the power to stop deserted her.

In that moment, with Judy Garland singing her heart out, Bea saw she had two choices. Give up drinking and find another way to gain confidence, perhaps through music and singing, or go on feeling sorry for herself, taking a drink to bolster her courage that led to another drink and yet another until she became so dead inside that she didn't care what happened to her.

In that split second Bea knew she must never touch drink again.

Chapter Twenty-two

Almost as soon as he had arrived, after transfer from Dover, Blackie had been asking the doctor at Gosport's Haslar Hospital when he could leave. The nurses had been jolly, and one or two had caught his eye for a quick kiss and cuddle in the laundry room as he'd become mobile again, but he wanted to be at home in Southsea. He needed to find the corporal's wife and tell her of her husband's bravery.

The girl who haunted his sleep, though, was the one in the photograph.

Never in his wildest dreams had he thought, after the months he'd spent while they dug shrapnel out of his leg, that today he'd be trudging the streets of Southsea. He called his limp, which showed itself when he was tired, his Dunkirk legacy. It meant he was no longer required to fight against Hitler. But he was alive, wasn't he?

Bomb sites, rubble and gaps in the streets told him how badly Portsmouth and Southsea had already fared. There were queues outside boarded-up shops but still people managed to smile.

The address on the corporal's letters in his pocket was burning a hole in his suit.

He was staying with Madame Walker and Herbert, who had damned near killed the fatted calf when he'd knocked on the door of their new studio up the road from the old one, which had been demolished by a bomb. 'Thank God no one was in there when the walls of my rehearsal rooms came down,' gushed Madame, who, in spite of rationing or because of it, had kept her figure.

Blackie had asked Herbert how the business was faring. 'The government closed the theatres and music halls, then opened them again after they discovered that the poor servicemen on leave had nowhere to go for relaxation. The Coliseum in Portsmouth is packed every night,' Herbert had answered.

Blackie shared one or two of his exploits with Herbert, but mostly he couldn't bear to be reminded of all that had happened. It would always be with him but it was better locked up inside his head.

Malc had died in the ambulance at Dover. Blackie had

held Malc's hand until the coldness of death had become apparent, then doctors had taken him away.

Now Blackie stood outside number thirty-three Victoria Road, staring at the stained mattress in the front garden. He raised his hand to the knocker and waited.

After a while he heard footsteps and the door opened.

Fluffy peroxided hair stood to attention around the woman's head, showing dark roots. A candlewick dressing-gown was stretched across ample curves. A cabbage-like smell swept out from the terraced house.

'I'm looking for Janice.'

Her voice was cigarette-raspy. 'You've found her, love. What can I do for you?'

Her dressing-gown gaped, but she didn't seem bothered. Blackie produced the letters. Officially it wasn't his job to return the communications to the sender: he should have handed them to the authorities. It might be a comfort for her to know Alfie had kept them safe.

But that wasn't the real reason he had sought her out. Blackie carried the photograph of the girl close to his heart and her likeness had eaten into his soul. How else was he to find her?

She put out a hand with chipped red nail polish and touched the envelopes. 'That's my writing,' she said.

A milk cart trundled along the street. He could see she was watching without really seeing it. He introduced himself. 'Come on in,' she said. She stood against the wall so he could pass along the dark passage towards the kitchen. He heard the door close behind him and the soft pad of her bare feet on the lino.

It was obvious she had been in bed when he'd knocked on the door. The fire was grey ashes in the grate. Several beer bottles stood on the table amid dirty glasses and a couple of overflowing ashtrays. A pencil stub lay on last night's *Evening News*. The small room was cluttered with heavy furniture. The ceiling, once white, was tobacco brown, and a damp patch along one wall spread downwards to the sideboard. She went to the window, pulling back the curtains, letting in some light.

She turned. 'Alfie's dead, isn't he?' She flopped into an old armchair. He nodded, sat at the table and put down her letters. Alfie and this woman had been romantically involved but she wasn't his wife. She hadn't been officially informed of Alfie's death.

She'd taken a packet of Woodbines from her pocket and slipped out a cigarette. She waved the packet at him and he shook his head. A match fizzed as she lit up.

'I ain't heard from him for ages. Not like him to not

write,' she said. She sighed, took a long drag and blew smoke towards him. 'Thanks for letting me know. Us not bein' married means I got no rights.'

He realized he was waiting for her to cry. She was stone-faced. She picked up a letter and turned it over in the hand that wasn't holding a cigarette. 'Has his missus seen these?'

Blackie shook his head.

She took another long drag on the cigarette. Blackie could hear noises coming from upstairs. He took out the photograph of the pretty girl and put it on the table. Somehow it didn't belong in this scruffy place and he hoped the woman wouldn't touch it, contaminate it. 'I believe this is his daughter?' he said.

She narrowed her eyes. 'Well, she's not my bloody kid. And not a kid no more.'

'Where can I find his wife?'

'How long's a piece of string? The bitch upped and left him before he went off to fight.' She shook her head. 'Dunno where she and the girl went.'

His heart dropped like a stone falling from a great height.

Her eyes were like two black currants surrounded by smudged mascara peering at him. 'I can write down where she was, last I knew.'

She leaned across and picked up the stub of pencil. As she

moved he caught the smell of her warm flesh, mixed with sweat and stale lily-of-the-valley perfume.

She tore the top off the newspaper and scribbled something, then passed the scrap of paper to him. Footsteps sounded loud on the stairs. 'Maybe a neighbour knows something. If you find her, don't tell her about the letters.'

As his fingers closed around the piece of paper, a bloke, face unshaven, eyes heavy with sleep, stepped into the kitchen, bringing with him the smell of stale beer and fags.

'What the 'ell's goin' on 'ere?' He wore blue-striped pyjama bottoms but no top, and his flabby stomach hung over the string at his waist.

'Nothing for you to worry about, Mike.' Blackie could tell that, for all the man's bluster, she had the upper hand. 'Go and put the kettle on. This bloke's just going.'

She walked down the passage with him. 'Did Alfie die easy?'

'Very easy,' Blackie said.

Chapter Twenty-three

'I said no talking!'

Mrs Wilkes gave a sigh, then stared at the choir facing her in the music room. 'You've made a magnificent effort in obtaining the uniform we discussed.' Her eyes roved along the two lines of women wearing knee-length black skirts and white blouses. 'As you know I'd have preferred black and yellow, but due to the shortages caused by the war I thought you might come up with all different yellows instead of the buttercup of St John's school colours. I must say, the black and white looks very smart. Well done, all of you. Where's Emily?'

A hand rose from behind Janet, a large, tall lady in the front row.

'Pish! We can't see you, dear. Change places with Janet.'

Janet's face went dark. 'I always stand in the front row.'

'We can still see you and hear your lovely voice from the

second,' said Mrs Wilkes, diplomatically. There was shuffling as the two women changed places. Janet's mouth set in a thin, disgruntled line. She was obviously unhappy about changing places. Mrs Wilkes shook her head. 'It's no good, I need to place altos to the left and sopranos to the right. We need maximum voice power, if we're to please the judges, and I want you to look good. Two rows, smaller girls at the front, taller at the back.' She hoped her tone said she meant business. There was a great deal of talking and moving about, but eventually two rows appeared of more or less equal numbers and heights.

'Well done,' she said, and licked her top lip. Bea, Ivy and Rainey were at the end of the second row. They were her best singers, and certainly the three most glamorous, but she couldn't very well make an example of them and put them at the front. That would cause uproar and she wanted harmony, not just in the singing but within the choir as well.

Obviously friends didn't like being separated. They got used to the sound of their neighbour's voice, but moving them around now to make the most of how they presented themselves would appeal to the judges and public. And even though 'my three girls', as she liked to think of them, were in the second row, they would also be singing in front of the judges as a trio.

She stepped back and smiled. 'That's better. Now we look like professionals. The positions you occupy will be your regular places for all performances. We'll run through the songs we're singing as a choir. Then you can return to your seats and get out your diaries. I have a couple of dates for you.'

A short while later, when the women had details of two appearances requested in different wards of The War Memorial Hospital in Gosport, Mrs Wilkes sat down at the piano and began to play. Every so often she looked at her choir as they sang. After a while she shouted, 'No! No! No! It looks and sounds terrible. I'd hoped you'd all have learned the words by now.'

Papers were rattling in some of the women's hands. 'I don't want to see anyone hiding their faces with the music. These are well-known songs. Words away!'

There were mutterings among the women but when she started playing again she was pleased to see that as they sang the choir was concentrating hard, their voices pure and clear. She smiled to herself and ceased playing once more.

'Now I want you all to look as though you're enjoying it. Put a smile on your faces, girls, please. At present you all look as if you're constipated.' After the giggles had died down she began to play again, and when she ended, she said, 'I think you'll do!' She looked down at Toto asleep under the piano. 'They're shaping up well, Toto. Very well indeed.' She smiled at her choir. 'Go home,' she said, 'and relax.'

As the choir filed out, chattering and laughing, Mrs Wilkes caught Rainey, Bea and Ivy before they disappeared with Jo and Maud.

She planted herself in front of Bea and said, 'Glad you're well again, Bea. We missed you.' She could see the blush rising from Bea's collar. Mrs Wilkes knew what had happened but she wasn't going to mention the gossip she'd heard. She'd also kept an eye on Bea tonight and noted she was quieter than usual, but the other two girls had been protective of her. She'd been worried Bea might leave the choir. That would have been a tragedy. Her voice was remarkable, and the three girls had charisma. 'You were in good form tonight. I'm very pleased with you,' she said. 'You practise together at home, don't you?'

Heads nodded. '"Bluebird" is a lovely song, Mrs Wilkes,' Ivy said.

'My neighbours bang on the wall about Bea's gramophone but no one bangs when they're practising in her bedroom,' said Maud.

'Thank goodness for that,' said Mrs Wilkes. 'It's a special song for three special girls.'

When the classroom was empty and Mrs Wilkes was

gathering her music together, putting it into the bag to transfer it to the bicycle basket with Toto, she realized she'd forgotten to tell them all that the tickets for the panto at the David Bogue Hall were selling well. She hoped to contribute a tidy sum to the Lord Mayor's Fund for Needy Gosport Children, the charity the choir had chosen.

So many little ones had become reliant on it because they had been orphaned by the bombing. She couldn't replace their parents but the contributions her choir received would hopefully put a smile on the kiddies' faces on Christmas Day.

But that was only one of her hopes for her choir. By gaining a certificate in the Fareham Music Festival she would prove to herself she could teach a group of women with untrained voices that anyone from any background could sing for the joy of it while bringing pleasure to others. Mrs Wilkes had never fulfilled her own potential as a concert pianist, but it made her happy to use her skills in teaching others to love music.

Those women weren't professional singers: they were wives, mothers and daughters. Some had lost husbands; some had lost sons; some had lost brothers. Some had been bombed out of their homes. But for one night a week they came to sing their hearts out and try to push the dreadful war from their minds. Three raids so far had made them all run for the school's shelter, yet when the all-clear sounded they elected to continue singing to give them the courage they needed to return home, if those homes still stood.

How many times had she stressed, 'Commitment means more than a beautiful voice'? Her choir had shown her they were committed. Each woman turned up regularly. Each listened without argument. And look how they'd presented themselves in their uniforms! She was aware that several little groups had got together, those who could sew and had machines, to help alter the black skirts that had come from second-hand stalls and rummage sales so that each could appear tonight in their St John's Choir uniforms. She was so proud of them.

Would the esteemed judges at the festival feel the same?

There would be stiff competition. Many choirs competed from all over the country. Many left disappointed. It was amazing that, with the war, the festival hadn't been cancelled. Who knew how long it would continue?

Toto gave a little bark, startling her out of her thoughts.

'Yes, Toto, I agree. There's no other choir quite like mine.' Toto could always be relied on to agree with her.

Chapter Twenty-four

Blackie watched Herbert put another log on the fire, sit back in the armchair and sigh. Then he smoothed his sparse hair and said, 'It poses a problem if you can't find the girl. She and her mother can't have vanished into thin air . . . unless, of course, they've been killed in the bombing.'

'The house they lived in is still standing but the neighbours were hardly a help. One old dear said she'd got up in the middle of the night to make tea and heard a car start up. A couple of days later the husband came back and all hell was let loose. He was throwing stuff around, drunk out of his mind, and yelling that the bitches had left him. She kept out of his way, she said.'

'Did you show the neighbour the picture of the girl?'

'Yes, and she recognized Rainey Bird. Said the picture was an old one – the girl must be seventeen at least by now.

Obviously if they ran away from him there must have been a reason.'

Herbert said, 'Are you sure *your* reasons for finding her are honourable? You're, what, nearly ten years older than her? Isn't she a little young for you?'

'It's not like that. I admit she's lovely but her father said she has the voice of an angel . . .'

'All fathers think their kids can hold a tune.'

'If she has a voice as good as her father said, I can make money out of her. You tried to put me on the stage but I'm as useless as a bucket with a hole in it. You also taught me to know talent when I heard it. Age doesn't come into it when you can hand stardom to a person on a plate.'

'Have you forgotten there's a war on? All the restrictions? And the music hall is dying.'

'Good singers are making it all the time. What about our Gracie Fields? And that skinny Italian, Frank Sinatra?'

'So you want to manage her? I still think you're wasting your time.'

Blackie looked at Herbert disparagingly. 'Think what you like but I've got a feeling about this girl. If it hadn't been for my damned leg playing up I'd have still been out searching. I was told by one neighbour that the wife didn't dare move far from home. If that's true, she was scared of him. Reason enough to run?'

'A friend could have found another place for them.' Herbert was pouring two glasses of whisky from a decanter.

'Apparently he didn't like her to have friends.'

'The *Evening News* advertises houses for sale and to rent.'

'I'd already thought of that. It might be possible to enquire with the regular letting agents. Somehow I don't think she'd have gone in for buying a house, do you?'

Herbert shook his head. He handed Blackie a glass and took a sip from his own. 'Then the obvious thing to do is go back to where she lived and walk the streets. Make enquiries where she would have used her ration books.'

Blackie thought for a moment. 'Herbert, you're a diamond!'

Herbert put his glass down. 'How about I come with you? There's every possibility you'll let your heart rule your head when you hear this girl sing.'

'You're saying you'll back me if she can hold a tune?'

Herbert smiled. 'Speculate to accumulate,' he said, pouring another drink.

Two days later the men were walking down Portsmouth's London Road into the city, passing the street where the family had lived. Ugly gaps along the road told Blackie the Germans were well aware of how important the south coast was with its factories, docks and shipyards. Hitler was doing everything possible to bomb Portsmouth out of existence.

Herbert made sure they took advantage of almost every café open in London Road. 'I don't want you coming back exhausted and in pain. Madame won't like that and she'll blame me. Anyway, people sit in cafés and talk, gossiping, and we might discover something to our advantage.'

Blackie stared at the man who'd tried to be a father to him. A well of emotion rose as Herbert added, 'We can also try the local schools.'

Blackie wasn't sure. 'She's old enough to have left full-time education.'

'She might have stayed on, you never know. It's possible another address was lodged so the authorities could keep track of the girl. Not all the schools closed because of the bombing and not all the youngsters were evacuated.'

'No teacher worth their salt would give out information to strangers about their pupil.'

'This is wartime, son. Things are different now. People are going missing all the time. Besides, we're not in the acting business for nothing. If you can't charm out an address . . .'

'You're forgetting something. It sounds like they ran to

escape a bully of a husband and father. They'll have covered all their tracks.'

'We won't know that until we search, will we? I think anyone with a heart will spill the beans when we tell them we're looking for Mrs Bird to tell her you were the last person to see her husband alive.'

Blackie had no answer to that.

A couple of days later Herbert was proved right.

'Brenda, get me the Gosport files.' The thin, bespectacled manager of Blandings estate agents used his long fingers to leaf through pages of handwriting in the ledger. 'I remember the woman in question,' he said, 'mainly because she was willing to take on a small house that was badly in need of updating. It'd been on our books for a while. We had a few other properties in Portsmouth but she asked for Gosport. The deposit was a cash transaction.' He peered at the pages. 'She told me she wanted to move to Gosport because she needed to be nearer her relations across the ferry. Nice little thing. Normally we don't like to let to women without a husband or father's signature as guarantor but the war has taken the men and she had the ready cash. In fact, she paid the deposit and a week in advance.' He peered at Blackie. 'You say her husband has been killed?'

'We need to reassure her that there'll be a pension.' He pulled the photograph of Rainey from his wallet. 'This is their daughter.'

The photograph seemed to be the turning point.

'Pretty girl. I never saw her, just the wife. I'll write down the Gosport address for you.'

Chapter Twenty-five

'Thank your lucky stars you're sharing this scrawny bird with me, but you can only eat it when it's cooled.' The small chicken was a present from a neighbour, a thank-you for helping his sausage-fingered daughter scrape through her grade-one piano exam. After it was plucked and cooked it looked more pathetic than ever.

Alice Wilkes glanced down at Toto. He was jumping up and down as though he was suspended on a piece of elastic. She picked up a piece of chicken and held it between her fingers to test the heat, then put the dog's bowl on the kitchen floor next to his water. 'Whatever would I do without you?' she said, scratching him behind one ear.

She covered the rest of the chicken with a piece of muslin and took it to the pantry. She wondered how different her life might have been if she'd had a family of her own, like so many other women of her age. 'I'm not really dissatisfied, Toto. How could I be? I love my job and my choir, and it's not as though my days aren't filled, but sometimes . . .'

She allowed herself to wallow in memories of the young musician and the walks they'd shared during the Great War, the war to end all wars, until a sharp bark from Toto told her he'd finished and wanted more chicken. She smiled down at him but shook her head. 'Tonight when we get back from Fareham we'll have the rest. Chicken for you twice in one day? You're eating better than most of the people in Gosport!'

The little dog followed her upstairs to her bedroom. From her wardrobe she picked out her heather-mixture costume. 'Not new, Toto, but good quality. I don't want to let my girls down.'

Yesterday had been the start of the music festival. Today Alice Wilkes's choir would be performing before the judges and a large audience. 'I'm going to wear the strawberry pink blouse with the frilly collar, a pair of black court shoes to match my leather music bag, and I've made sure the piano's been tuned,' she told the dog. 'Several of the judges are well-known musicians, Toto. I read that in the *Evening News*. It'll cover the event because the Mayor of Fareham will be there.' Toto jumped up on the bed and wagged his tail.

Those who attended were expected to sit through all performances so, although her choir would not be performing until eleven o'clock, she was glad she'd ordered the charabanc to take them to Fareham with plenty of time to spare. At five in the evening they would return to Gosport, with or without certificates of excellence. Last night at a special practice she'd warned the choir, 'If you're not there when the charabanc is ready to leave, we'll go without you.' All the hard work they'd put into their medley of songs told her they'd be on time.

Her trio wouldn't be singing until after lunch.

Of the eight choir acts competing, she had heard three before and the competition would be fierce. 'If we don't win a place I'll never put my choir through this again,' she said to Toto, running a brush through her wiry hair. 'We'll stick to raising money for good causes.'

'Had a letter from the council yesterday.' Maud linked her arm through Jo's as they walked along Forton Road. The three girls were in front, chattering, and each was carrying her freshly ironed costume in a string-handled brown-paper carrier bag.

'There should be a place for Granddad at Bridgemary after Christmas,' Maud continued. 'He's at the top of the list for a lovely room in a lodging house where the owner has nursing experience. Part of me is relieved but another part of me doesn't want the family to be separated. I hoped the council would give us a bigger house so we could all have a bedroom to ourselves. I could still care for him then.'

'You mustn't turn down what they offer, Maud. Because of the bombing, there's so many people crying out for homes. And you do need a break from the old man, Maud.'

'A break? I've forgotten what that is. To be able to sleep through the night with only Hitler's bombs to worry about would be marvellous. But Solomon is family and I owe him a debt.'

'He might feel better amongst people of his own age.'

'We never stop worrying, do we? I think it's built into a woman to worry.' Maud gestured towards the three girls. 'Bea's still not herself, you know.'

Maud didn't know how she'd managed to carry on with her everyday tasks when all she'd wanted to do after Bea's unlucky experience was hold her daughter close and take away her pain. Eddie was like a rock to them all.

'Do you expect her to be?'

Maud shook her head. 'Ivy and your Rainey have been towers of strength. But it's like she's withdrawn into herself. I'd give anything to have her being cheeky to Eddie again.'

'It's early days yet. Besides, them three have been practising so much for this day and the panto, none of them have
had much time to think about anything else.'

'I wish I could have got Bea to stay on at school and take
typing and shorthand like your Rainey and young Ivy.'

'You can't make kids do anything they don't really want
to do, Maud. Just be thankful she managed to stop with the
drink before it really got hold of her.'

'We had a neighbour who couldn't help himself. Sometimes
he wasn't able to get his key in the door when he got back
from the pub and we'd often find him asleep in the garden
in the mornings.'

'What happened?'

'What d'you think happened? One morning he was found
stiffer than a board.'

'The charabanc's there!' Ivy shouted back at Maud and
Jo. Maud saw choir members being shepherded on by Mrs
Wilkes, Toto barking about her feet excitedly.

'Some have brought their husbands,' Jo said. 'Didn't Eddie
want to come?'

'Someone had to look after Granddad,' Maud said. 'Good
morning, Mrs Wilkes.' She began hauling herself onto the
charabanc. 'Oh, we've been saved places,' she added – a
blonde woman, one of the choir, was frantically waving

at them and pointing to seats. Maud stared along the aisle, taking note of which relatives had come along in support. Ivy's mother wasn't there.

'I wish we could leave,' Jo said, and dug her elbow into Maud, who was taking up most of the seat.

'Don't wish your life away,' Maud said. 'We'll be off as soon as Mrs Wilkes has finished checking we're all here. Then we must concentrate on the festival and on winning.'

'I feel like a schoolkid in this hall,' said Maud. 'Where are the girls?' She looked at the three empty chairs. 'This place even smells of school milk.'

The cold hall was only just beginning to warm up. In front of her was the stage where shortly she would stand and sing. It wouldn't be like a concert where she could sing for the joy of it. No, this time she had to remember to enunciate her words properly, to smile, to be professional . . .

'Getting changed into their uniforms in the lavatory, I expect, like we've just done,' Jo said.

Maud thought of the smell that had nearly choked her as she'd exchanged her skirt and jumper for the St John's uniform back in the Ladies. She glanced down at the carrier bag at her feet. 'I wish this was all over,' she said, making herself as comfortable as she could on the hard chair. 'The judges are coming in.'

Maud glanced to where Alice Wilkes was sitting, Toto held fast on her lap. She was staring at the small procession walking sedately along the side of the stage to a long table set with glasses and a jug of water, with a row of chairs behind it.

A yellow Labrador guided the man holding its lead to a chair and waited patiently beside it.

'He's blind,' said Maud, stating the obvious. 'He's been through some nasty times – look at his scars.'

'He's also a composer,' Jo read from her programme. 'This says he lost his sight in the Great War. Being blind doesn't stop him listening carefully to music and words, does it? They must all be worthy judges or they wouldn't be here.'

'Even the Mayor?' Maud winked at her.

'Well, he's a decoration in that gold chain, isn't he?' Jo dug Maud in the ribs again.

Maud watched as a representative introduced the judges individually. Each stood up and said a few words. The blind man was introduced as Graham Letterman and began to speak. A thud from further along the row of seats told Maud that Alice Wilkes had dropped her music bag, along with Toto, who gave a surprised yelp. Rainey was helping to pick up the sheet music, clearly trying to make as little noise as possible.

Mrs Wilkes's face was chalk-white. Maud leaned across Bea and said, 'What's the matter with her?'

Suddenly Mrs Wilkes took a deep breath, then clutched the music Rainey handed her. She looked at Maud and smiled an apology. Maud thought she saw a light in her eyes that hadn't been there before. She dismissed it as nerves.

Having sat through several choirs and their offerings, Maud wished the festival was over. 'I hate it when the judges scribble things down while people are performing,' she said. 'It makes me think they've done something wrong.'

'Sssh!' Mrs Wilkes said. Then she gave the signal for her choir to rise and walk to the steps that led to the back of the stage. 'Performing on a proper stage here will get you all in the mood for the panto at the David Bogue Hall,' she said, when they were all standing behind the plush curtains. They'd all been threatened with dire consequences if they talked to each other.

The St John's choir silently lined up.

'We don't say "good luck" because it's unlucky. Instead we say "break a leg". So, break a leg girls.' Mrs Wilkes left the stage to take her place at the piano. Maud saw the daft smile on her face and wanted so much to mention it to Jo but didn't dare.

There was polite applause after their introduction. Four piano bars to count and their medley of First World War songs began.

'It's a Long Way to Tipperary' was followed by 'Pack Up Your Troubles in Your Old Kit Bag', and then the choir harmonized and divided voices to sing both songs at the same time, finishing together. Someone in the audience began clapping too soon but the accolade was drowned out as 'Over There' came next. The familiar joy was rising within Maud as she sang. A quick glance at Jo, who looked as if she was smiling for England and singing as though her heart would break, gave her a further boost of happiness. All eyes in the hall were upon them and suddenly Maud found she could forget about Granddad, about food shortages, about the war as she sang her heart out. Maud's favourite 'Roses Of Picardy' followed, the sadness of the words catching in her throat, and then they were into 'Keep the Home Fires Burning', lusty voices imploring Britain to remain strong until our brave boys returned from war.

All too soon it was over. The clapping stopped and Maud saw the judges still scribbling away. Mrs Wilkes nodded at the women to come down from the stage and go back to their seats. She had a smile on her face a mile wide, thought Maud.

While the next choir readied themselves, Mrs Wilkes passed her thanks along the row of her girls. 'I couldn't have wished for more,' she added. Then, 'In ten minutes there'll be a break for tea and rock cakes, after which it'll be the solo singers and small groups, then prize-giving, and it's over for another year. Maybe it will be cancelled until the war's over. Who knows?'

'I wish I knew why she keeps staring at the judges' table,' Maud said.

Chapter Twenty-six

'Are you sure this is the right address?'

Blackie knocked again on the front door. 'Course I'm sure, Herbert.' But he glanced again at the piece of paper in his hand, then stared at the number on the door to make sure.

'Excuse me.' The voice was paper-thin and belonged to a skinny white-haired woman peeping out from next door.

Herbert walked up to her. She had a headscarf and three iron curlers clamped at the front of her thin hair.

'Are you looking for Mrs Bird?'

'We are,' called Blackie, following him. If he was to take a deep breath and blow, the woman might disappear, he thought.

'She's got the day off work today. Gone to Fareham to sing in the music festival. It'll be in the papers, you mark my words.' Blackie instantly recognized a lonely lady who loved to talk. He and Herbert were sitting ducks. 'I often hear her practising her singing. These walls are like paper, and she loves singing, she does. On Wednesday night she's singing at the David Bogue Hall in Stoke Road. It's *Snow White*, starts at seven.' She smiled, showing ill-fitting false teeth.

'And her daughter?' Herbert's voice seemed loud.

Blackie didn't need to take the photograph from his inside pocket to show the woman. This was the right address: this was where Alfie Bird's family lived.

'Oh, you mean Rainey. She's singing there, as well. Lovely voice, sings like an angel.'

Blackie stared at Herbert. They'd found who they were looking for.

'No wonder they're called rock cakes,' said Ivy. 'I'm lucky I've got any teeth left. If it hadn't been for your mum bringing sandwiches I'd be dying of hunger by now.' She pushed open the door to the Ladies and stopped dead in her tracks, causing Bea to bump into her back.

'What's the hold-up?' Rainey sounded cross.

'Come in, there's room for all of us,' said the small curly-haired blonde applying more lipstick to her overpainted mouth. 'You three must be Alice Wilkes's girls. You're on after me in the second half.'

The sound of a chain being pulled and a lavatory flushing in a nearby cubicle cut into the silence.

Rainey was the first to come to her senses. For this Ivy was glad because she didn't know what to say to the apparition in front of the speckled mirror now patting her bleached sausage curls. 'Yes, that's us,' Rainey provided. 'And you are?'

Ivy saw a tight little smile curve on the blonde's heavily Pan-Stik-smothered face. False eyelashes like tiny black fans blinked in front of blue eyes. The smile hadn't reached them.

'My dears! Don't you ever look at programmes? I'm Little Annette.'

When no one said anything, a look of annoyance passed over the woman's face. 'I'm number-one girl on the circuit. You'll have to do well to gain a place when I'm performing.' She smoothed down the pink ballet dress that emphasized her stick-thin body.

Ivy heard Bea snap, 'Girl? You must be thirty if you're a day!'

The atmosphere in the Ladies dropped to freezing point.

Annette, with a look of pure hatred, glared at Bea's reflection in the mirror, then swept her mascara and hairbrush from the wooden shelf and into her little pink handbag. She sashayed out, allowing the door to bang behind her.

A young woman, dressed in black relieved by a red scarf

at her throat, stepped out of the cubicle. 'Whoops! I think you've made an enemy there,' she said.

'Who the hell was she?' Bea asked.

'Little Annette, former darling of the music halls. Her agent keeps her in the public eye any way he can. Especially now she's not earning. Because of the war, many of the theatres are either closing down or using acts to cheer the troops.'

'But she's old!' Ivy knew Bea couldn't help herself.

'Little Annette she started out and Little Annette she'll be until the day she hangs up her ballet and tap shoes. I'm Gloria Gold,' she said, smiling at them. 'I know who you three are because I'm acquainted with Alice Wilkes. She's a good teacher and a good woman. She must think you three have something special to offer if you're singing without the rest of your choir.' She ran a hand over her straight dark hair. 'I was in the hall when you all sang. It sounded top-hole.'

'Thanks. That's a jolly nice thing for you to say,' Ivy told her, as Bea pushed her aside and went into the cubicle.

Gloria looked at her wristlet watch. 'I must go,' she said. 'See you later.'

The door slammed behind her but opened again immediately and a young girl came in, blonde plaits curled around her head, like the skater and film star Sonja Henie. Ivy looked at Rainey, who shook her head: the conversation was now at an end.

After the break, the hall was filling nicely again, and when the girls and the rest of the choir were seated, Ivy leaned across to talk quietly to Mrs Wilkes. Toto stretched his head to lick her fingers. 'Hello, precious,' she murmured, then to Mrs Wilkes: 'We met Little Annette in the lavatory—' She got no further.

'I hope you didn't make fools of yourselves. She's an established singer, or was. Not in the public eye now. Ingénue she is not, but she can make things difficult for you, if you cross swords with her. I hear she's hoping for a wireless career.'

Ivy thought of the woman's stick-like arms and legs, the dreadful child's dress. 'But—'

'But nothing,' Mrs Wilkes snapped. 'She's on before you. Watch how her every action is timed to the split second. Watch the knack she has of holding the audience in the palms of her hands. She may not be a young girl but she'll have you believing she is.'

Ivy sat back in her seat. Perhaps Mrs Wilkes was right: they might learn a lot from Annette's performance.

Twenty minutes later, standing behind the curtain, Ivy smiled at her two companions. Mrs Wilkes hadn't lied. Annette's piece had gone without a hitch. She was mesmerizing. She'd walked onto the stage as though she owned it. Her voice had been as clear as a bell and her dance steps lighter than Fred Astaire's. She'd had the audience believing she was a young girl singing and dancing. Ivy was enthralled. The applause practically shook the building.

'And now for something completely different . . .'

The curtains went back, a hush enveloped the auditorium and, after a nod from Alice Wilkes at the piano, Bea's sweet voice began the folk song.

The tune, the words, their meaning and the three voices in perfect harmony filled the hall.

Ivy dared to take a look at the judges. They were watching, not scribbling on their writing pads. The sadness of the song overwhelmed her. She looked to the back of the hall and, as her voice rose for the final verse, she saw her mother, who'd told her she couldn't spare the time to come to Fareham.

Della was sitting in the back row smiling at her, willing her to sing, to do her very best, love spilling from her eyes. Even the glass beads in the head of the fox fur slung around her neck glinted brightly.

Chapter Twenty-seven

Mrs Wilkes stood on the step of the charabanc and announced, 'I'm extremely proud of you all. Second place in the two classes is amazing.' She smiled at Ivy, bent down and whispered, 'Did you see what I meant about Little Annette's performance? Faultless. She deserved a first.'

'She's a nasty piece of work.' Ivy glared at her. 'She's one of those people who climb over everyone else to get to the top.'

Mrs Wilkes looked agitated. 'Pish! No, my dear, the woman is on her way down and she knows it – everyone does. But in this business we look after our own. Jealousy caused her nastiness to you. I maintain you should be nice to the people you meet on the way up because you're sure to meet them again on the way down. Now –' she looked around the charabanc '– let's have a rousing cheer for everyone's hard work.'

When the choir had quietened she said, 'The photographer told me that the report with photographs will be in the *Evening News* tomorrow night. No doubt we'll be bombarded with queries about performing at all sorts of places before Christmas. Don't forget your costumes on Wednesday for *Snow White*.'

She made her way along the bus to where Jo and Maud sat together. The last of Maud's fish-paste sandwiches lay on her lap. Toto jumped up, putting his paws expectantly on Maud's knee. Maud broke off a piece of sandwich and he wolfed it. 'Maud, I need to ask you a favour. If I give you the list of travellers, they're all present and correct, could you see them safely off the charabanc? The driver has promised to drop everyone at the ends of their roads. I'll see you all at the David Bogue Hall for our big performance. Remind everyone there's no more rehearsals at St John's. I have a little unfinished business in Fareham.'

Maud took the sheet of paper and the pen offered to her and Mrs Wilkes smiled. 'Thank you,' she said, and made her way off the vehicle. The driver started the engine. 'Wave to Mrs Wilkes,' shouted Maud, and as they moved off, the small woman was left clutching her dog outside the hall.

*

Alice stepped back inside. She had no idea how she was going to do this. Should she wait? Should she try to find him? Suppose he had already left by a back exit? What if his family was with him? She was taking a big chance in following her heart after all these years.

'Excuse me,' she ventured, to an elderly man in blue overalls sweeping the parquet flooring near the stage. 'Can you tell me if all the judges have left?'

He stopped what he was doing and wiped his hand across his nose. 'Didn't I see you with two acts earlier?'

Alice nodded, but before she could speak, he said, 'It's no good you moaning if you don't think the judging's fair. Won't get you anywhere.'

'No, it's not that. It's personal.'

'Oh,' he said. He used the broom to point to a door at the side of the hall. 'They usually have a cuppa in there before they leave and most have already gone. The mayor was collected.'

She interrupted, 'The man with the dog? Has he left yet?'

'No. He lives in Fareham. Bess makes sure he doesn't come to any harm.'

Alice's heart dropped, like a stone. She'd been so overwhelmed to think she might be in the presence of the man she had cared for so long ago that it had never entered her head his wife would be waiting.

'Bess?' The name escaped her.

'Graham Letterman's dog.'

And now her heart was beating wildly. The dog! His guide dog! Of course! And she knew only too well how a faithful canine friend could love their owner more than life itself. Beneath her arm Toto wriggled.

'I don't want to be a nuisance.' Even as she spoke Alice knew that nothing in the world would stop her entering that room. Letterman? Graham Letterman. She'd recognized the name from the programme. Of course, she had never known his surname. In the music business Graham Letterman was deeply respected.

'If you wants a word with him I should knock now.'

'Uh! Thank you.' Alice shifted Toto to a more comfortable position and knocked sharply on the door.

'Come in.'

Alice's heart swept skywards. She would know that familiar voice anywhere. How she'd sat among the audience in the hall, her ears straining to pick up every word he had said, and hadn't rushed up to make herself known to him, she had no idea. Except, of course, she had to be sure.

Her free hand turned the brass handle, the door opened and Alice went inside.

The man was in the process of replacing his dark glasses.

The same long fingers with oval nails. Blue-veined now, and something else, scars on his hands as well as on his face.

'Can I help you?' he asked. He was now pulling his coat on.

The dog watched her, eyes shining expectantly. Toto wriggled in the crook of her arm.

'Let him down,' the man said. 'Bess won't hurt him.'

Alice couldn't help it: 'Oh.' The word slipped from her lips.

'I have no sight but my other senses are heightened,' he said. Alice set Toto on the wooden floor and he immediately bounded towards the Labrador, which, her harness around her, sat quite still while Toto made a complete fool of himself nuzzling and licking her. After a few moments the Labrador gave Toto a brisk nudge, as if to say, 'That's enough,' whereupon he settled by the side of his new friend, his tongue lolling from his mouth.

'Now . . .' began the man, then paused. 'Do my scars upset you?'

Alice was amazed he could tell she was staring at him. But it wasn't because of the gouges in the hollows of his cheeks or the puckered flesh that she was staring: it was the pure wonder that this was the man she'd fallen in love with so long ago and who had disappeared from her life.

It was his voice. She knew and loved every inflection in his speech. At first she hadn't dared believe it was really him. Faces change but voices stay the same.

'Graham,' she said.

Just the one word, his name, and he felt for the chair at the desk and sat down heavily. 'Alice?'

She put out a hand across the table and traced the back of his fingers.

'Oh, my God,' he said. 'It's you?' It was a question as well as a statement.

Alice allowed her hand to cover his. 'It's been a long time. I thought . . .' What did she think? That he was dead? That he no longer wanted her in his life? Her mind flew back through the years to the bandstand at Stokes Bay, the music, his smiles, the touch of his hand.

'How wonderful to hear you again. Have the years been good to you?'

A knock at the door interrupted him and the elderly cleaner said, 'Will you be much longer, sir? I need to lock up.'

Graham clutched at Alice's fingers as he rose from the chair. 'Come with me,' he said. 'There's a little café along the road. I'll buy you a cup of tea. That's if you want to, of course.'

Alice allowed herself to move with him, then bent down and Toto jumped into her arms.

'I'm just off,' Graham shouted, towards the door. 'As ever, thanks for everything.'

He and Bess were obviously known in the café and the two dogs sat contentedly beneath the table.

'So you're the Alice Wilkes with the choir and the three girlies who each gained a second place?'

Before she had time to answer a tray was set upon the table with tea and crockery for two people. Alice smiled at the young woman, who asked, 'Want some water for the dogs?'

'Kathy, that would be lovely,' Graham said, pulling a handful of coins from his pocket and allowing the girl to choose the amount. 'Take a tip for yourself,' he added. With a small smile at Alice, the girl did as she was told.

Alice set out the cups and poured the tea. She set a cup of tea near to his fingers and guided his hand to the saucer. The young girl came back with an enamel bowl full of water, which she set down beneath the table. Almost before she'd walked away, the dogs were lapping.

How Alice had longed for just this moment, to be with him. Yet now she was, she felt powerless, unable to speak, to ask questions, to say what was on her mind. It was as if a chasm lay between them that was impossible to cross.

His hand slid over the table and found hers, which thrilled her. She also felt guilt that he should be touching her when he had a wife. But she had already known he was married when she'd decided to approach him, hadn't she?

He said, 'I didn't think you'd want to see me like this.'

She said, 'I thought you were dead.' They'd spoken at once. There was a pause, then Alice said, 'Tell me what happened.' She thought she would rather listen to what he had to say than explain about her own life, the life that had taken away her girlhood and planted her in middle age. And suddenly she was relieved he couldn't see her as she was now but would picture her as she had been.

'I was taught gunnery and photography in the Royal Flying Corps. I was billeted at Hastings and went out as an observer with my squadron on the Western Front. Even from the beginning while flying over the front there was heavy fighting. I was in a Bristol F2B fighter, facing the tail. I'm not sure if I ever shot anything but I gripped that gun, pointing it up and around and down.' He paused, as though remembering was an effort. 'The enemy always came at you from behind, never the front. I had to take photographs with a semi-automatic camera fitted inside the cockpit's floor. I was shot or, rather, the plane was hit, and I'd no idea whether we were over enemy lines or not.' She could see beads of sweat on his forehead. 'There was a cornfield and we landed and I hit my head. I remember the flames, the smoke, and then men running towards me, but most of all I remember the smell of burning flesh, then nothing until I woke in a French hospital.'

She didn't speak, knowing it was better for him to get the retelling over with.

'For a long time I had no memory of what had happened. It came to me in bits and pieces. I was transferred home to Blighty. My wife came to see me. I could tell by her voice that my burns upset her. She also gave me the terrible news that our elder son had been killed. She never returned to the hospital. We lost touch. It was to be expected, I suppose. The other fellows in the sanatorium said it happened frequently.'

His silence spoke volumes. Alice wanted him to carry on.

'My music saved my sanity. I needed to get past the changes in my hands, my fingers. My skin would never allow me to play as before but I could teach. So that was my aim. I could still compose. Bess is my eyes and she opened a whole new world for me.'

Then he smiled and Alice saw the young man he used to be.

'Last year my younger son discovered my whereabouts and brought my first grandchild to see me. My wife had lied to him, telling him I'd perished. She didn't want him to see the thing I had become.'

'But that's so cruel.'

'She thought she was protecting him.'

'Where's your wife now?'

'She died a few years ago. On her deathbed she told my son I hadn't been killed in the war after all.'

Alice was appalled at the cruelty his wife had heaped upon him. He spoke again: 'Alice, I'm not going to say I haven't thought about you. I have. The more my memory returned the more I wanted to see you again. But look at me. I have nothing to offer any woman.'

His hand felt for the cup again and he raised it to his lips.

Then he said, 'It feels good talking to you, Alice. How have you fared over the years?' She told him. He listened as she'd always remembered him listening to her, full of interest, so she was able to talk freely without feeling he wanted her to hurry and finish.

Eventually she plucked up the courage to say, 'It would be good to meet you again.'

'I don't need pity, Alice.' He was frowning but he smiled suddenly and said, changing the subject, 'Those girls of yours have a bright future.'

Now Alice was on very firm ground. She told him about

her choir. Beneath the table the dogs were sitting close. It looked as if they had become friends. If only she and Graham could recapture a little of what they'd once shared, Alice thought, she would be the happiest woman alive.

Chapter Twenty-eight

'Bert, I was so proud of Ivy.'

'So you ought to be, Della, though why you didn't go up to Fareham with all the others . . .'

'How could I? Without me around, she can be herself.' Della shook off the fox fur and laid it on the seat beside her.

Bert surveyed his empire. Although it was early in the evening he was surprised Ivy wasn't back yet from singing in the Fareham Festival. He was longing to hear from her all that had happened.

As usual there were only a few customers in so he felt no qualms at closing early on Wednesday to watch the pantomime. He'd have liked to see Ivy, Bea and Rainey sing this afternoon. He'd had no idea that Della intended to go but was sincerely glad she had shown her daughter how much she cared.

'That girl loves the bones of you!' He set down the cup of strong tea in front of her on the Formica counter. He thought of how Ivy had railed against the young thug who had accosted her because of her mother's profession. Della really had no idea how protective Ivy was of her. 'A second place, eh?' He felt as pleased as if he'd had a part in Ivy's success.

He served an elderly woman, who took ages to sort out her money. As he shut the till, he said, 'A letter came for Ivy today.' He reached behind him and took a long brown envelope from the cluttered shelf.

Della grabbed it. 'It'll be the results of her typing and short-hand tests.' She turned it over almost as though she expected to read the letter through the envelope. Then she transferred it to her handbag. 'I'll give it to her tonight and let's hope it's not bad news. Don't want to spoil her happiness today.'

'How can it be anything but good news, all the work she's done?' Sometimes, Bert thought, Della could be so negative. He smiled to himself. He'd rather have a negative Della than no Della at all. He realized she was talking to him.

'Shut your eyes and only open them when I say.'

He obeyed her instantly. He heard her climb down from the stool and walk to the stairs. He heard the rustle of paper.

'What you playing at? Can I open them now?' He waited for her to answer.

'There you are. Don't say I don't ever get you nothing.'

Bert opened his eyes. On the counter a long object was wrapped in newspaper. Della was still talking.

'I got to Fareham early but when I saw the programme I went for a walk. I didn't want to stick out like a sore thumb in the audience, did I?' He didn't answer because he was busy unwrapping the paper. 'There was a market with farmers. Animals in pens and cages, that sort of thing. In a big black shed there was stuff piled on the ground, house clearance, I reckon.' Now Bert had removed the last of the paper. 'I saw that and knew I had to buy it. It's a little thank-you for everything you do for us.'

Bert couldn't speak. He pressed his lips together in an effort to stop his emotions spilling over.

The highly lacquered black cane was in the shape of a furled umbrella. He touched the glossy surface, which was covered with diamanté. Even though he could feel and see encrusted grime he knew it was a very special thing.

'There's some glass stones missing but I didn't think you'd worry about that, and I know it's a bit scratched . . .'

'Della, it's beautiful.' He picked it up. It was as light as thistledown. His heart was overflowing that she should think of him on such an important day as this.

'It's not a bloke's cane, is it?'

He put the treasure on the counter again. 'It's a stage prop,' he answered, 'most likely used by some lady in show business . . .' He walked round to where she was again sitting on the stool and took her in his arms. The warm smell of flesh and her perfume made him feel like a young man again.

'Don't be daft. I knew you hadn't got one like it.' She struggled free. He saw he'd knocked her silly little hat with the veil and feather so it didn't sit straight on her dark hair. She stared at him. 'After watching her today with the other two, I got a feeling she won't need the back-up of a secretarial career.'

'Who got first place, then?' He thought he ought to ask as he began rewrapping his present. He'd put it beneath the counter until he closed up.

'Some strange song-and-dance creature. She was good, I'll give her her due, but she didn't have the freshness of our girls.'

'Maybe the judging was fixed. Stranger things have happened, Della.'

'I don't believe Alice Wilkes would have anything to do with something that wasn't quite right. I also think the girls will go on to greater things.'

'Della, it's a bit of fun that's all, and getting the girls' names in the *Evening News* is a bonus. D'you want another cup of tea?'

She shook her head. 'You wasn't there, Bert. You didn't feel the magic in that room, like I did . . .' Della tailed off. She became thoughtful, then said. 'If my Ivy wants to go further with this singing lark, I'll be behind her all the way. But I can't be a millstone around her neck.'

Bert could see she was getting upset. He'd asked her many times to let him take care of her and her daughter, but the silly independent woman wouldn't have it.

'Bert,' she said, 'just think how awful it would be for Ivy if she became a big star and then some newspaper wrote all about her and told the world about the way I earns my living. I just couldn't bear it if that happened. She'd lose all the respect, all the glory . . .'

'Della, you're running ahead of yourself. They won second place in a local music festival, nothing more, nothing less.' Bert understood Della perfectly well. They both knew it could be a very cruel world for young girls who wanted to go on the stage.

'I felt like I owned the stage,' said Bea. She bent her head forward and went on brushing her blonde hair, then looked up at Ivy. 'How did you feel?'

All three girls were in Bea's bedroom going over the day's activities.

'Sick before we went on. I was convinced I was going to forget all the words and make you two look daft.'

'But how did singing to all those people make you feel?' Bea chucked the hairbrush onto the bed and shook her hair away from her face.

'Like I wanted to throw out my arms and say, "Here I am. This is what I can do,"' Ivy answered, then glanced at Rainey. 'I could sense you beside me willing me to add to the magic, and I wanted to make it perfect for us.'

'Today has been the most wonderful day of my life.' Bea picked up a tumbler of home-made ginger beer and swallowed a mouthful. As she replaced it on the chair she said, 'After everyone had clapped, I felt like I was walking on air.'

'It was a great feeling,' admitted Rainey. 'Much better than singing with the rest of the choir, not that they aren't good, but I felt the three of us were really part of one whole thing, like segments in an orange.'

'I'm surprised you can remember what a blinking orange looks like,' said Ivy. 'Seriously, though, I've decided it's what I want to do. Sing!' She was animated.

'Just as well because on Wednesday we do *Snow White* and get to sing as a trio again,' said Bea.

'But I want more than singing in hospitals and halls for

charity. I want to sing and make money from it. I want singing to be my career, my life,' said Ivy.

'I want that, too,' said Rainey. 'It's what I've always wanted. Do you think Mrs Wilkes knows how we can take this further?'

'She's got a really good reputation as a music teacher but I think school work, and all that goes with it, is as far as she can take us. At one point in her life she probably dreamed of a career for herself, playing not teaching. How come she didn't get it? She must know about the pitfalls.' Ivy was looking at Bea.

'We can ask if she thinks we're good enough.' Bea was thoughtful. She knew there was something that had to be addressed. The other two wanted to carry on singing as a trio. Were they wondering if she would let them down?

'Something happened to me this afternoon. I realized I was hardly out of my childhood but already I've been wasting my life. When we started to sing I knew what a selfish fool I'd been.' Bea saw her two friends were watching her intently. 'I've already lost what I had with my brother. It'll be a long time before Eddie trusts me again.'

She paused, then began again. 'My little problem grew into a bigger one, and it had been going on for a good while. I thought I'd managed to keep it secret until . . . until . . .' She faltered. 'What I'm trying to say is that I want people to be proud of me, not look down their noses, but proud like they were this afternoon in Fareham. I know it might be only a dream but I want to be like you two and try to do something with my life.'

Bea was crying.

'You idiot,' said Ivy, going towards her. 'We're a trio, and that means three of us, all for one and one for all.' Bea felt Ivy's arms go around her and then Rainey enveloped them both.

'I've got something to tell you,' Rainey said, pulling away. 'I found out today when a letter came in the early-morning post that I've passed my exams. Mum wants me to get a job in an office.' She looked at Ivy. 'You should find a letter waiting for you when you get home.' She suddenly looked distressed. 'I don't want to hurt my mum but all my life I've sung. I want to go on singing. Somehow we have to find a way. Let's talk to Mrs Wilkes before we do the panto next Wednesday.'

'Not before the panto. She'll be worried and het-up. Afterwards would be better,' said Ivy.

'Just a moment,' said Bea. 'Suppose all three of us have exaggerated our own importance and think we're better than we really are?'

For a moment there was silence. Then Ivy said, 'Well, there's only one way to find out, isn't there?'

Chapter Twenty-nine

Graham turned the key in the door but allowed Bess to nose her way into the small house first. She wouldn't rush: she'd wait until she was sure he had caught up with her, then stand patiently while he took off his coat and hung it on the newel post.

In the small scullery he made tea and took the prepared tray back into the living room where he set it down near the door leading out to the conservatory. It was his favourite seat. Even in winter he believed he could feel the promise of sun to come. Bess, now he'd unfastened her harness, gulped at the fresh water in her dish in the scullery, then settled beside his chair.

In the small house Graham felt secure. Every inch was familiar to him.

It had been a shock, Alice reappearing from his past, and

her presence in his life would take some getting used to. He smiled, thinking of the dogs together.

'You liked that bossy little thing,' he said, and his hand felt for the softness of Bess's coat.

He mulled over everything in his mind while drinking his tea. Then he cleared away his tray and took from the pantry Bess's dinner – he had prepared it before leaving the house. That seemed an age ago now.

For a minute he listened to Bess eat, then went back into the living room and removed his violin from its case on the sideboard. It felt familiar and beloved. He had long ago stopped despising himself for his imperfect playing. His fingers felt for the bow.

The tune formed itself into the piece he had composed many years ago, which he had entitled 'Alice'.

'There's a letter for you upstairs in our room.' Della gave Ivy a hug as soon as she stepped into the café. 'You were wonderful today, all of you.'

'Yes, well done.' Bert was busy with a frying pan.

Della took a deep breath of the familiar smells of cooking.

'Mum, I was so glad to see you there.'

Della saw Bert glance at her and smile. She felt embarrassed. 'Well, don't keep me waiting. Go and look at your letter.'

'I think I know what it is. Rainey's passed! Her letter came this morning.'

Della could see Ivy was excited for her friend. She turned to Bert. 'I should have left it down here.'

'No,' Bert said. 'It's best she reads it in private.' He was turning fried bread.

Della could hear Ivy's footsteps on the bare boards of the stairs. She pulled herself onto a stool in front of the counter. 'I hope to God she's passed. If so, she can leave school now and find a good job away from Gosport.'

Bert looked at her. 'You can't mean that. There's plenty of decent places here for her to work.'

'The further she goes from the south coast, the less my reputation will follow her. In this place she'll be reminded of her roots, of me, and she'll be put down at every turn.'

'You're being stupid.' He transferred the golden fried bread to the plate and set it on the hob to keep warm. 'There is something you can do.'

'What?'

'Give up the life. You've done what you set out to do, make sure she got a good education . . .'

'How would I live?'

'With me.'

'What? Even now you'd ask me to stay?'

'I already have, haven't I? Tell that bastard Jim you won't be working for him any more.'

Della couldn't answer for the noise Ivy was making.

'Mum! Mum!' She clattered down the stairs, the letter in her hand. 'I've passed!'

'Good girl! I knew you would.'

Bert looked pleased.

Della hadn't expected Ivy to look glum, but suddenly she did. 'Mum, there's something I have to tell you.' She took a deep breath. 'I did this course for you and I appreciate everything you've done for me, keeping me on at school when I could have been working but . . . When we got back from Fareham, the three of us got talking and we –' her voice wobbled '– we want to sing.'

'Just how am I supposed to keep you while you wait for this magical career to happen?' Jo stared across the kitchen table at her daughter. She wasn't angry but she was upset. 'Being in the choir is a bit of fun. You can't let what happened today go to your head!'

She rose, pushing the kitchen chair back across the lino. 'I know you was singing before you could walk, Rainey, but if you think the money from your Saturday job is all you're going to contribute, you've got another think coming!'

She marched into the scullery and filled the kettle, then lit the gas beneath it. She needed tea after her daughter's bombshell. Rainey wasn't going to sit on her bottom and wait for a fairy godmother to come along. Certainly not when she had passed her exams, allowing her a decent office job! Jo was about to poke her head around the scullery door and yell that if Rainey thought they could use the money she'd got from the sale of the car she was seriously wrong! Immediately that thought entered her head she was ashamed. Rainey didn't have a nasty bone in her body. She knew that money was put away in case something serious happened.

Jo leaned her head against the scullery's cold wall. She could hear no sounds coming from the kitchen. It wasn't often she yelled at Rainey, and she knew she'd upset her. She sighed and watched the blue and orange flames lick at the base of the kettle.

Of course Rainey wanted to sing. It was what she'd always wanted. That girl had been a tower of strength, and it was because of her that Jo had a job she loved, a comfortable home and had met Syd. Syd, who was gaining Jo's trust so much that she'd bought him a ticket to see the pantomime. It was Rainey who had given her the courage to escape from Alfie. She deserved something in return for saving her mother's sanity. Jo took a deep breath of the stale food and gassy smell of the scullery.

She peeped around the open door. Rainey sat with her knees up in the armchair, her head in her arms. Jo thought her heart might break to see her child like that. She walked over and put her hand on Rainey's shoulder. 'Sorry,' she said. 'I've spoiled what should be one of the happiest days of your life.' Rainey lifted her head, her vibrant hair a perfect frame for her tear-stained face.

Jo said softly, 'I'm an absolute cow!' She took another deep breath. 'But I promise that if you take a job, any job – it doesn't have to be in an office – I will do everything in my power to help you get what you want. We've got some money we can use to show you three girls off to the best advantage with matching clothes and such—' She got no further for Rainey had thrown her arms around her neck and was practically smothering her with kisses.

Chapter Thirty

'I'm sorry, all the seats are taken.'

Blackie looked at the elderly woman sitting at the little table inside the doorway of the David Bogue Hall. She wore a shawl over her coat and a pair of fingerless gloves that enabled her to count the coins from a biscuit tin into piles.

'How about I pay double the price to see *Snow White* and we don't have a seat but stand at the back?' Herbert had pulled from his wallet a ten-shilling note and placed it in front of her.

Her beady eyes stared back. 'Got someone in the choir, have you?'

Blackie thought quickly. 'We didn't know you could get tickets in advance, and my sister will be so disappointed. We've come a long way.' He hoped she wouldn't ask the name of the fictitious sister.

The woman sniffed and wiped her nose with the back of her knitted glove. Then she inclined her head towards the end of the passage where a cacophony of noise was coming from behind a blackout curtain.

'Mind you pull them blackout curtains across. We don't want them Jerries seeing what we're up to.'

In the smoke-filled auditorium the air reeked with the smell of warm bodies. Red velvet curtains were pulled across the stage.

'There's no orchestra,' said Herbert, 'only a piano.'

'What do you expect? It's a local production. This isn't the Albert Hall.' Blackie propped his arms on the rail at the back of the rows of chairs. In his hand was the photograph.

'And I fear you've brought me on a wild-goose chase,' said Herbert.

'Our trip won't be entirely wasted,' said Blackie. 'Don't forget, there's a woman and her daughter in the cast, who might be happy to know their husband and father carried this photo until the day he died.'

'Less noise, please,' Alice admonished her choir. She was a little tearful. Surrounded by her girls in their costumes, cobbled together from items picked up in second-hand shops and begged, stolen or borrowed from their own families, she thought they looked superb.

The dwarfs were sure to raise an audience chuckle. Seven pairs of enormous foam-rubber feet strapped to the knees of the actors lined up and waiting by the side of the stage was a sight to see. Green trousers, baggy red tops tied with string and green hats with red woollen pom-poms completed their outfits. As they wouldn't be going on straight away, they knelt and chatted excitedly. Alice saw Ivy pass a cylinder of rouge along the line. 'Mrs Wilkes says we need rosy cheeks,' she said.

'What a waste of make-up when there isn't any in the shops.' Nevertheless Marlene dipped her finger in the powder and smeared her face before she passed it to the next.

'It belongs to Mrs Wilkes and she doesn't use it,' said Bea. She had on a false beard made of cotton wool. Several wore spectacles.

'Like I said, what a waste,' Marlene repeated, adding, 'This blinkin' shovel's stickin' in me side.' All of them had small garden tools wedged in their string belts, except Ivy who, as Sneezy, had an enormous white handkerchief pinned to her top. On the boards beside each of them seven jam-jars, 'borrowed' from the local WI, contained a painted red flame. These were their lanterns and each had a string around its neck so they could carry it. Alice thought how wonderful it was that every choir member had rallied round to do their best.

'I don't know why you're moaning,' said Rainey. 'Us three have to get changed at half-time into our choir outfits so we can sing, then afterwards dress up again.'

'When I said, "Be quiet," I meant you lot as well,' said Alice, moving closer while Toto wove excitedly in and out of her feet. 'We've got a full house,' she added. Then, 'In a few minutes I'm going out to announce you and the show will begin. I can't play the piano and prompt you when to come in so listen carefully for your entrance.' The dwarfs nodded. 'Snow White and the other performers are entering from the other side of the stage. When I play the working-song music put smiles on your faces. Make a grand entrance. I've every faith in you,' she said, then slid around the side curtain and out of sight of the cast, the little dog at her heels.

The audience quietened, allowing Alice to tell them who they were and that the performance proceeds would go to charity. There was loud clapping and she had to calm them down. 'I hope you've all read the local paper tonight,' she said. 'This choir gained a second place at the Fareham Festival.' She waved her hands to stop more clapping. 'After the interval, when tea will be served from the kitchen hatchway, our show will continue with a special treat for you.' Alice gave a broad smile. 'My trio of girls will sing the song that gave them second place too, "The Bluebird Song". Now, without further ado, *Snow White*.'

This time she didn't stop the clapping that roared in her ears as she descended the small steps to sit at her piano.

Ivy, as Sneezy, would be leading the dwarfs onto the stage. Her heart was pounding with fear and anticipation. Her mother and Bert were in the audience, probably expecting great things of the choir and her. She supposed these feelings were normal for anyone waiting to go on. She thought of all the time they'd spent getting ready, the practising, worrying, learning the words. The pantomime had brought the choir closer together . . . Suddenly she was aware of a terrible smell engulfing her. 'Can you smell that?'

Now she could hear muffled giggles.

Rainey said, 'I'm ever so sorry. I think that Spam I had for my dinner had been sitting in the cupboard too long.'

'I'm not about to offer the choir a contract to appear at Portsmouth's Coliseum,' said Herbert, in the interval. Blackie could see he was bored. Not so the audience: they were enjoying every moment. Of course it probably helped that the people watching were mostly relatives of the singers.

'You laughed like a drain when the dwarfs came on,' said Blackie. 'Anyway, this is a damned good cup of tea included in the price of the ticket . . .'

'I paid through the nose for them,' Herbert moaned. 'And because everyone's in costume we still have no idea which parts are being played by your girl and her mother.'

'We soon will when we go back in the hall and sit down.'

'Stand up,' Herbert reminded him.

Just then a whistle was blown that seemed to signify everyone should return to their seats. Blackie and Herbert waited while people pushed and shoved around them, holding back and finishing their tea. After all, neither had a chair to get back to. When they went into the auditorium the audience had already begun to clap the three young women standing in the centre of the stage. All three were smiling but Blackie could see they were nervous.

The plump woman with the little dog introduced the girls as 'my trio' but Blackie recognized the girl in the photograph immediately.

Herbert gave a low whistle. Blackie glared at him. 'I should have realized she wouldn't be a kid any longer.'

The girls began singing and a hush came over the hall.

Blackie looked at Herbert. His face was impassive but he was staring intently. Blackie was listening to the words. The girls seemed to be in a world of their own. When the song finished and the last note had been sung, the hall erupted with noise.

Herbert was quiet. Blackie nudged his arm and asked, 'What do you think?'

Herbert turned his head. Blackie could see his eyes were bright with tears. He blinked them away and said, 'Never mind your girl, we should sign up all three.'

Just then the air-raid siren wailed.

Chapter Thirty-one

'You're going the wrong way!'

'No, I'm not, Herbert. The crowd's rushing out into the street. I'm making my way to the back of the stage to find those girls.'

Herbert was now muttering and cursing, as people pushed past them wanting to get to the air-raid shelters.

Blackie had reached the steps at the side of the stage that the small round woman had used earlier. He bounded up, closely followed by Herbert. Standing for so long had made Blackie's leg ache but he wasn't about to give up on finding the girl in the photograph now he was so close.

Backstage was deserted. Clothing and props had been left where they'd fallen. It was also pitch black. All the lights had been turned off.

'Wait for me,' Herbert said. 'I can't see as well as you.' One of the back doors had been left open.

'Can you hear that?'

'Hear it? I can see them now.' Herbert was standing in the doorway. Searchlights had picked out planes and already ground fire was leaping towards the enemy. Blackie could hear the bombs whistling down and watched as walls of dust and flame swept into the sky. Although they were not close he ducked every time.

'Shut that bloody door,' he yelled. 'We can't go out in that – we'll never find the shelter now.'

Herbert kicked the door closed and for a second or two there was peace, until a dog's bark broke the silence.

'It came from in here,' said Blackie. He walked into the wings and was amazed when a trapdoor lifted in the stage floor.

'You'd better get down here with us if you don't want to be blasted to kingdom come,' said the frizzy-haired woman who'd been announcing the programme. 'Can't leave our patrons to fend for themselves.'

'That sounds remarkably fair of you, dear lady, and I can't thank you enough for the shelter you're offering us,' said Herbert, quickly gathering his thoughts, stepping forward and beginning to lower himself down beneath the stage.

When Blackie, too, descended, it took him a while to realize, despite the initial silence, that the cavernous space was filled with people chatting and laughing. Candles in jam-jars gave a dull light.

Blackie was about to ask why he had heard no noise until the sharp bark from Toto, when the frizzy-haired woman, as if anticipating his question, said, 'Insulation. We're well insulated beneath the stage. This is my choir and family friends,' she said, waving her hand. 'I'm Alice Wilkes.' She'd hardly got the last word out when Toto barked again. 'And this is Toto,' she added. 'The Jerries have rather caught us on the hop.'

Ever the gentleman, Herbert put out his hand. 'No time for surnames. I'm Herbert and –' he gestured to Blackie '– this is my young friend Blackie.'

Blackie shook her hand. It was stuffy in the bowels of the stage.

'Don't stand about,' Alice said. 'Find yourselves some seats.'

Now his eyes had become more used to the dull light, Blackie saw plenty of discarded props, curtains and old chairs with which he could make himself very comfortable.

Alice peered at him. 'Pish! I see you have gypsy eyes, very lucky, most unusual.' She pointed across at a fair-haired young woman and said, 'Go and sit with Jo. She'll tell you all about the pantomime. Did you see it?'

Again there was no chance to say anything as she'd moved on to talk to Herbert. Blackie sat next to Jo and gave her a weak smile. 'Hello, I'm Blackie. Does anyone ever get a word in edgeways?' He nodded at Alice.

Jo said, 'She's our music teacher so it's natural for her to tell us what to do. We're used to it.'

He sensed her nervousness and tried to make her feel more at ease: 'We really enjoyed the show, what we saw of it. The dwarfs were very funny but the high point was the three girls singing that old folk song.'

'Oh, I'm glad you enjoyed it. My daughter's the one in the middle with the startling auburn hair.' She moved her carrier bag to the floor to give him more room on the narrow bench. She was wearing slacks and a long-sleeved brown jumper. He could see bright material poking out from the bag.

'Really?' Was that all Blackie could manage? Everything was suddenly moving too fast. This wasn't the time to take out the photograph and begin talking about the last moments of her husband's life, then move on to her daughter's possible career.

A moment of silence had sprung up between them. He

looked at her. The greenest eyes he had ever seen stared back at him from a heart-shaped face. Her hair, a soft blonde, was hanging to her shoulders in a sort of bob but the front was messy and she kept pushing offending strands out of her eyes. He had the strongest need to touch it, lift it away from her face and tuck it behind her ear. He suppressed the desire, knowing how unseemly it would be.

He remembered her neighbour had said both mother and daughter sang in the choir. 'And do you sing?' he asked.

'I'm sure I didn't make much of an impression up there on the stage,' she said, 'but, yes, I'm in the choir, if only to make up the numbers.'

He thought it was a cue to laugh, so he did. 'And does your husband sing?'

Her face took on a pinched look. 'I don't have a husband,' she said. He caught the note of bitterness that spoke volumes. He thought of the dead corporal's letters from another woman and the single photograph of his daughter that he had carried until the day he had died.

It was beginning to make sense now. This woman had left her home and her husband, that much he knew. If the army, like him, had had trouble tracing her, it was possible she wasn't even aware her husband was dead. He could hardly blurt out who he was and his reasons for looking for her at the very moment bombs were raining down outside, could he?

He looked across to where Herbert was sprawled on a rumpled velvet curtain, the white dog on his lap, talking animatedly to Alice Wilkes.

It was in that moment his problem was solved for a tall man appeared at his side and said to the woman, 'One of your lot has discovered a Primus, while another's been under the other side of the stage to the kitchens and got hold of the makings for tea.' He looked at Blackie. 'No doubt you could do with a cup.'

Blackie had the strangest feeling the man had come not to offer tea but to mark his territory, for he did the very thing that Blackie had longed to do. He gently picked up the wayward strands of hair from the woman's forehead and tucked them behind her ear. She smiled, and Blackie thought that smile was like a ray of sunshine after a storm. It also showed the two were well acquainted with each other. He felt the man warranted a reply. 'Yes, please,' he said.

'Maud's looking for you,' said the man to the woman.

'It was her that moved from the seat beside me,' she said, 'but I'd better go and find her.' She made to rise. 'Blackie, this is my friend Syd. He owns a garage.' She turned to Blackie. 'I didn't ask about you,' she said.

Blackie said, 'I've recently left hospital, got knocked about a bit in France.' He couldn't tell her now why he was really there. He consoled himself with the knowledge that he had found the right woman, and that her daughter was the girl in the photograph. And he knew where they lived.

'Oh, I'm sorry,' she said. 'Will you be expected to return?'

'No,' said Blackie.

'Bad show,' said Syd. 'You must tell me what happened. Jo,' he insisted, 'don't forget about Maud.'

Blackie thought quickly. Syd was steering Jo away from him. Why? Did it show a spark of jealousy in him?

Syd and Jo were standing facing each other.

It was now or never.

Blackie swiftly took the photograph from his pocket and slipped it inside Jo's carrier bag. He sat back comforted by the knowledge that no one had seen a thing.

Chapter Thirty-two

It was nearly nine the following evening when Blackie knocked on Jo's door. He would have liked to come earlier but the bombing on Wednesday had taken its toll. Portsmouth had been hit hard. He'd spent most of the day helping Herbert survey his premises and studio, which had been hit. Luckily they had been empty at the time so no one was hurt. Madame always went to the shelter immediately the siren sounded. Blackie thought the damage was irreparable.

Despite his overcoat, he shivered. November wasn't the kindest month. He had begun to think no one was at home when he heard footsteps. Apologies were already on his lips as Jo opened the door. 'I knew it was you! The photograph of my daughter, how did you come by it?'

'Shall we talk indoors instead of out here?'

'If it's money you want not to tell him where we are, you're out of luck.'

He knew then that she had no idea her husband was dead. Worse, she thought he had come to blackmail her. He had to put his arm against the front door to stop her shutting it in his face. 'Hold on. It's not what you think.'

'You know what I think, do you?'

'I think you're very angry but even more I know you're scared and there's nothing to be frightened about.'

She stepped back and allowed the door to fall ajar. Blackie heard another door open nearby. 'Quick! Get inside,' she said. She grabbed his arm and pulled him across the doorstep. 'My neighbours are kind but so nosy.'

It smelled of lavender polish and of something delicious cooking in the oven. As he followed her to the kitchen he said, 'That smells heavenly.'

'My friend Maud got hold of some mixed fruit she split with me so there's a bread pudding in the oven for when Rainey gets home.'

'I remember Maud,' he said.

'You'd better sit down.'

He did as he was told. Then she asked, 'Are you going to explain how you got hold of my daughter's photo?'

He looked around the comfortable kitchen. He could see

someone had put a great deal of effort into making the shabby room look nice. 'Can I sit by the range?' he asked. He rubbed his hands together, as if to prove he was cold.

'Please yourself,' she said. 'Only don't take all night making up your mind to talk because I want you out of here before my daughter comes home.'

He sat in the armchair. Where to begin? he asked himself. At the beginning, of course.

'Your husband, Alfie, was in a foxhole with me in France.' He stopped. He had her full attention. Her beautiful eyes were fixed on his own.

Suddenly she spoke: 'He's dead! That's what you've come to tell me, isn't it?'

Her voice had risen alarmingly. He had no idea what he would do if she burst into floods of tears. He was quite certain now she had run from Alfie and had had no contact with the army. Momentarily Blackie remembered the strangeness of the corporal, his apparent withdrawal from what was going on around him, his unexplained presence in the lookout post. Blackie took a deep breath, amazed at the woman's stillness.

'He died saving me and killing the enemy.' Blackie had already decided he wouldn't elaborate. He stared at her. She still hadn't moved. 'He told me his daughter sang better than Vera Lynn.'

Blackie was surprised when a smile appeared on her lips. 'He always thought that,' she said. 'Did he tell you anything else?'

When Blackie shook his head, she seemed satisfied. 'So you weren't billeted with him?'

Again he shook his head. 'We weren't together long.'

'I think I need a cup of tea,' she said. 'Do you?'

Relief washed over him that she wasn't dissolving into hysterics. 'I'd love one,' he said. 'Do you want any help?'

He didn't imagine she was unable to make a pot of tea, of course not, but he wondered if she needed someone with her when she finally realized her husband was dead.

Anticipating his thoughts, she said, 'I'm not going out there to scream and shout and cry. Our marriage had gone beyond that point.' She disappeared into the scullery and he heard the gas popping, then the rattle of the teapot and crockery.

He sat gazing around the room, remembering the estate agent who'd told him the place was cheap because it was in a deplorable state. Well, it was a little palace now, he thought. There were so many questions he wanted to ask her but he knew it wasn't the right time and he needed to talk to her about her daughter, Rainey.

He heard the oven door swiftly open, then close again,

and the spicy scent of the bread pudding wafted in. He was trying to remember when he'd last eaten it when Jo came into the kitchen carrying a tray.

'I don't want you to think I'm some hard-faced bitch because I have no tears yet for Alfie.' She put the tray on the table, then sat down on a kitchen chair.

He took a deep breath. He didn't think that at all – in fact, he marvelled at her control, and the clear and concise way she spoke to him. No wonder the garage bloke wanted to keep her for himself. 'I don't, and that's not the only reason I'm here.' Say exactly what you need to say and no more, he admonished himself. His eyes followed her movements as she began pouring the tea. She pointed towards the sugar and milk. He chose only milk.

'There's more?'

'Alfie told me she could sing. Last night I heard those three girls lift the hearts of all those people in the hall. How old is Rainey?'

'Seventeen, same as Ivy the dark one. The blonde is older—'

He interrupted: 'The man I was with, Herbert, is an impresario. He and his wife run a theatrical business, and their acts play all over the world.'

'Stop. You're trying to tell me he wants to put my daughter on the stage?'

'Herbert and his wife are like parents to me and . . .'

Jo began laughing. When she stopped, she said, 'Let me get this right. You want me to let you take my girl and send her halfway around the country, singing?'

He nodded.

'Have you been talking to any of the girls?'

Now he was confused. 'No,' he said.

'Drink your tea,' she admonished, leaving hers on the table and going out into the scullery. He heard her open the oven door and put something down. Then she came back into the kitchen, throwing an oven glove onto the table. 'Sorry, I didn't want my bread pudding to burn.' She picked up her cup and drank the contents. 'Right, you start at the beginning.'

'Can I first ask a personal question?' He took a deep breath, then blew out his cheeks, expelling the air. 'Syd? Are you and he . . .'

She shook her head. 'I don't know what it's got to do with you but we're very good friends. He's helped me to stand up for myself . . .' Her voice tapered off. 'Without his help I'd never have regained the confidence I'd lost after . . . after . . .' She took a deep breath. 'Put it this way, a year ago I would never have had the courage to talk to you like this.'

She turned away from him, seemed to regain her

composure, then looked at the mantel clock. 'My Rainey will be home soon. I don't want you here when she comes in. She's a child who'll jump at the chance you say you can give her. But I'm not so easily hoodwinked. I want to think about your offer. She's a minor, remember. I'd like it if we can talk some more. Another time, another place?'

Blackie felt as though his heart was about to explode with happiness.

Chapter Thirty-three

'Of course it's a golden chance for the three of them, but how do you know it's not some kind of trick?'

'You trust me, don't you, Maud?'

'You, yes. That chap with the odd-coloured eyes could be sending pretty girls into white slavery.' Maud banged a cushion into submission. The two of them were alone in Maud's kitchen.

'I thought of that,' said Jo, 'which is why I've been doing a bit of detective work. I went to see Alice Wilkes. That dog's moulting and I got covered in white hairs. Anyway, I asked about the studio Blackie mentioned and she was dumbstruck.'

Maud's eyes were wide.

'She said that Herbert never told her he was married that night when we were all under the stage but his wife is famous and responsible for some of the best-known artists in the country. And, yes, they brought Blackie up . . .'

'Well I never!' Maud said. 'But is he the right Blackie? He could be an imposter.'

'Apparently not. Mrs Wilkes was thrilled to bits about the possibility of the girls going on to bigger things. She showed me Mrs Walker's name in the phone book. She said, if I wanted, I could telephone her and verify Blackie's character there and then.'

'Did you?'

'She did! I was a bit too nervous but when the woman said Blackie had spoken about the girls, Mrs Wilkes passed the phone to me.' Jo heard Maud's intake of breath. 'Well, I told her I thought the girls were too young to go gadding about.'

'You never!'

'Yes, I did. Guess what she said?'

Maud shook her head.

'She said she agreed with me and she thought it would be a good idea for me to be their chaperone.'

'You mean, you go an' all?'

Jo nodded. 'I told her I have to work and she said I'd get paid as soon as the trio started earning money.'

Maud threw her arms around Jo. 'Have you said anything to Rainey?'

Jo shook her head. 'The three of them want this so badly it hurts them. But I need to know everything is above board, and that you agree, and that Della, Ivy's mum, is all right with everything. I'm going to meet Blackie to find out exactly what's going on and what's required of us all.

'I'd told Rainey I'd do everything I could to help her but she couldn't sit on her bum and wait for it to happen. I told her to get a job. She said she didn't want to work in an office. All that studying and passing exams and she says office work isn't for her!'

Maud said, 'I never liked Bea working in Woolies with them other girls.' She found another cushion to fluff up.

'Hopefully they'll get good money if they become established but they can't afford not to work until that happens. When I tell Rainey what's going on, and I'm not breathing a word to her until I know all the ins and outs, I'll tell her she's to carry on working wherever she can until Blackie is positive they have a proper act and someone somewhere is willing to pay them.' She paused. 'Well, tell me what you think.'

'You've got it covered. But we need to talk to Della, see what she says.'

Jo said, 'Of course. If those girls are willing to train with Madame Walker between working it'll prove they really do want to sing.'

Maud agreed. 'Best to keep it all to ourselves at present. I know Eddie won't like Bea gallivanting about. Not after what happened down the Fox.'

'If you want my opinion, Maud, your Bea has seen the error of her ways. Anyway, I'll keep my eyes on what's going on. Now, isn't it about time you put the kettle on?'

As Maud moved towards the scullery, she added, 'Your Syd's going to have a lot to say about this. You know how fond he is of you.'

'I'm going to do what's best for my Rainey. Me and Syd aren't joined at the hip, Maud. He's been a Godsend to me this past year, and it's because of him I've learned how to stand up for myself, but if he doesn't like me meeting Blackie to discuss things, that's up to him!'

When she was walking home Jo thought of two people she had to share the secret with: the Harringtons. There was plenty of time to do that, though, after she'd met Blackie tomorrow night and talked some more. Perhaps Mr Harrington would allow her to work shorter hours. The girls had to come first and she needed to keep a watchful eye on them at all times. Jo loved her job in Alverstoke but she loved Rainey more, and until money came her way she had to keep working.

She pulled her coat tighter around her waist. It was going to be a cold evening. She hoped the enemy planes wouldn't come again tonight.

Jo sat across the table from Blackie, staring into his mesmerizing eyes.

He'd picked her up by car from her house, and for once she was glad Rainey was out with her two friends. They'd gone to Bea's to listen to the gramophone. Her brother had bought Glenn Miller's 'In the Mood' for her and she played it continually. She had pushed back the bedroom furniture and they had practised the jitterbug. Maud had told her they were doing a better job of helping the downstairs ceiling fall down than ol' Hitler's bombs.

It had been a long time since Jo had sat in a posh restaurant. Here in Southsea, sitting at a table looking across the sea, she felt as though she was in another world.

A chandelier lit the white-clothed tables set with shining cutlery. A four-piece band played in a corner. A few couples were dancing to the music. She could smell a profusion of expensive perfumes. Jo was glad she'd put on her long black dress. It was the first time she'd taken it out of the cupboard since she'd lived at the house. She was happy it still fitted her, if a little too tightly, but she'd had to wear her everyday coat because it was the only one she possessed. She'd felt self-conscious handing it to the cloakroom girl to hang among the fur coats and stoles.

They'd already eaten. Jo couldn't remember when she'd last had such a succulent serving of liver and bacon hot-pot, with dumplings cooked separately. She knew he wouldn't start talking about the girls until he felt he had wined and dined her sufficiently. He glanced at his watch. Jo couldn't help herself. 'Fed up with me already?' She smiled at him.

Those glorious eyes crinkled at the corners and he answered, 'Far from it. I've asked Madame to join us and she should be arriving soon.'

Jo's heart began to race. So, this was no trick: her daughter was at last going to realize her ambition. As if on cue a handsome woman with her hair piled in becoming curls, wearing an expensive woollen two-piece, was shown to their table by the head waiter. Herbert accompanied her.

'Don't get up,' said the woman. 'We aren't staying long.' Herbert gave Jo a huge smile. Blackie stood to give Madame a hug, then the waiter pulled out a chair and seated her. She turned to him. 'A bottle of something good, please, and put it on my account.'

Jo was in no doubt she was well known in this establishment.

'Let's get straight to business,' the woman said. 'You know my husband and this dear boy.' She nodded at Blackie. 'He's told me all about the girls and yourself.' Jo wondered how that was possible: she'd been careful not to reveal too many facts about her past. She let the woman's words pass.

'Blackie thinks your girl and the other two have immense possibilities for a singing career, entertaining troops.' Jo was about to say this hadn't been talked about at all, when the woman added, 'Before I put my name on a dotted line, I'd like to see the goods, so to speak. It's not that I don't trust my dear Blackie's judgement but it is, after all, *my* reputation at stake.' Jo's head was still whirling with the phrase 'entertaining troops'. 'I don't intend to spend money that's not going to give me a good return.' Her sharp eyes bored into Jo's. 'You do understand, don't you?'

Jo's mouth was dry. She took a sip of the wine the waiter had poured. When these people got their teeth into something, they were like a dog with a bone, she thought. She took another sip and a deep breath, then said, 'These are young girls with little experience of the world and I don't want them to be taken advantage—'

Madame interrupted, 'But I thought you were to act as their chaperone? I rarely move from Southsea, these days, so if you're backing out I shall have to hire someone else.'

'No, no!' Jo said. 'Of course I agree.' She thought she saw a look of relief cross Madame's face. 'Everything is moving so fast I can't keep up. The girls need the security of work now. Their families, me included, can't afford to keep them on the off-chance they might eventually make money singing.'

'Good! Working for an employer will instil some backbone but I need to see them perform. So, shall we say Thursday afternoon at three, my new studio?' She looked at Blackie. 'You can deal with everything, can't you, dear boy?' She stood up, then turned to Jo. 'I see you and I are going to get on well.' Herbert gave Jo another smile. She realized he hadn't spoken a word throughout their meeting. He and Madame left.

Jo swallowed the rest of her wine. 'Well, I think you and I had better talk,' she said to Blackie.

Chapter Thirty-four

'You'd better come in,' Jo said.

Blackie looked at his watch. 'It's getting late.'

Jo opened the door of his car and stepped out onto the pavement. She could hear the gramophone softly playing dance music. 'They're still up.' She rattled the letterbox loudly.

Blackie joined her at Maud's front door as Maud opened it. When she saw Jo, she smiled. 'Come to take your daughter home?'

'Yes. But I hoped the three girls would still be here. Blackie would like a word with them, and you, of course.'

Maud motioned them in from the cold and led them down to the warm kitchen. 'Make yourselves comfortable. I'll fetch the girls down from Bea's bedroom.' She went up the stairs.

Blackie sat at the table, stretching his long legs in front of him, and Jo shrugged herself out of her coat and took the armchair near the fire.

'Eddie not in?' Jo called.

'Out with some girl. They've taken Granddad for a pint,' Maud shouted back. Jo heard voices, the gramophone's silence, then chatter and bustle as Rainey, Bea and Ivy tumbled into the kitchen.

''Lo, Mum,' said Rainey. Jo saw her glance warily at Blackie. He didn't seem at all perturbed, but gave her a dazzling smile. Rainey perched on the arm of the other armchair that Ivy and Bea had claimed. 'I remember you. You sheltered from the bombing with us beneath the stage at the David Bogue Hall.'

Ivy chimed in, 'There was an older man with you . . .'

'That's right,' Blackie said. He turned towards Maud, who'd subsided onto a kitchen chair. 'Do you mind if I talk to the girls, Maud?'

Maud shook her head. 'Not at all. It'll be good to get it out in the open.'

Jo saw Bea frown at her mother's words, and said quickly, 'It would be better if your mother was here as well, Ivy, but I'll go down to the café first thing in the morning to talk to her.' Now Ivy looked mystified.

Blackie said, 'To cut a long story short, my name's Blackie Wilson. The man I was with under the stage is Herbert Peters, the husband of Madame Nelly Walker.'

'I know who she is. She puts people on the stage.' Ivy's voice rose. 'Quite so,' agreed Blackie. 'Herbert and I heard you three sing and we'd like to manage you. Your voices together are like nothing we've heard before and we think you could do a lot for the war effort, cheering the troops.'

Blackie's voice was lost beneath the screams and shouts of the three girls.

Jo saw him looking at her, a smile on his handsome face. She smiled in return, allowed the noise to continue for a while, then stood up and shouted, 'Quieten down!'

Faces turned towards her, voices hushed.

'Right! I take it that you girls are in agreement?' Before she'd got the last word out the noise started up again, so she put up her hand to silence them. 'There's a lot to be talked through and we'll get to it all in good time.' She looked at Ivy. 'You need your mum's permission, so nothing will happen without that. If all this goes ahead as planned, it could be a while before you actually earn money. You need jobs to tide you over.'

'Not in an office,' said Rainey.

'Not necessarily in an office,' admitted Jo.

'The armament factory's hiring,' said Maud. 'They always need people for shift-work and the money's good.'

'I'm not going back to Woolies,' Bea put in. 'But I wouldn't mind Priddy's. Wouldn't it be nice if we could work together? Wherever we work we can tell them we're only staying to earn money until we become famous.'

'I don't think so,' said Rainey. 'They wouldn't hire us, and we'd make enemies among the other workers.'

Jo broke in: 'I would hope you'll give your all to any job at the same time as rehearsing the stagework.'

Blackie put his hand up. 'First and foremost, Madame Walker needs to hear you sing. Thursday afternoon at three o'clock. If she doesn't think you're worth it, you can forget about fame and fortune. Meanwhile, Jo will answer any questions you have. But if Madame does take you on you'll find yourselves working harder than you've ever worked in your lives.'

There was a sudden silence, broken by Maud, who'd risen to poke the ashes in the range. Blackie watched her, then stood up. 'I think we should go back to our homes and think things over,' he said. 'It's getting late.' Jo nodded, glad he had made that decision. 'Do you want a lift, Ivy?' he asked.

'Please,' she replied.

Jo stood up, gathered her coat from the back of the chair

and said, 'I'll be round in the morning early, Ivy, to talk to your mum.' She'd guessed that Della wouldn't be at home now.

'Do you think she'll give her blessing, Ivy?' Blackie looked concerned.

'She'll worry about the future. She hoped I'd work in an office.' She sighed. 'But she knows I want more from life.'

'I won't get a wink of sleep tonight,' said Bea.

As Blackie made his way to the door, he said, 'Remember, it all depends on how you present yourselves to Madame on Thursday.'

In the back of the car Ivy and Rainey talked excitedly. Jo heard them mention Priddy's, the armament factory, but mostly their chatter was about songs and what clothes to wear. Jo caught Blackie looking at her and mouthed, 'Thank you, for everything.'

Blackie pulled up outside the closed café. Before he'd opened the door for Ivy to get out, Jo saw Bert appear in the doorway. 'I was getting worried,' he began. He was still wearing his greasy apron.

Ivy jumped out of the car and ran to him. 'I've got something to tell you,' she said, tucking her arm through his and guiding him back inside.

*

Jo relished the silence as Blackie drove her and Rainey home. Silence that was broken when Rainey spoke.

'So,' she said thoughtfully, 'you and Madame Walker's husband, Herbert, happened to come to the David Bogue Hall on the night of our production of *Snow White*, heard us three sing and that's how it's all started? It's like a fairy-tale – like Lana Turner being discovered buying a soda in the Top Hat Malt Shop and now she's a famous actress!'

'Yes,' said Blackie.

'No,' said Jo. You could almost touch the silence that followed, she thought. Sooner or later she knew her clever daughter would start to wonder exactly what had triggered the girls' sudden good fortune.

'Well, Mum, what is it?'

The ominous silence intensified.

The car was turning into Albert Street.

'Blackie, it's time Rainey knew the full story. Do you have time to come in and talk?'

There was concern in his eyes when he turned to look at her. 'I think it's for the best,' he said, pulling up outside number fourteen.

The kitchen was warm and welcoming as Rainey, Blackie and Jo sat round the table. Jo's heart was pounding. She had put off telling Rainey her father was dead because she didn't want to see the hurt in her eyes. In the short while since she had heard the truth of Alfie's death she had wanted to find the right moment to tell Rainey. Now the time had presented itself.

Jo listened as Blackie told Rainey of Alfie's bravery. Rainey's eyes filled with tears, and Jo breathed a sigh of relief that, despite everything, Rainey had loved her dad.

'I wanted to find you so I could tell you he saved my life. I'm glad I did because I now know the authorities hadn't any idea of your whereabouts. Rainey, your father told me you had a wonderful voice, and he was right.'

Jo left her chair and went to her daughter. She put her arms around her, half expecting Rainey to shrug her off because she hadn't told her the truth straight away.

Somehow Blackie had anticipated this: 'Your mother's been waiting for the right time to tell you the truth.'

Jo could feel Rainey shaking and she wanted to take away her daughter's pain. Rainey looked at her. Her voice was little more than a whisper when she said, 'He did love me, after all, didn't he, Mum?'

The smell of fried bread and bacon made Jo's mouth water as she sat on a stool at the counter in Bert's café with Della at her side, swamped by a huge fluffy dressing-gown.

'You don't mind if Bert hears everything, do you?' Della said. 'He's like family, see.'

Della looked worn out, thought Jo. It was barely seven in the morning. Bert had had to wake her.

This hour was the only time Jo could fit in her visit to Ivy's mother. She wanted to cycle home to find out how Rainey had fared. Her daughter had got up at the crack of dawn to apply for a job on the nightshift at Priddy's armament factory and Jo had to get to the newspaper shop.

'This is one of Bert's busiest times of the morning.' Della scratched her head. 'Breakfasts are his speciality. Do you want anything to eat? The eggs are fresh and there's some tasty bacon.' She put her hand across her mouth and whispered, 'Bert's well liked in the black market.'

Jo shook her head. The cup of tea in front of her looked as if it had been made with tar.

Della yawned, showing small, very white teeth. 'You'll have to excuse me. I'm normally in bed asleep at this time. You said you've got news about the three girls taking up a singing career?'

Jo explained about her meeting with Madame and Blackie. When she'd finished, Bert caught her eye and winked. 'You'd really do that, look after them girls?'

'My Rainey's seen things she ought not to have done, but she's no age to be mixing with stage folk.'

Della chimed in, 'Too right!'

'Don't you put the boot in before you know all the ins and outs, Della. This is what young Ivy's always wanted,' said Bert.

Jo thought Della with her mascara smeared and no heavy lipstick looked like a young girl. Now Della's eyes seemed to cloud as though something was worrying her. 'Of course you'll be wondering, but if they get through their audition I'll look after her.' Jo picked up one of Della's hands. 'If you're not happy about this, though, and would prefer her to work somewhere else, fair enough, but it's the three girls Madame Walker wants because their voices are so distinctive.' There, she thought. She could do no more.

Della had disentangled her hand from Jo's and was stirring her tea. Jo thought she looked very sad for someone who had been given good news.

Bert put money into the till and handed out change to a customer. The wireless was playing dance music and already there was a fug of cigarette smoke in the café. He wiped his hands down the side of his apron. 'Della, give your girl the chance you never had.'

Della looked at Jo, who saw the brightness of tears as Della answered, 'Yes. And thank you.'

Alice Wilkes threw her blue two-piece on the bed. It wasn't right. She couldn't put on an outfit she'd often worn on those summer Sundays when she'd sat at the bandstand with Graham. Of course, it didn't matter what she wore, not really. He wouldn't be able to see her or her clothes. But that wasn't the point: she wanted to look as good as she possibly could for him. And a summer dress wasn't suitable for late November. She finally decided on a warm lambswool jumper and a tweed skirt.

'Get off, Toto!' she admonished. He was playing with her black shoes and she didn't relish a shoe hunt before leaving the house. She picked him up. 'We're going to see your new friend, Bess. You'll like that, won't you, my little one?' Thinking of Bess brought Graham back to mind. 'You don't know how I've longed to see him again,' Alice said, smiling at her little friend. She placed him on the floor, where he sat and stared at her with sorrowful eyes.

The telephone call had been short yet straight to the point. 'Alice, can you meet me on Sunday at the usual place, usual time?' He hadn't waited for a reply but had ended the call.

At first she'd stood by the telephone, thinking he might call back.

Then she realized how much courage he must have summoned to ring her. She stared into the mirror. 'Where did I go, Toto? When did that slim, pretty young girl with her heart and head full of dreams disappear?' A greying, frumpy woman stared back. In her blue eyes Alice could still see the hopeful, youthful self. She might look different on the outside, but inside she hadn't changed at all.

And neither, she hoped, had Graham.

Della sat in front of the mirror. Hands trembling, she spat on the tiny brush and rubbed it along the small black block so she could begin coating her eyelashes with mascara. She hated the way she looked tonight. A face puffy with crying stared back at her.

It had come at last. A possible new beginning for the daughter she loved more than life itself. Part of her wanted fame and recognition for Ivy but she feared it would slip through her daughter's fingers when the trio made the headlines, as they surely would, and Della's means of making a living came to light.

'My girl is doomed even before she steps on the ladder to success,' she told her reflection.

She glanced at the clock. It was time to meet Jim in the Fox. No doubt he had already lined up customers for her services. The manager of the pub threatened to bar him permanently for soliciting, but every so often Jim gave him a backhander, which shut him up.

Since Jo's appearance in the café that morning, Della hadn't been able to think straight. Mechanically she'd gone about the business of daily life. She'd not slept – how could she? Of course, she could go to Jim and tell him it was all over, that he'd had the last pound of her flesh. Let the younger girls make more money for him.

She was frightened. Of course she was. She was money on legs to Jim.

He'd accompany her to the massage rooms in the flat opposite Gosport's bus station and the long night would begin. She knew she couldn't tell him of Ivy's good fortune and that she now wanted a different life for herself. He'd beat her up, that was a dead cert. He'd done it before when he thought she'd stepped out of line. Not that she'd told Bert, of course not. She'd simply slapped on more Pan Stik to hide the marks and put a smile on her face.

Jo was going to tell the girls the good news. She said Della should be at Maud's when they heard. Blackie would be there, too, so they would have a clear picture of what was expected of them and what he could offer. But that was the last thing Della wanted, to be sitting in someone else's house, as if she was one of them. She declined. Anyway, she knew the facts, and when Ivy arrived home she would be excited and tell her all over again.

Did Della think any of the girls would opt out of being managed professionally by Madame Walker? No: singing was all they ever talked about.

Della put the finishing touches to her mouth with her brightest red lipstick, dabbed Californian Poppy behind her ears and slung her fox fur around her shoulders. Its glittering eyes looked at her reproachfully.

'No Jo today?' Syd asked Mr Harrington. He waited in the shop for his change for the newspaper.

'Had to let her go early, some family commitment,' came the answer.

Syd pocketed his change, grunted a goodbye and walked back to his garage. He glanced at the car to which he was fixing windscreen wipers and decided to step outside for a cigarette. The indicators needed looking at, too, but a smoke might just put him in the mood to carry on. He took a deep breath of the oily air, a smell that, usually, he couldn't get enough of, but today he felt a bit lost.

No doubt Jo was seeing the dark-haired chap with the odd eyes. He was a nice enough bloke but why had she needed to go out for a meal with him? How could Syd afford such niceties as meals out in smart places? Syd had planned on asking her if she fancied going to the Criterion picture house to see *The Old Maid*: he knew she liked Bette Davis. No chance now – the cinema changed films tonight.

Syd took a long drag on the Woodbine. He had seven cigarettes left in the green packet. He'd have to make them last. He didn't like the Turkish ones. Decent fags were difficult to get hold of now, just like the jobs on cars were dwindling. Petrol rationing was putting his livelihood at risk. Luckily his was the only maintenance garage in Alverstoke and the affluent society who lived there, doctors and naval people, were still running their cars. He'd be out of business otherwise.

He missed Jo: that was the problem.

She'd been like a scared rabbit when he'd first met her, but she had come out of her shell now. She'd explained what she was prepared to do to make sure the young girls came to no harm and he was proud of her. But it was Blackie he was worried about, filling her head with ideas Syd couldn't compete with.

Chapter Thirty-five

Ivy yawned as the four of them stood outside the unprepossessing locked building in Southsea. Although she was excited she was also tired. It had taken an hour to travel across on the ferry to get here and would take another hour to get home. She'd managed a little fitful sleep but after this meeting with Madame Walker, which might change their lives, there was a nightshift to do at Priddy's armament factory. The sooner she got away from the fumes and dust that stained skin yellow, the happier she would be. But that miracle would only happen if Madame liked their voices.

Ivy had been pleased when Rainey had rushed round to the café to tell her she'd secured a job at Priddy's and that they were still hiring workers. She and Bea had applied and been immediately taken on.

All night long she poured concentrated explosive powder

into shell cases that were then hooked to a conveyor-belt to be checked by the manager. Priddy's supplied ships, aircraft and troops with the explosive equipment they needed in the fight against Hitler. Although she'd worked there just a few days, Ivy hated the noise of the machinery, the powder that got into her throat, making her cough, and her eyes, making them sting.

She agreed that it might be a long time before they fulfilled their ambition to sing on the stage so meanwhile they needed to work. She hoped with all her heart that today would be the turning point in their lives.

'Someone's coming,' said Jo.

The heavy oak doors opened with a creak and Blackie stood aside to admit them. 'Madame's already here,' he said. He stood aside so they could all troop in. 'Don't forget what we spoke about the other night. Lots of smiles.'

'He sounds like Mrs Wilkes,' said Bea. Ivy had noticed how unsure of herself Bea was. She'd hardly spoken on the way over, and as she'd sat holding her penny ticket on the ferry boat, her hands had been shaking. Rainey was the one in control. It was all so exciting. The only thing that worried her was that her mother was content to allow her this chance to go ahead, yet she didn't seem as excited as the other two mothers.

They walked down a long parquet-floored hallway and into a large room, where about a dozen chairs faced a small stage.

Madame was already seated. Blackie went over to the piano and sat down. No one seemed to be talking among themselves. It reminded Ivy of being in school again.

'Take off your coats,' Madame instructed. 'Let me see if I can differentiate between you. Bea?' She gave Bea a long stare through dark-rimmed spectacles. Then she smiled. 'Hello, my dear.' Ivy thought Bea looked like she was going to the guillotine. Madame then peered at Rainey. 'Ah! Rainey, I'd know you anywhere because of the photograph.' Ivy had shed her coat and now stood next to Bea. 'So you must be Ivy.' Ivy nodded. She felt as if she ought to curtsy to the woman dressed in grey velvet and smelling of some flowery perfume. 'Welcome,' she said. 'Let's start as we mean to go on. I like the look of you all.'

Ivy smiled at Jo, who was sitting down with her back so straight a board might have been propping her up.

'Get up on the stage,' commanded Madame. 'You have music, dear boy?'

Blackie nodded.

Ivy knew Mrs Wilkes had lent the copy of the folk song to Jo especially for today. 'Look as though you're enjoying this,' she hissed, as they climbed the steps to the small stage.

The music began and the girls sang.

Ivy tried hard, while giving full rein to the emotions the song evoked, to judge how Madame was feeling but her face betrayed nothing. As the piano notes faded, Jo stood up and clapped, looked about nervously and sat down, obviously embarrassed. The girls stood silently awaiting Madame's reply.

'It's a beautiful song but it's not how I see you.'

Ivy's heart plummeted. She didn't like them!

Madame was talking again: 'I see you dressed in uniform, perhaps, singing songs with more pep in them. I want you as entertainers, cheering our dear boys to victory, not willing them to cut their throats because of the sadness in those words. Cover songs are fine. Singing songs that other artists have had success with means singing music that is familiar, loved, even. We'll see how it goes. Oh, yes, we need a name for you as a group. I gather all three of you are blessed with bird surnames, Herron, Sparrow and Bird?'

Ivy thought her heart would spring out of her chest with excitement: they'd be like the Andrews Sisters or Judy Garland, when she'd sung with her siblings as the Gumm Sisters. She nodded frantically at her benefactor. 'I've given it a great deal of thought,' said Madame, 'and wonder how you'd feel about the Bluebird Girls?'

For a moment there was silence.

Ivy looked at her two friends, who were practically wriggling with delight. Of course they loved the name.

'Does that mean you'll represent us?' Ivy couldn't help herself.

'Of course,' said Madame. 'But you'll take instruction from Blackie.' She looked along the row of chairs at Jo. 'Are you happy with this, my dear?'

Jo said, 'More than happy.'

'I do understand it's not feasible for you to travel here daily,' Madame went on. 'After all, you have jobs that are important to our country. I've made arrangements for the hall in Gosport, the one that was hired for the pantomime, to be available for you to use for practice.'

Jo spoke up, 'We can't afford to pay for it.'

'That's all taken care of. I'm backing the Bluebird Girls until they're earning. That doesn't mean I'll be paying any of you wages.' She gave a tight smile. 'I'm not a charity. All of you are working, and if you want to make a success, you'll need to understand it's not handed out on a plate. Jo, Blackie will advise you. He'll hold the purse strings for music, stage clothing, make-up, travel . . . If I consider it worthwhile I'll get you a recording contract.'

'You spoke about them entertaining troops,' Jo reminded her. 'Will there be danger?'

'My dear, they have to be polished before even I will entertain this. But you can rest assured they and you will be looked after as well as any of the entertainers who amuse the troops. The Bluebird Girls will be a morale-booster to our dear boys.'

Ivy was glad that Jo had thought things through and was asking the questions her own mother might worry about. Just imagine, she thought, they could be stars! She looked at Rainey, who was plainly dumbfounded, and Bea, white as a sheet. Jo had one last question. 'When will they earn money?'

'My dear, that depends on our three girls. The harder they work, the luckier they will be. I shall book the girls into a revue at our local theatre, the King's. We'll see how it goes from there. Again, Blackie will coach. I understand you're used to appearing in front of audiences?'

Ivy thought about the patients in hospitals Mrs Wilkes had staged shows for. They were a captive audience. She nodded at Madame, who stood up, holding on to the arms of her chair. 'If you're happy with my terms I'll arrange for a contract,' she said. Ivy watched Jo's face. Clearly she agreed.

'Blackie will take you back to Gosport by car. I don't want to make any of you late for work. Iron out any queries with him.'

Blackie stood up and accompanied her outside. The door swung closed on them.

Rainey was jumping up and down on the stage. Ivy began to cry and Bea stood as still as if she had been magically turned to stone.

'Well, girls,' said Jo, rushing onto the stage and throwing her arms about them all, like a hen gathering her chicks. 'You are on your way!'

Chapter Thirty-six

Ivy was glad that their first stop was Bea's house. Bea went straight indoors to get ready for work, chattering excitedly to her mother and Eddie, who was already home. Granddad was taking a nap. Eddie said he didn't want him to wake so he braved the cold to come out to the car, threatening to gag Bea if she didn't keep the noise down.

'Jo,' he said, 'I'm so pleased about everything and I'd like to thank you, and you, mate –' he grinned at Blackie, who'd stepped out of the car to light a cigarette '– for giving Bea a chance.' He lowered his voice and whispered through the window Rainey had wound down, 'Jo, Bea will do well, I'm sure. Look, it's no good beating around the bush, she's fragile. You know that, don't you? This singing business has happened so quickly and it's only a few months since that – that . . .' He couldn't finish the sentence.

Ivy watched Eddie run a hand through his blond hair. She knew he meant Bea's unfortunate mishap at the Fox.

'I know you worry about her,' Jo said, 'but I'll look out for her.'

Ivy added, 'We'll all look out for her.'

Eddie's eyes held Ivy's. Suddenly a jolt ran up Ivy's spine, like an arrow, riveting her with helpless attention to Eddie's concerned face. He moved back onto the pavement. It was as if he had suddenly remembered something he had long forgotten. Ivy turned away and wound up the window. Her heart was thumping.

Blackie had opened the driver's door and reclaimed the front seat. 'He's a nice bloke,' Blackie said cheerfully. Ivy could smell the fresh cigarette smoke on him.

'Yes, he is,' Jo answered. 'Can you drop Ivy off next?'

As the car drove slowly down the street, Ivy watched Eddie in the side mirror. He stood on the pavement, frowning and looking at her until Blackie turned the corner.

Rainey was talking non-stop about the costumes she thought would suit all three of them, but Ivy's head was in a whirl. What had happened between her and Eddie back there? Somehow it was as if they'd been seeing each other for the very first time. Whatever it was, she knew he, too, had experienced it.

She heard Jo ask, 'When shall the girls start practising?'

Blackie said, 'When Madame suggests something it's usually done and dusted. Tomorrow would be good for me.'

He turned his head briefly towards Jo, who answered, 'Perfect. Now I know the definite amount of time I need away from Harrington's, I can sort out something more permanent there. I might offer to do the morning newspapers so I can leave earlier in the afternoons.'

'Do you think your boss will agree?'

'I can ask,' said Jo. She turned to Ivy. 'Can you let Bea know tonight that we'll start practising tomorrow?'

Ivy nodded.

When the car arrived in Gosport town and pulled up outside the café, Ivy shouted her goodbyes to Jo and Blackie. She'd be seeing Rainey again later for the nightshift. She'd already decided she could easily walk to the David Bogue Hall and be there at the designated time. Jo had planned the practices to fit in comfortably with the girls working nights and getting some sleep. It made a big difference not to have to make their way to Southsea every day on ferry boats and buses.

Her face fell as soon as she walked into the warm, smoky interior and discovered her mother wasn't there.

'Sit down, love, I'll do you something to eat and a nice cup of tea and you can tell me everything. Don't go asking about your mum. She went out about an hour ago.'

Ivy could see from the stains on Bert's blue and white striped apron that he'd had a busy day. She was more than disappointed to find her mother wasn't waiting to hear all that had happened that day. She sat down in her usual seat just inside the door.

Bert came from behind the counter carrying a cup of tea. 'How did you get on, love?'

She smiled shyly. 'We're to have special rehearsals to sing popular music, new clothes, maybe make a record . . .'

'Whoa, hold your horses,' he said. 'That's too much for my tired old head to take in.'

She laughed at him. 'It's too much for me an' all. They want to make us into stars.'

'And what will we call you? The Gosport Girls?'

'That's good, Bert, but not good enough. We're to be the Bluebird Girls.'

He let out a low whistle. 'You're having me on?'

Ivy shook her head. 'No. It's like I'm going to live in a different world.' She sighed. 'Where's me mum? Why isn't she here so I can tell her all about it?'

*

The cold air nipped at Alice Wilkes's stockinged legs. Toto bounced along beside her, happy to be out in the fresh air, every so often stopping to sniff at the exciting new smells he encountered.

The curt telephone message from Graham weighed on her mind. She was happy to have heard from him. Many times, after searching the telephone book for his number, she'd been on the verge of ringing him. Prudently she'd decided to allow him to recover from the shock of their meeting after such a long time and allow the next move, if there was to be one, to come from him.

As she crossed the road towards the beach, she wondered again why he'd chosen not to elaborate on their meeting place or the time.

The trees were bare, the ground hard underfoot. Here and there a holly bush showed its shine and the promise of red berries. She could hear the sea now, rolling in and pulling back over the pebbled beach as if there was no war, no Germans hoping to invade. Did the government really believe stringing barbed wire along the stones would deter Hitler?

And then she saw the sea. Despite the weak sun, the water was a murky brown stretching towards the Isle of Wight. In the distance, near the bandstand stood a figure with a dog.

Her heart began to beat faster. He'd come to meet her! Alice had no intention of shouting to him. She wouldn't need to do that: the dogs would tell each other and Graham that she'd arrived.

The bandstand was battle-scarred with the years. Once painted a bright white, it was now a flaking, forlorn ghost of its former self. The deckchairs, once colourful and filled with cheerful men and women, children playing at their feet, were no more.

Bess wagged her tail. Trapped by her harness, she was trained not to show emotion. Toto ran around her, then Graham bent down, felt for the little dog and asked, 'Pleased to see us?'

He stood up again and faced Alice. 'I'm sure it's all changed but I'll always remember this place as it was.'

Alice looked at him. She didn't see his scars, just the man she'd fallen in love with all those years ago.

'I hoped you'd come,' Graham said. 'I hoped you'd remember.'

'How could I forget?' Alice said. Now she understood the brevity of his call. He wanted her to have remembered their special Sundays, just as they had never eluded him.

Graham said, 'I've prepared tea at home. Bess and I would like it very much if you and Toto would join us.'

Alice said, 'Toto and I would be happy to do just that.'

Chapter Thirty-seven

'You've already got three bookings for tonight.' Mandy was outlining her mouth with a fuchsia lipstick, a mirror propped up against the telephone.

Della sighed, then turned the ledger to see who had booked in to use her services. First was Paul Harris.

'I can see you're not happy, Della. What's the matter? Making money upset you?' Jim took off his Homburg hat and threw it at the coat-stand. It landed neatly on a peg.

'Clever sod,' said Mandy. Her black roots were showing through her blonde hair.

'Paul Harris's breath stinks like a sewer,' Della grumbled.

'Well, I'm not asking you to kiss him . . .' Jim gave a belly laugh.

Mandy giggled.

Jim liked to think he was sharp with the repartee, thought Della.

She looked out of the window at the bus station. A number three was just leaving for Fareham. She wished she was sitting on it instead of waiting in this knocking shop for a fat, greasy bloke whose breath smelled of onions. She had been trying to pluck up the courage to tell Jim she no longer wanted to work for him. Ever since she'd met him in the Fox tonight, where he'd had her usual port-and-lemon ready on the bar for her, she'd wanted nothing more than to say, 'I want to devote myself to helping my daughter achieve the career she deserves. Jim, it's over.'

The words wouldn't come. Didn't come.

After she'd finished her drink, he'd walked her with propriety down the street towards the ferry. With every step she took she tried in vain to make the words form in her mouth.

Della hated herself for leaving the café before Ivy had come back from Southsea. Her daughter had been worried they wouldn't like her singing. But Blackie, with the funny eyes, and that Madame wouldn't go to all the trouble of inviting the three girls along for a talk without good reason. Ivy was destined for something Della had never dreamed of and she was frightened that the way in which she earned her living would hold Ivy back. If Della could get out of the business now, before the girls hit the big-time, then with a bit of luck her past wouldn't be raked up.

So, rather than talk to Bert and wait for Ivy, she'd taken a walk over to Walpole Park. She'd sat on a freezing bench where the swans were huddled together for warmth on the boating pond and decided what she would say to Jim. She stayed there, thinking, until she felt like a block of ice.

She would tell Jim tonight, then walk away from her old life.

Only it hadn't worked out like that. She'd forgotten how scared she was of him. Now she glanced at the clock on Mandy's desk.

A row of five chairs were placed along the wall for the men to sit and wait if the girl of their choice was unavailable. The three bedrooms, behind closed doors, contained beds, chairs, dressing-tables and a small cupboard, which held the necessary tricks and tools of the trade.

Of course prostitution, living off immoral earnings, was illegal. But Jim didn't worry about that: a great many worthy members of the police force and the local council had sampled his girls for free. Again Della stared at the clock.

'The hands won't turn any faster with you staring at it,' said Jim. He'd already poured himself a whisky.

Della opened the door to her room. 'I need a word with you, Jim.'

He followed her in. She moved to the window. Here at

the back the view was of the rear of Woolworths and their overflowing rubbish bins. She saw it had started to rain. Drops chased each other down the dirty window.

Jim came and stood next to her. 'Gonna be a filthy night, Della.'

'I'm not doing this no more. I've had enough.'

She felt the blow before she saw him raise a hand. Then the trickle of blood ran from her nose and she watched, mesmerized, as a drop, bright red, dripped onto the clean white sheet. Then she almost choked as the blood, metallic, reached her mouth.

The flat of his other hand smacked her.

Della staggered under the force of the blow. One of her clip-on ear-rings flew to the lino. She put up her hand to her head and felt the dampness of more blood.

'Get yourself cleaned up. You got a client coming soon. I won't have my girls looking like trollops.'

Della bolted from the room. She knew she was unsteady on her feet and feared any moment that she'd trip on the stairs. She burst out into the cold rain and ran as fast as her high heels would allow along Mumby Road. A couple of times she stumbled on slabs broken during the bombing. She used the back of her hand to stem the flow from her nose, and even in the darkness she could see the blackness of blood on her skin.

She'd been hit before, of course she had. But Jim would sort out an over-enthusiastic punter – most of the time he was around when the girls were working. As for him punching her? She knew this was his way of saying he owned her. He would expect her to return to the brothel and apologize to him, after she'd cleaned herself up, of course. Then life would go on as before.

But she didn't want that life any more. What she wanted was for Ivy to be proud of her. She wanted to support the girls, like Jo was doing. She didn't want her Ivy to be labelled by the gutter press as the singer with the prostitute mother. If she could give up her way of life now, she knew Blackie and probably Madame would do everything in their power to make sure their money-makers were squeaky clean. That meant they'd nip in the bud any rumours that their families were less than wholesome.

Ahead she could see the corner of North Street where the café stood in darkness, the blackout curtains doing their usual excellent job.

Ivy would be at Priddy's now, working the nightshift. If Della could pass along the hallway and the ever-open doorway that led into the café she could get upstairs before Bert saw her and began to interrogate her. Bert always worried about her when she worked.

There was no sound from the wireless as she pushed against the street door. That meant the café was quiet tonight. Della took a deep breath and moved quickly. She didn't dare glance into the café but took the stairs, running like a mad thing.

'Della? Is that you?'

She heard his footsteps on the bare wood at the bottom in the hall but she didn't look down or answer him.

Quickly she inserted the key into the lock and she was inside her room, shutting the door behind her, leaning against the cold wood and taking deep breaths. Slowly she slid to the floor as her tears came thick and fast.

After a while Della realized Ivy had drawn the blinds before she'd left for work. She got up, put on the light and went to the mirror.

She gasped at the state of her face. Not only had Jim marked her but, because the rain had plastered her hair to her head, she looked like an old woman. With fresh tears pricking the backs of her eyes Della went to the sink, filled the kettle and lit the gas.

She would have a strip wash, dry her hair, attend to her nose, which hurt like hell but she didn't think was broken, take a Beecham's Powder and get into bed. She'd be there in the morning when Ivy came home and she could apologize then for being out earlier.

Della made a pot of tea as she undressed. She hung the sodden fur on a hanger, then put it high on the dado rail to dry off. After attending to her face – already the bruising was coming out below both eyes and it was tender to the touch – she washed with her favourite Imperial Leather soap that Bert had given her, and put on a clean nightdress. Her head felt as if someone had embedded an axe in it so she sat on the bed and, from the drawer in the small table, she took a Beecham's Powder. She always kept a good supply – at twopence each they were a godsend in easing her many headaches. She poured the white powder into her tea. She undid another, then another and stirred them into the cup. She made a face at the bitter taste but it wasn't that bad – she'd tasted worse. When she'd drained the cup she refilled it from the pot, added milk and more powders. Soon the pot contained nothing but used tealeaves, and a nest of powder-wraps littered the floor.

Della didn't know why she hadn't thought of this before. With her out of the way, Ivy could look forward to a much brighter future.

Chapter Thirty-eight

It was pointless staying open any longer, thought Bert. The rain kept customers away. He put up the closed sign and bolted the café door. The side door was always left unlocked for tenants.

He would make a sandwich for Della, he decided. He'd caught a glimpse of her – she'd come home early for once. Surely she'd want to know how the meeting in Southsea had gone for Ivy.

A few minutes later he was trudging up the stairs to the top floor with a plate of sandwiches. He banged on her door. 'I got something to eat for you, Della. Cheese and pickle, your favourite.'

When there was no answer, he thought perhaps she was already asleep. But he couldn't erase the thought that she was home much earlier than usual. He knocked again. Then he noticed the strip of light shining from beneath the door. Della was very particular about the blackout: she wouldn't leave a light burning unnecessarily. His forehead creased with worry. Something wasn't right.

'Open this door, Della!' It was a command. He fumbled at his belt for his pass-key and let himself in. It was the empty Beecham's Powders papers he saw first. When he looked at Della sprawled in bed he let out a cry. 'No!' Her face was swollen, she had two black eyes and her nose was like a prize fighter's.

He was at the cupboard where Della kept her food, searching, knocking down tins of condensed milk, pushing aside a tin of cocoa. He found what he was looking for: the loaf of salt. He scraped a goodish pile into a cup and added water, stirring it in. At the bed he scooped up Della and forced the rim of the cup to her mouth. 'Swallow, damn you!'

The salty water trickled down her chin and onto the sheets. Her whole body was limp. What if she'd taken something more than the powders? He feared he could be too late.

'No, no, no,' he moaned. Bert tilted Della's head back and forced open her mouth, then tipped the salty mess down her throat. For a moment she didn't move, then a gush of warm vomit rushed at him, soaking his shirt and dripping everywhere. Della opened her eyes. They were like bright slits in the black puffiness of her face.

'Thank God!'

Then he was back at the sink scraping away at the salt block.

When he returned to her she was vomiting again, using her elbow to hold herself steady while the watery substance fell to the floor.

'Drink this.' He held her and forced her to empty the cup whereupon she was immediately sick again. She sat in her own mess until he dragged her out of the bed and said, 'Now walk! Then you can have some more to drink.'

Now she managed to croak, 'No!'

'Yes,' he said. 'You tried to end it all, and that's a crime. Suicide's an offence against the law.' He gazed into her ravaged face. 'That Jim did this, didn't he?' She tried to push away from him, but he was holding her too tightly. He marched her to the sink and forced her to down another cupful he had prepared. Again she vomited. He held her hair back,

'I told him I didn't want to do it no more.'

He couldn't answer her but he used a tea-towel to wipe away the snot and slime on her face. 'I think we might have got rid of it all,' he said. 'Thank God I came in when I did. How d'you feel?'

'Like I could murder a cuppa,' she said, her voice hardly more than a whisper. 'Without salt!'

He smiled at her. Della's nightdress was sticking to her and she smelled deplorable, but she was there with him, and she would be all right, and that was all that mattered. He looked at the shambles of the room. 'If I go downstairs to get the takings and collect fresh bedding, can you be trusted to clean yourself up? I won't be long. Then we can have that cup of tea.'

'I didn't really mean to—'

He cut her off. 'We'll talk after I've cleared up this mess.'

Bert stripped the bed and, with the sheets dragging along behind him, he went downstairs. If he soaked them in the big copper, he could wash them later, he thought. He cashed up, putting all of the money in a blue bank bag except for tomorrow's float. He was planning to go up to his own room and bring out some clean pillows, sheets and blankets to sort out Della's bed.

The street door flew open so hard it banged against the wall. Jim thrust himself into the passageway. His clothes were soaked with the rain and his hat brim was dripping. He was taller than Bert, younger. 'Where's the bitch?'

He wasn't drunk, but he had been drinking – Bert could

smell the whisky on him. He knew there'd be no reasoning with the angry man.

Bert backed into the space behind the counter and put his takings on the shelf for safekeeping. 'If you mean the woman you beat up, she's not here,' he said quietly.

'Where is she? I've lost a lot of money tonight because she's had some daft bee in her bonnet—'

'It ain't daft not wanting to sell herself no more.'

'She's here, I know it.' Jim stared up the stairs. He wasn't listening to Bert. 'I'll make her pay.'

Bert unhooked the sheathed swordstick and walked back into the passage. 'Get away from them stairs. Them's people's private rooms up there and I told you long ago it's out of bounds.'

'You gonna stop me, old man? Gonna whack me one with your walking stick?' He grinned at Bert. 'If I kick that away you'll topple over.'

He aimed a kick at Bert. The casing from the blade fell to the floor and Bert slashed at Jim's outstretched leg. Jim's foot didn't reach its target because the blade sliced through his trousers. In an instant, beads of blood swelled into the long split of material.

'You fuckin' cut me!'

'Now get off them stairs and sling yer hook!' Bert growled,

glaring at Jim. He waited, willing him to step down. He didn't want more trouble but there was no way the bloke was going up to Della's rooms. Bert could feel himself sweating even though the passage was cold and the rain blowing through the open door made it colder still.

Jim had lost interest in Della and the reason he'd come to the café, and instead was bending over, examining his bleeding leg. 'You're a bloody madman,' he said. But he was now off the bottom stair and limping towards the street door. 'I'll get even with you for this,' he said, stepping into the rain.

'Just so long as you remember Della don't work for you no more,' Bert called, and kicked the door shut.

He walked unsteadily into the café and rinsed his face and hands at the sink. After a while he stopped shaking enough to pick up the cane and plunge the sword back into its casing. He'd never cut anyone before. He felt sick at his actions.

When he had the takings in his hands again, he climbed the stairs. His next job was to clean up Della's room. It wouldn't do for Ivy to come home and find her mum in a mess like that.

Chapter Thirty-nine

Ivy picked up the two-pound bomb she'd been filling with explosive and hooked it onto the conveyor-belt. She hated the stink of the lemonade-like powder that misted the air, settling everywhere and yellowing the strands of her hair that she couldn't tuck into her white turban. She watched as the container made its way above the long bench to the next stop on its journey to completion, then to be used by our boys to win the war against Hitler. A warm feeling swept over her as she thought about their audition with Madame Walker that afternoon.

'A Nightingale Sang in Berkeley Square' was blaring out of the wireless, raising the morale of the workers in the armament factory.

Ivy yawned and started filling another bomb case. The job was exacting and dangerous. Meg, working beside her, a shrivelled conker of a woman, started coughing. Ivy paused until her fit had passed. The TNT caused all manner of ailments but the pay was good and Meg had a family to feed.

Priddy's Hard, the armament depot at Gosport overlooking Portsmouth harbour, was in its usual nightly hive of activity.

The buzzer sounded. 'Thank God for that,' said Ivy. She took off her gloves and scratched at her head beneath the turban. 'This thing makes my head itch something terrible.'

The machinery had stopped. It was time for a break.

Bea, in blue dungarees, was standing behind her. 'Shall we go outside for a breather?'

'Good idea,' said Rainey.

'You can't,' said Meg. 'It's pissing down with rain.' She left the three girls with a triumphant look on her face.

'One day I'm going to swing for her, miserable cow,' said Bea.

'You'd be unhappy, too, if your old man got blown up at sea, leaving you with six kids to bring up,' Rainey pointed out.

'Stop it, you two. We've got nothing to be unhappy about,' Ivy said. 'Let's find somewhere quiet so we can talk.' She already had an Oxo tin in her hands that contained sandwiches Bert had made.

'If we don't go out we don't have to change,' said Bea.

No nail varnish, no hair-grips, wedding rings taped up, a complete change from outdoor clothing to work clothes that was supervised by an overseer.

All three, along with their blue dungarees and white turbans, which denoted the department in which they worked, wore substantial boots with safety soles.

Rainey started laughing.

'What's so funny?' Ivy asked.

'We are,' Rainey said. 'We've been told to think about blue stage costumes. Well, look at us, we're already wearing them!'

They entered the canteen, which smelled of sweat and food, and found a quiet corner. As the girls sat down, Ivy said seriously, 'Rainey, I think you should keep your voice down. We can't let on about this to anyone, especially not the women we're working with.'

Bea, who was just about to head towards the counter to buy teas, stopped in her tracks. 'Why not?'

'We've already talked about this, Bea. We'd look pretty silly if things didn't work out, wouldn't we? And there's so much austerity now that it might cause jealousy if there's a possibility we could earn good money. We do have to go on working here for now, you know,' said Ivy.

Bea grinned. It looked like the penny had dropped.

'Right,' she said. 'We talk to no one, except the people closely involved.'

Rainey, who had taken a bite of a sandwich that was more Marmite than cheese, nodded in agreement. 'I'm sorry for being so thoughtless.' She, too, tried tucking her waves beneath the front of her turban. Ivy knew she wasn't happy because she had found green strands: the chemicals did that to red hair.

'My mum's as excited as I am about everything,' said Bea, softly, then went on her way towards the tea queue.

'How about your mum?' Rainey asked Ivy, swallowing bread hastily.

Ivy sighed. 'She's over the moon,' she said. She had no idea why her mother hadn't been waiting at the café to hear her news. It had hurt to know that Della had preferred to be somewhere else on such a special day. Of course Bert had been lovely, excited for her, fussing around her, like a mother hen, but she'd so looked forward to telling Della. She blinked back a tear – if she needed to wipe her eyes they'd become inflamed and itch like mad with the tiny grains of powder floating about. Ivy took a deep breath. 'I do wonder if we'll be able to keep it up, all the rehearsing and then coming here every night.'

Rainey, who had earlier confided to her friends of her

father's death and Blackie's search for her and her mother, said, 'It's all I've ever wanted, to sing, you already know that. My dad wasn't all a father could be but he's made this chance possible by giving Blackie that photo.' She stopped talking as two women walked by the table, then continued: 'If we want it bad enough we can make it happen.' She looked towards the tea queue and groaned. 'It's that one we've got to keep our eyes on.' She inclined her head.

'Sometimes I think Bea's got no more sense than a sardine.' Ivy watched Bea giggle as one of the packing lads tried to fit both his large hands around her tiny waist. He was brawny and his dark hair was a mass of shiny curls.

'She should be served next, thank goodness,' grumbled Rainey.

'Yes,' said Ivy. 'I'm not jealous of the attention she gets, she's like a man magnet, but I could do with a cuppa.' They stared at each other and started laughing.

Ivy let herself in at the side door. Earlier tonight she'd thought the shift at Priddy's would never end but now the morning was beginning to lighten. She smiled at the sounds of the birds singing their early chorus. She only ever noticed sparrows, pigeons and seagulls in the Gosport streets but hundreds were singing their hearts out now.

The women on the line had been talking about the extra Christmas rations the government were allowing: four ounces of sugar and two ounces of tea. She and the girls were more excited about having Christmas night and Boxing Day night off. That meant two days they didn't have to work at Priddy's. The bomb factory wasn't closing because the war was stopping for Christmas: the need for armaments was just as important but the management had sent round a missive offering extra work to those employees who were willing to come in.

Ivy wondered if the boss would be as helpful in the New Year when she, Bea and Rainey might be appearing in the revue and would need time off.

There was a strong smell of bleach everywhere. She saw the stairs had been freshly washed. Upstairs the smell was stronger. She began to open the door.

'That you, Ivy love?' Her mother's voice startled her. Della was usually asleep when Ivy returned from work.

'No, it's Frank Sinatra come to take you away from all this,' Ivy said.

Della was standing at the stove waiting for the kettle to boil. She saw her mother had washed her hair. She looked around the room – indeed, it looked as though she'd had a spring clean in December.

Ivy took off her coat and shoes and sat on her bed. 'You must have come home early to clean this lot up,' she said. She watched as Della made a pot of tea.

'I felt bad I wasn't here for you.'

'Well, you're back now so that's all that matters.'

Della turned round with a cup of tea in her hands for Ivy.

'What's the matter with your face?'

Ivy was at her side, taking the tea, putting it on the draining-board and peering at her mother.

Della gave her a wonky smile. 'I told Jim I was through with the game and he didn't like it.'

'Have you been to the hospital?' Ivy's eyes were full of tears. 'The police should be told. Have you . . .'

Della turned her gaze on Ivy. Her words were clear and concise. 'The police might help Jim but they'd take no notice of me. Anyway, Bert sorted Jim out. Then he sorted me out.' She tried to smile but her split lip made it impossible and she winced. 'The main thing is, I'm never going back to that flat down by the bus station.'

Ivy pulled her mother in for another hug, mindful that she was hurt.

'I'm going to help out downstairs.' Della was still being hugged so her voice was muffled by Ivy's jumper.

'Let me look.' Ivy pushed Della away and scrutinized her

face. 'Well, it'll heal,' she said. 'Listen. It's time for some changes here. I'm determined to make money and I'll look after you. You don't know how pleased I am that you've said goodbye to that man.'

'There's something else I must tell you. I don't want no secrets between us two, ever.'

Ivy stared at her. Della was now sitting on the bed beside her. 'I wasn't in my right mind when I came in out of the rain, looking like something the cat dragged in. And . . . I took quite a few Beecham's Powders. Then Bert came and, well . . .'

Ivy let the words sink in. She couldn't imagine her mother feeling so down that she would do a thing like that. Something hard, like a stone, settled in her heart. In a moment they would talk more, and she would share with Della the happiness she'd felt earlier. Until that moment, Ivy knew she had never really understood her mother. But now everything that had passed before was gone and a new beginning was opening for both of them. Everything would be all right.

Ivy put her arms around her mother's neck and whispered, 'It says on the Beecham's packet "Why suffer? They act like magic to end the pain." But I'm sure they only mean you to take one.'

Della guffawed, got up and went to the sink. She picked up the two cups and said, 'Better stick to tea, then.'

'He can go in next week,' said Millicent Meadows. She wore a heavy brown coat and had a headscarf tied beneath her sharp chin. 'He'd be settled before Christmas. Of course you'll need to transport his bits and pieces to Lavinia House.' She began checking her notebook. The heat in the kitchen was making her cheeks glow.

'I am bloody here, you know!' Solomon stared at the woman from the council. 'Talking about me as if I don't bloody exist!' Maud saw him shake the *Evening News* he'd been reading as if he was wringing its neck.

'She's doing us a favour, Granddad. And when me and Eddie took you to Bridgemary to see the place you fell in love with it, didn't you?'

Granddad grunted, the woman looked happier and Maud sighed.

'I heard you got on well with Gertie Adams in the next room,' the woman said to Solomon.

'What's it to you? That woman's got a bit of go in her,' he said. He cleared his throat and spat into his handkerchief.

Maud raised her eyes heavenwards. Gertie had appeared immediately they'd put the key into the door of Solomon's room. It was like she'd been asked to show them around, thought Maud.

'This is the living room, and the bed is in that alcove there.' The sprightly white-haired woman had waved her arm. 'You don't need to cook no food, as we got Mrs Ford, a proper cook to do that. You won't go hungry here. There's a cleaner as well, Sunshine by name and sunny by nature. She'll do bits and bobs of shopping if you need it.' She'd floated about pointing to this and that. 'The toilets and bathrooms are three doors away. If you feels a bit unwell or thinks you can't manage to get to the toilet knock on the wall for me . . .' At this she'd burst out laughing, showing sparkling white false teeth. 'Let's face it, we all gets funny turns, don't we? But we don't have to trail down the bottom of the garden to have a wee. Day or night Mrs Manners is on call. Trained nurse. Ever so nice she is.'

Granddad had stared at her, open-mouthed.

'I'm next door,' she repeated. 'If you wants a chat. But in the evenings we all sits down in what's called the Leisure Room, comfy in there, and nice and warm. Listens to the wireless, plays crib or cards, they gives out tea and biscuits . . .'

Gertie got no further for a middle-aged woman in a pinafore had come in. 'Thank you, Gertie, you've saved me the job of showing them about.'

Gertie had grabbed Granddad's arm and whisked him away to introduce him to some of her male friends in the Leisure Room. Surprisingly, Maud remembered, he'd gone like a lamb to the slaughter.

Now she smiled at Mrs Meadows. 'Mrs Manners said it's usually quiet there. Except for Gertie. But I'm wondering if Solomon wouldn't prefer to spend Christmas with us and move in in the New Year.'

'No, I wouldn't, love,' Granddad said. 'To tell the truth, now I've made up me mind, I'd like to be in there for Christmas cos Gertie's brother's coming to stay in the family room. He used to play football for Pompey, and we worked out I went to school with him. Be nice to talk over old times.'

Maud looked at Millicent Meadows. She didn't want to tell this woman how much she'd miss Solomon and that she'd hoped the council would rehouse the whole family in a bigger place so she could go on looking after him. Nor would she tell anyone that when she'd closed the front door on her she'd go upstairs and have a cry. But it wasn't like she'd never see him any more: he could easily get the bus down to her and she, Eddie and Bea would pop in regularly.

'I suppose that's settled, then,' Maud said.

Chapter Forty

'Bea, Rainey, you'll have to sit in the back of the van. Jo and Ivy, you're in the front with me.'

'Why do I have to get in the back, Eddie? It's all dusty,' Bea moaned.

'Well, just watch where you're sitting. You've got eyes in your head, haven't you?'

It was nice to hear Eddie and Bea bickering again, thought Ivy. She was very conscious she had to squeeze up on the bench seat close to Eddie to make room for Jo. They were lucky to be getting a lift to the David Bogue Hall.

'It's nice not having to walk,' she said, when at last Eddie had finished checking the van's doors ('I don't trust Bea to shut it properly from the inside') and climbed into the driver's seat, moving his feet towards the van's pedals. 'No bother, I'm on my way down to the town hall to see the planning committee and I can drop you all off.'

He turned to smile at her and her heart started thumping. She was squashed close enough to smell his woody cologne. He looked nice today, dressed up in a dark suit, she thought. He ran his fingers through his blond hair but it sprang back across his forehead again.

'Why are you seeing them?' Jo asked. Ivy thought she looked pretty today, in a warm cherry-coloured wool jacket beneath which she had a grey blouse and grey slacks. She'd also made up her face, unusual for Jo. She wondered if it was for Blackie's benefit.

'I'm stuck for labour with the young blokes away fighting. Always the same. If I can get hold of the materials, I got no men. I'm due a big shipment of cement so I'm hoping to start building with the other things that have been delivered. It'll be the first phase of family council housing in Bridgemary.'

'Does that mean some of the Gosport families that have been bombed out will be rehoused?' Ivy asked. She could hear giggling coming from the back of the van. Bea and Rainey were all right.

'Eventually,' he sighed, 'When the bombing stops. Meanwhile I got enough work with making good the bomb damage. The council are talking about us taking on some of the prisoners of war currently held in St Vincent Barracks as labourers.'

'How do you feel about that?' asked Jo.

'If it works out, I'll be happy. I expect some of the men will be glad to be working. No one likes being locked up.'

'But they're our enemies,' said Jo. Ivy saw her mouth was now a thin, hard line.

'Most of them are young blokes brought up to fight for their country, just the same as our lads.'

'You'd really employ Germans?' Jo's forehead was furrowed with disbelief.

'All I'm worried about is building homes to help families live somewhere decent, Jo. That and earning a living. It's been hard on Mum having Granddad living at home. Someone's always had to babysit him.'

'But Germans?' Jo didn't like to think of the enemy who had destroyed English homes being trusted to rebuild them.

'Look, Jo, when the farmers lost their labourers in the Great War they got land girls. The Women's Land Army did wonders. Lots of people didn't think it would work, but it did then and it does now. Everyone has to pull together in this blasted war.' He took his eyes from the road and smiled at her. 'Don't forget we got three girl factory workers in this van! If women can work like men, why shouldn't prisoners of war work as well?'

Jo said, 'Won't they escape?'

'How are they going to get out of our country without passports?' Ivy thought she was clever to point that out.

'I always knew you were the bright one,' said Eddie, giving her a blinding smile.

Eight words directed at Ivy by Eddie and her heart was thumping so loudly she was sure he would hear it.

He pulled up outside the hall and, before he opened the back doors to free Rainey and Bea, Eddie went round to the passenger side of his van and helped down Jo, then held out his hand again, this time for Ivy.

She wondered if he, too, felt the electric current tingle against his skin as she did when their fingers touched. Looking into his eyes, she was sure he had. He opened his mouth to say something but no sound came, and he held on to her just a little bit longer than was necessary as she climbed down from the van.

'At least the caretaker's opened up,' said Jo, as she pushed open the door and went into the hall. 'It seems funny just us being in here.' She realized she was talking to herself for the three girls had gone straight to the kitchen.

Memories of the interrupted pantomime came flooding back. They were so lucky the hall hadn't been damaged. A couple of nights later there had been another full house when Mrs Wilkes had encouraged her girls to perform again for free.

'Hello, everyone.' Blackie's rich voice rang out from behind the curtain at the side of the stage.

'Oh, hello,' said Jo. 'I never noticed a car outside.'

'I came across on the ferry,' he said. 'I remembered you said you could walk here, so to save petrol I left a bit earlier and used public transport. You look nice.'

Jo felt her face colour. She wasn't used to receiving compliments. Syd always agreed she looked all right, but it had been years since she'd had a compliment from Alfie.

'Need to see if there's a tape measure in the kitchen,' he said. 'I forgot to ask Madame . . .'

She didn't hear the rest of his words as the door closed on him. Why had Alfie suddenly sprung to mind? When she had first heard about his death, she had given way to tears alone in her bedroom. A loss of life was such a waste. She remembered the early days when they'd spent as much time together as they could. She had been so very young. Getting older had made them grow apart. She mentally shook herself. She was looking back at her marriage through rose-tinted spectacles. The memories of black eyes and broken bones came flooding back.

She was here today to keep an eye on the girls. Because of Blackie, Rainey had a chance to do something good with her life. So why was she alone in the hall, the girls in the kitchen – and what on earth did Blackie want a tape measure for?

'Mum! Come and take our measurements, will you?'

Rainey stood in the doorway, smiling.

Blackie brandished a tape measure. He shrugged. 'I found it in the drawer. It's not something I can do, is it? And if I let them do it themselves we'll get some right funny numbers of inches.'

Jo went over and took the tape measure from him.

'You stay in the kitchen. It's warmer in there,' he said. 'I need all their measurements for clothing, including arm and leg lengths, bust, waist, everything.'

'I think I know what you mean,' said Jo, hastily.

'Madame is set on air-force costumes, with hats, also long evening gowns in blue with elbow-length gloves, so when I said all measurements, I meant all measurements. I'll stay in here until you've done that.' He moved back into the hall. 'I'm going to run through on the piano some of the music they're to sing.'

Rainey could hardly contain herself. 'What are we singing? Tell me!'

'I'll play them through when you come out of the kitchen!' He looked at Jo. 'Is she always like this?'

'Only when she's excited,' said Jo. 'Do I get new clothes, too?'

'Oh, we will have our little joke won't we? The answer is no.'

In the kitchen the tea was already made. Jo sent Ivy out with a cup for Blackie while she set about measuring the girls and writing it all down with a separate page for each of them.

Jo had no idea where Madame could get the materials but she'd already said it wouldn't be a problem. No doubt she had dressmakers as well. Of course, the air-force uniforms would need to fit well. The girls would also have to have fittings. None of that was Jo's worry. She could hear piano music, and excitement swelled within her.

A little later, mission accomplished among much giggling, Jo trooped her charges into the hall.

'They're like excited puppies,' said Blackie. 'Are they like this at choir?'

'This is different, isn't it?' said Jo. 'Though Alice Wilkes is extremely proud of them.' Blackie was sitting at the piano. He'd discarded his jacket and the empty cup was on the floor.

'We'll all have to do her justice, then. These are the songs I want word perfect, with dance steps.' He handed Ivy some song sheets and Rainey and Bea stared at him.

'Dance? Who said anything about dancing?' Bea's eyes were wide.

'Not like ballet and tap, simple movements. I'll be your choreographer.'

'What?' It was Bea again.

'I'll show you how to move. We don't want you all wriggling around any old how, do we?'

'Mum! Look at these songs!'

Pages were thrust into Jo's hands. 'An Apple for the Teacher', 'Our Love', 'We'll Meet Again', 'Tea for Two' and 'Over the Rainbow'.

'We can't sing "Over the Rainbow"! That's Judy Garland's song!' Bea was indignant.

'You can sing any song I think you can sing,' Blackie said.

'But we won't be as good.'

'You'll be different, not better or worse. You'll sing it your way. Or, rather, the way I suggest you interpret the song. Each of you will be the main vocalist in a certain song, with the other two backing her up.'

'But there's five songs and three of us . . .' Ivy was curious.

'That's because I haven't been able to get hold of the

music for one of them.' The girls were suddenly silent. 'I've got on order Billie Holiday's "God Bless the Child". You all have wonderful voices but we need a really sultry voice for that one. I'd like you to sing it, Ivy.'

'Do you think I could?' She looked bashful.

The shout of 'Yes!' was deafening.

'Right,' said Blackie. 'I remembered that none of you can read music. Not to worry, some of our favourite singers can't either, Billie Holiday for one. So I've done what Mrs Wilkes does and printed out the words. Learn them, practise when and wherever you can, together if possible. But we'll run through those five now.' He looked at Jo. 'Have we time?'

She nodded. 'We have about an hour and then we must leave, else the girls will be late for work.'

'We'd better get cracking then, hadn't we?' Blackie said. 'It's not long until the New Year.'

All eyes were on him, as he said, 'Oh, didn't I tell you? Madame's booked the King's Theatre for a revue in January.'

Chapter Forty-one

'I do like Bette Davis,' said Jo, as she took the port-and-lemon that Syd was handing to her.

'I know you do. That's why I suggested we see *The Letter*.' He gave her a big grin, then settled down beside her in the Alma pub. 'I haven't seen much of you lately, and when I go into the paper-shop, Mr Harrington usually tells me you've left early.'

Jo gave a big sigh of relief that she could enjoy the drink and a chat with Syd. She was tired. 'It seems like the days don't have enough hours in them now.'

'I miss you.'

Jo took his hand. It felt soft. She saw he had scrubbed the grease from all the crevices and dug out the oil from beneath his fingernails to look as presentable as possible for her. 'Oh, Syd,' she said, 'I need to supervise what's going on with my Rainey, and Ivy and Bea, and I have to earn money as well.'

'When eventually they make their debut, or whatever it's called, you'll have more time.'

'Hardly,' she said. 'That's when my job will become harder. I'll need to keep an eye on . . . What do they call them? Stage-door johnnies. You know, men who prey on girls, send them flowers, turn their heads . . .'

'I know what kind of men they are,' he snapped.

'Well, you know what I'll have to contend with.'

He said moodily, 'I suppose that means you'll have to travel all over the place.'

Jo dropped his hand. 'Of course!' She realized she'd been sharp with him.

'I'll never see you then.'

Jo ignored that remark. 'Don't let's spoil a lovely evening by squabbling. I'll have to be home soon – I've got to be at the paper-shop by half past four in the morning for the delivery of the dailies.'

'If it's money you need, I can help you . . .'

She shook her head. 'I have money put by. You helped me sell the car, remember? That money's got to stay where it is until Rainey and I are desperate. The girls are working hard so their families don't go short. I have to do the same.

Besides, I need to go with the girls for my own peace of mind.'

He took a long drink of his pint. Jo picked up her glass and sipped. The air in the pub was thick with cigarette smoke and the smell of the beer had given her a headache. More than anything she wanted to be at home in bed.

Syd put his pint glass on the table, which was scarred with ring marks. 'I suppose that Blackie goes everywhere too?'

She put down her glass and stared at him. She took a deep breath. 'I'm tired, Syd. You've been a good friend to me. But I can't have you worrying about where I should go and who I might be with. I don't want to hurt you, but I took a lot of that stupid jealousy from Alfie. I can't take it from you.'

She got up, pushing the table aside and went to the bar door, then out into the street where the fresh cold air was like balm. As she walked past Watt's the greengrocer, she was aware he hadn't followed her.

She liked Syd, she really did. He'd helped her get where she was today, given her the courage to stick up for herself. She loved him for that.

But never again would she answer to any man!

Chapter Forty-two

'Oh, I do like that Cheeky Chappie's chatter,' said Edna. The women at Priddy's were crowded around the noticeboard where the usual goings-on in the area were pinned up for the workers' perusal.

'He gets a bit near the knuckle sometimes, doesn't he? But who better to start the New Year off at the King's?' Mo said. She scratched at her turban. 'He comes from Brighton, you know.'

'It's those funny clothes he wears that make me laugh,' said Edna. Rainey saw she was reading a poster: 'Max Miller, Song and Dance Man. One week only'.

'Who else is appearing in this revue, then?' Mo asked.

'There's a strong man, a magician, a woman with poodles, a dancer called Little Annette, and in the second half before Maxie-boy it's the Bluebird Girls.'

'Who are they? Is there a picture?' Mo asked.

'No, there's a picture of Max Miller but the others are just names.'

'Shall we book and go? I get a bit fed up with pantomimes, don't you?' Mo said.

Rainey put a hand across her mouth. She'd expected to see an advertisement in the *Evening News* but she had never thought to see a poster advertising the show at Priddy's! Of course, she should have realized: Blackie and Madame were doing everything in their power to make a success of the girls. And at their first appearance onstage there would be critics and newspaper people who could make or break them. Rainey shivered. Everything was moving so fast now. The days were whizzing by with work, rehearsals, fittings, practising and more practising every moment they could. They were always hungry, always tired.

Mo, Edna and some of the women had moved away from the noticeboard so Rainey was able to stare at their stage name printed in blue. She shuddered as she looked at Little Annette's. So, they were going to meet her again? Fancy them being on in the second half as the lead-up to the great and famous Max Miller! Would they meet him backstage?

She didn't think Bea or Ivy had seen the poster yet. She'd

left them in the room where they filled the shell cases. It was quiet in there at their break-time. Everyone poured into the canteen, glad of a change of scene. It was too cold and too dark to venture outside, and, besides, there was all that palaver with changing clothes and boots.

Rainey had just visited the lavatory, and as she walked quickly back to Ivy and Bea she marvelled that each of them had become word perfect in all the songs. It was the dance steps that bothered them. She thought of earlier that day at the David Bogue Hall.

Bea had kept leading with the wrong foot, exasperating Blackie.

'I'm going to write "left" and "right" on your feet,' he'd grumbled.

'I'm sorry! I'm sorry! I'll try harder,' she'd cried.

He'd made them go over and over the simple steps until at last she'd got them right.

The air-force costumes had been sent over today, along with hats, matching underwear, shoes and stockings. Somehow Bea had put on an inch around the waist so a note was pinned to the skirt for the dressmaker to let it out.

Rainey couldn't get over how professional both Bea and Ivy looked in costume. It didn't seem to sink into her brain that she was dressed identically and looked good, too. Until

Blackie took the big mirror off the wall and propped it up so they could see themselves full length.

'We look real!' Bea had shouted.

Ivy had pinched her arm and Bea had squealed. 'You are real, you dozy cow,' Ivy said.

Blackie had made them go into the kitchen and change back into their ordinary clothes. 'I want the three of you dressed in the glittery gowns for the very last number only. You'll have to get changed at the side of the stage. Are you all right with that? There will be people about but you can't be prudish—'

Bea broke in: 'You should see some of the funny places we've got changed when we've done concerts with Mrs Wilkes. We've undressed in hallways with people walking up and down, hospital corridors when the visitors are arriving and, once, in a public library where people were changing their books!'

'What she means is they don't mind,' chipped in Jo. 'I'll be there to make sure the changes run smoothly.'

'Good.' Blackie still looked troubled. 'There is one problem.'

'What's that?' Jo had asked.

'You girls are on stage all the time, so there will be no break. Somehow we'll have to work out how you get into the right glittery dresses so you end up dressed, on the stage at the same time, to sing the last number, "Over the Rainbow".'

There had been silence and Rainey had practically heard their brains ticking.

Jo had said, 'How about if, during the second to last number, they come off the side of the stage to me, one after another, always leaving two girls onstage singing? I quickly help with their costume changes. Then they'll all be ready to stand together centre stage for "Over the Rainbow"?'

'Yes, that could work. We'll try it when the dresses are here.' Blackie smiled at Jo.

'Just a minute, you said "right dresses". Aren't they all the same?' Ivy frowned.

'Oh, didn't I tell you?' Blackie said. 'Madame has had the three gowns made up slightly differently for each of you. You'll love them, I can promise, the sequins glitter like stars, and you'll be—'

Rainey stopped thinking about earlier and came down to earth with a bump. Moaning Minnie was announcing an air raid!

Should she turn and run to the shelter with the mass of workers now shoving against each other in the corridor and trying to escape the building? Or should she carry on to the workroom where she hoped to find Ivy and Bea?

All for one and one for all, they'd said, hadn't they? She decided to go back to Bea and Ivy.

Everything went dark. Rainey hoped her mother was safe. They'd been promised a Morrison shelter that would fit into their kitchen but it wasn't going to be delivered until next March. Jo hated the Anderson: it was cold and dark.

Bodies banged against her and, although they had been told to walk quietly to safety during raids, the workers, scared, cried out and ran into her. She could smell the fear in the air. If one bomb hit this place, she thought, there'd be nothing left.

Heavy blackout blinds covered the windows but Rainey could make out searchlights streaming across the sky. She'd heard on the wireless that the Germans were leaving London alone to concentrate on bombing other main cities, Birmingham, Manchester, Southampton, and that meant Portsmouth as well.

The crowds pushing to move in the other direction to her had thinned now. She was able to walk quite quickly along the passageways that, even in the dark, she knew well.

At last she reached her workroom. The sounds coming in at her from the shelling were frightening. In the doorway she called, 'Ivy? Bea?'

The large room seemed to move so she grabbed hold of the doorpost to steady herself. The terrible thud surprised her, but no more than the amazing sight through the windows of a wall of water from the creek outside, rushing up into the air like some giant water spout. There was a huge sucking noise and a shower of drops cascaded down the side of the building and its windows.

Then came the explosion. Terrified, Rainey held on to the doorpost as though it was her lifeline. She covered her eyes as glass blew inwards from the windows, but peeped through her fingers to see one of the wooden jetties suddenly jump into the air and the wood fall like a shower of straw into the creek.

Then came a deathly silence.

Her eyes were smarting with the chemical dust floating in the room and her ears were now filled with a ringing sound. Even so, she heard a tiny voice call, 'Rainey?'

She allowed herself to slide to the floor. With her arms around her knees she made herself as small as possible, willing the noise in her ears to go away and her shaking body to still.

'Rainey?'

She flinched as she felt the hand on her shoulder. When she lifted her head she saw Bea standing over her. Her arms flew around Bea's legs. 'I thought you were gone,' she said. Now she was crying and she had to wipe her nose with her sleeve for the great gobs of snot that were pouring unheeded and mixing with her tears.

And then Ivy was there, pulling Rainey to her feet.

The three girls stood locked together. Flakes from the ceiling fell about them like snow. The ringing was lessening in Rainey's ears and she said again, 'I thought you were gone.'

Ivy said, 'We knew you'd come back for us.'

Bea said, 'That bloody big bomb went in the creek and blew up our landing stage.'

Rainey began to laugh.

Chapter Forty-three

'Sounds like a herd of elephants above us,' said Jo. She stirred her tea.

Maud wiped her hands on her wraparound pinafore before she answered. 'They're overjoyed to be practising their dance steps especially as Priddy's shut up shop for a couple of days to clear up.' She raised her eyes towards the ceiling.

'I can't believe no one was hurt in that blast.'

'Boats were smashed and there were dead fish everywhere in the water and in the yard. It stinks, I was told. They've got to renew the landing stage, but apart from broken windows, everything else held.'

Maud shoved a plate towards Jo. 'Try a sponge biscuit. I made them myself using the extra Christmas sugar I won't be needing. I can't believe that Madame woman has invited us all to a Christmas dinner at her place. That's a surprise.'

'You'll come?' Jo took a mouthful of biscuit, chewed and swallowed. 'These are tasty,' she said.

'I can cook, you know,' said Maud, tartly. Then she grinned. 'Course we'll be there. A dinner for free is not to be sniffed at.' She pushed an escaping pin back into her hair to keep her fringe out of her eyes. 'Granddad's not coming.'

Jo stared.

Maud shook her head. 'Now he's properly settled in his new place he won't be budged. That neighbour of his, that flirty Gertie, has got him enthralled! The ex-footballer brother of hers is like a magnet to Solomon and he can't wait to see his old mate again. You know Gertie got him – Solomon, not her brother – to go on the bus to see a medium? That's what this Helen Duncan calls herself. It was in a Spiritualist church. The place was full, Granddad said. She told him his wife was watching over him. Fair took his breath away that did. His Eileen didn't make such a good job of watching him when she was alive. She never knew what pub he was in!'

Jo nearly choked on her second biscuit. 'So it'll be you, Bea and Eddie?' She'd taken a swallow of tea to wash it down.

'Eddie's not keen but I told him we've got to support the girls. Anyway, in the New Year he'll be up to his eyes in work.'

'What about them German prisoners?'

'He's got a load of them coming to work for him up at Bridgemary.'

Jo wasn't sure how she felt about that.

'Alice Wilkes has dropped out. She's preparing a special meal for a friend,' Maud said. 'It must be a really special friend an' all for her to turn down an invitation to Madame's, mustn't it?'

'I suppose so. I'm bringing Syd.'

'I thought you and he . . .'

'Madame said we can invite a close friend. I thought it might make up for the way I was short-tempered with him.'

Maud sighed. 'It's up to you,' she said. Jo thought the look on her face spoke volumes.

Just then a car's horn sounded out in the street. Jo ran to the bottom of the stairs and shouted, 'Hurry up, girls. Our lift to the David Bogue Hall is here.' She struggled into her coat in the hallway and was relieved when Ivy, Bea and Rainey came out of Bea's bedroom and hurried down the stairs.

Jo turned back to her friend. 'Maud, love, thanks for the tea and biscuits. Blackie's going to drop us off again after practice. I expect we'll be later, though, as there's no work tonight for the girls. Blackie said he'd have a surprise for us today. I wonder what it is.'

It wasn't long before the three girls were in the back of Blackie's car and Jo sat in the front.

She asked, 'What's the surprise, then?' She could smell his spicy cologne.

'Wait and see,' he said.

'Have the blue dresses arrived?' Rainey asked.

'Again, wait and see,' Blackie said.

He wouldn't say anything, but whenever he caught Jo looking at him, he turned briefly to smile at her.

Blackie pulled up outside the hall and allowed them all to get out of the car, then drove around to the back where there was a large car park.

Ivy, Rainey and Bea crowded around Jo as he pushed open the door.

The sound hit her straight away. In the hall there was a small band! A young man was playing the piano, a very large man tuning a trombone, another sitting at a set of drums and a tall good-looking man, with a trumpet, waving at their entrance.

Jo and the girls were watching and listening to them running through 'An Apple for the Teacher' when Blackie came in, rubbing his hands because of the cold outside. 'I see you've found my surprise,' he said. He shivered. 'Thank God it's warmer in here.' He nodded a hello to the band.

Bea said, 'Dresses? Did you bring the dresses? Were they in the car's boot?' She didn't allow Blackie to speak. 'What are they doing here?' She looked towards the musicians.

'In the kitchen,' he said, 'is the answer to the first question and to the second. You won't be singing to my piano-playing when you're onstage. You'll have musicians, maybe these boys. I thought you needed to get used to singing with proper backing. I know you're not working at Priddy's tonight, so you'll sing along with this excellent band. But . . . you will sing until you get it right. Or they get fed up with you and decide to go home.'

'When do we try the glittery dresses on?' Bea frowned. 'If we're singing and singing, you might forget.'

'I shall not forget, Bea, because when I think you're all in tune with the music, I'll have the three of you dressed, and making sure you know exactly where and how to stand. Have any of you ever sung with a band before?'

Jo saw her three charges shake their heads.

'Just as I thought,' said Blackie. 'Let's get started.'

Jo saw that the three girls were fired up with excitement. Rainey and Ivy immediately took off their coats and climbed onto the stage.

Bea said, 'I'm cold.'

'You can't be,' said Jo. 'It's warm in here. Don't start being a prima donna.'

'What's that?' Bea asked, reluctantly taking off her coat to reveal a sweater tight across her ample breasts and slacks that emphasized her rounded bottom. One of the musicians gave a wolf-whistle. Mollified, Bea joined the others on the stage.

'A prima donna is someone who thinks the world revolves around her! And I'm sorry, Bea, but you're all equal in this group.' Blackie frowned at her. Bea tossed her hair back and pouted.

Blackie walked to the front of the stage, turned and put up a hand to stop the band playing, looked at the three girls and said, 'You, the Bluebird Girls, open in a famous theatre in a little over a fortnight. Money and time's been spent for your benefit. I appreciate you've already worked very hard, but it's not enough! I must have one hundred per cent from all of you. Do you understand?'

Jo bit her lip. For a moment there was silence as the girls digested his words. Then Blackie said, 'Madame is giving you the chance of a lifetime. You can be stars! You can be shining lights in this damn war!' He shook his head. 'You have talent. Let me bring it out!' There was another pause, longer this time, then the red-haired man at the drums started clapping, the rest of the band joined in and the tension was broken. Blackie looked at Jo . . . and smiled.

Chapter Forty-four

Della turned the slices of bacon in the big frying pan. She wore one of Bert's ample aprons, which swamped her tiny frame. A pall of cigarette smoke hung in the air, mingling with the cooking smells.

She looked at Bert reading the invitation card.

'It says you've been invited for Christmas to eat with Madame, Blackie and Herbert. It says plus one, not Ivy, she's already been invited.'

'I can't go. I'll get Ivy to apologize . . .'

'Della. You have to go. These people are reaching out the hand of friendship to family members of the Bluebird Girls. You'll hurt Ivy's feelings if you don't support her.'

Della left the bacon to pour a large mug of tea and set it on the counter in front of Bert so he could take the money from the customer who'd requested it.

Until the postman had brought in the letter, she'd been quite content cooking and listening to the Bakelite wireless spilling out dance music. The hum of voices and the cosy atmosphere inside the café was soothing.

Again she turned the bacon and breathed in its beguiling scent. 'How am I supposed to get there when there's no buses running that day? Besides, I've got nothing suitable to wear. And what can I talk about? I got nothing to say to posh people.'

'You get on all right with Blackie, and the others are no different.'

She forked the bacon onto a large plate and set it on the hob to keep warm. 'You could be my plus one,' she said.

He turned to her. 'I'd be like a fish out of water there.'

Della caught sight of herself in the window. Her cheeks were rosy with the heat in the café. 'You could wear that suit you got for your mate's funeral. I'll press it.' She felt quite positive now. 'And, really, I've got loads of pretty dresses.'

'The ferries are running, Sunday service mind, but I could order a taxi.'

'Do you really think Ivy'd want us there? I don't want to let her down.'

'Stop putting yourself down, Della. You are as good as

anyone else who'll be there. You wouldn't have got an invite if you wasn't.'

Della looked at Bert and smiled.

The members of the band had congregated by the bar in the White Horse, drinking pints, smoking and eating the Spam or Bovril sandwiches Blackie had bought. Every so often the sound of laughter issued from them. Ivy, Jo, Bea and Rainey sat in an alcove. Blackie had a small whisky on the table in front of him, and Jo had half a shandy. Blackie had asked the girls what they'd like to drink, had dismissed their unsuitable requests by the time he'd reached the bar and returned with lemonades. Jo noticed Bea pull a face when she tasted her drink. On the table there were the remains of another plate of sandwiches.

Jo stared at the green and red decorations. Some were a bit dusty, but the paperchains were obviously new for their colours were brighter. It looked very Christmassy, she thought. She'd not had time to think about decorating their house. She looked at the long pendulum wall clock. She hoped Blackie would remember that she still had to be up at the crack of dawn to take delivery of the daily papers at the Harrington's. Already it was dark outside.

'I like what you've done so far today, girls,' he said. 'When

we return to the hall you can try on the blue dresses. Then –'
he smiled '– I'm giving you time off because it's almost
Christmas.' Bea squealed and Ivy banged the table. Jo knew
relief was written all over her face. Rainey looked at her and
mouthed, 'Thank goodness.'

'I'll see you all at Madame's place on Christmas Day. Now,
are you all sure you've got transport?' Blackie asked. He was
paying for another round of drinks for the musicians, who
had also finished for the day.

The girls started chattering about who they were going
to Madame's with and it became quite noisy. Jo hadn't asked
Syd yet but she knew if he accepted he'd be indignant to be
offered a lift and would insist on driving himself, her and
Rainey. 'I'm sure we're all right but if things become difficult
can I beg seats in your car?' she asked Blackie tentatively.

'Just give me a ring, Jo.' He suggested they go back to the
hall across the road.

Immediately they were inside Blackie said, 'On the
morning of the first matinee performance I want you four
at the King's Theatre for early-morning rehearsal. We'll go
through the show exactly as it will – or should – happen in
the afternoon.' Bea opened her mouth but he anticipated
what she was going to say. 'All the other acts will be there.
It's to give you a feel for the theatre.'

Jo saw Bea close her mouth. Something inside Jo told her that if any of them was going to act up it would be Bea. She dismissed the thought. She wasn't being fair to the girl.

Blackie sent Jo and the girls into the kitchen. 'The clothes are in a dress bag hanging on the back of the door,' he said. 'Come out when you're ready.'

Jo almost couldn't believe the time would come when she would see her own daughter, Rainey, singing on the stage of one of the most famous theatres in the south of England. She was so proud of her.

Then she chuckled: every surface in the kitchen had articles of female apparel slung haphazardly over it.

She heard Rainey say, 'This is so beautiful.'

'Can I look?' Jo had turned her back on them, knowing they'd prefer her not to gawp. After all, there wouldn't be much privacy later at the side of the stage, so she'd give them what she could now.

'Oh!' The word fell from her mouth.

Where had her charges gone? Two gorgeous young women in tight-fitting sparkly blue gowns stood in front of her. Rainey's dress had a high neck but only one short sleeve, and below it she wore a pair of dark blue satin high heels. She was in the process of pulling on elbow-length satin gloves. Ivy's dress was slightly more full in the skirt with a heart-shaped neckline and a waist that pinched to a hand-span. She had similar shoes and gloves.

Bea was red in the face and struggling to fasten her sleeve-less dress with the plunging neckline that emphasized her generous curves. Jo couldn't help herself, 'My God, that dress fits you like butter!'

Bea blew out her cheeks. 'Thank you but I'd feel better if I could do it up!'

Jo turned her round. 'Breathe in,' she said, and with difficulty hooked and zipped it up. 'I'll send it back with a note asking the dressmaker to let it out a bit. In the meantime, between now and the New Year, don't eat!' Bea slipped on the high heels. 'You all look wonderful,' Jo said. 'Now go out into the hall and watch the men's jaws drop!'

Chapter Forty-five

Jo thought Syd looked very smart in his best suit. He caught her looking at him while he drove and smiled at her. The atmosphere was still a little strained between them but she knew he was doing his best to be extra cheerful. She was pleased because if there was one thing she couldn't abide it was a man who sulked. She'd had too many sulky silences in the past with Alfie where she'd had to walk on eggshells.

The weather was cold but it was dry and sunny, and Jo was happy the awful winds at the beginning of the month had dropped.

'Did you bring a gift for the hostess?' Syd asked.

'We couldn't afford to buy ourselves anything. And I certainly haven't got a present for you, Syd. There's nothing in the shops.'

'You can share the big box of chocolates I bought from Harrington's,' Syd offered. 'I'll say it's from all of us.'

Jo looked at Rainey. 'Would that be a very large and expensive box with a kitten chasing a ball of wool on it?' Her question was directed at Syd.

She was still looking at Rainey when Syd answered, 'It is.'

Jo put a hand to her mouth and whispered to her daughter, so Syd wouldn't hear, 'That box has been in the shop since before the war started!'

Jo had been to Madame's studio but never to the house.

Surprisingly, Syd had to park on the road with other cars behind and in front. Further up she spotted Eddie's work van.

A main road followed the beach at Southsea, winding its way down to South Parade pier. The road where Syd parked ran parallel to the beach road and it was there, set back in gardens, that tall detached houses stood.

Her first thought was, no wonder she and Blackie had so little in common apart from the girls. If he lived here he was far above her station in life. Not that she was ashamed of her little rented terraced house in Gosport, certainly not. It was clear, though, that Blackie was used to better things.

Jo and Rainey got out of the van before Syd came around

to help them. Rainey stood awestruck. 'Fancy living here,' she said. 'And they've got that big studio in the heart of town.'

'Make a lot of money and you, too, could live in a place like this,' said Syd. He was holding the box of chocolates.

The gravelled driveway ended in a large wooden porch. Jo was just about to use the lion's head knocker when the door was opened by Herbert, with a smile that practically sliced his face in half. 'Welcome,' he said. 'So glad you could make it. You're our last guests to arrive.' After taking their coats and hanging them in a cupboard by the front door, Herbert led them towards double doors, which were opened wide. Before Jo saw her friends she heard Maud's strident voice obviously answering a question.

'The choir is a lifeline to us. For an hour or so we can forget the war. You get out of it what you put in, and the money we collect helps those worse off than ourselves. Alice Wilkes is a saint.'

Jo raised her hand in greeting to the room full of people but her eyes were drawn to Madame. She made her way over to the imposing figure sitting in a velvet chair near a huge open fire. 'Thank you for inviting us.'

Madame, dressed in grey, her hair elaborately set, said, 'I'm so glad you could come, my dear. You won't mind if

I don't get up? My joints are pretending they don't belong to me today.' Jo smiled at her, shook her head, and saw the kindness shining from her button-black eyes. 'Go and talk to your friends, my dear. I'm sure you've all lots to speak about. Chat away to friends of mine too. Just some people in the business who wish you well.'

The fire crackled. Jo noticed sprigs of holly tucked about the huge oil painting above the fireplace. She gasped – the girl in the painting was incredibly beautiful, her dark hair hanging about the shoulders of her décolleté gown, her dark eyes shining with vitality.

Jo looked down at Madame, who smiled. 'Yes, I was beautiful once,' she said. 'And I know it's important to grab happiness when it comes your way.'

Jo wasn't sure what her answer to that should be, but luckily Syd held out the chocolates and said, 'Thank you for allowing me to come.'

'Dear boy, how very kind of you,' said Madame, her eyes twinkling almost as brightly as they did in the painting.

Jo looked around for Rainey and saw all three young women talking animatedly near a large sideboard where drinks were set out.

'Go and help yourselves to drinks,' Madame said. 'We're not standing on ceremony today.'

'Thank you,' said Jo, and hurried over. She didn't want Rainey, Ivy or Bea to make fools of themselves.

'No drinking!' Her words were sharp.

Rainey looked at her mother in surprise and alarm. 'I was just about to pour orange for us,' she said.

'I'm sorry, love,' said Jo, chastened. A figure materialized at her side.

'Is a little wine allowed at the buffet?' Blackie stood next to her.

'Buffet? Not a sit-down meal?' The words left her mouth without Jo thinking. Blackie was looking incredibly handsome in a well-cut dark suit. He was staring past her and asking, 'Whisky or a beer?'

'A beer would be fine,' said Syd. 'Jo doesn't encourage Rainey to drink wine.'

Jo was about to snap that she could speak for herself when she thought better of it. Syd was only echoing her own words. Though it wasn't Rainey she worried about, but Bea. The less said about that the better, she thought. Blackie was unaware of Bea's digression from the straight and narrow, and she'd like it kept that way.

Blackie handed round drinks, poured her a port-and-lemon and was talking about the meal. 'Madame doesn't venture into the kitchen much nowadays so the food has been prepared by a caterer.'

'I'm sure it will be lovely,' said Jo. She smiled at Blackie, then moved across the room to talk to Maud, who was standing alone, Eddie having sought out the three girls. He was hanging on Ivy's every word.

'Bit posh in here,' said Maud. She patted her hair, curled especially for the occasion. 'Did you see those signed photographs of music-hall stars covering the walls of the hall?'

'Not really,' Jo said. 'I was more interested in not tripping up and making a fool of myself.'

'Never mind about you making a fool of yourself! Will you look at that Della? How does she have the nerve to wear that moth-eaten fox fur today, of all days?'

Jo looked over to where Ivy's mother was chatting to Madame. They appeared to be deep in conversation. Jo saw Madame wave Herbert out of the room. Mystified, she edged away from Maud, leaving Syd to chat to her.

Bert stood with a pint in his hand. 'They seem to be getting on well,' Jo said to him.

'That's not the half of it.' Bert smiled. 'The old woman's sent her hubby upstairs to get something.'

Before Jo could ask any more questions, back into the room came Herbert, with a red fox fur slung over his arm.

'It's gorgeous!' Della promptly dumped her own fur in Bert's free hand and swung the glossy, shiny-eyed auburn one about herself. She raised her shoulder and the magnificent fur caressed her neck. She closed her eyes in ecstasy.

'Keep it, dear girl. It suits you far better than it ever did me,' said Madame. Della promptly bent down, threw her arms about the woman's neck and kissed her papery cheek.

'Well, I never,' Jo heard Maud exclaim.

Herbert rattled a spoon against a glass and everyone stopped talking to pay attention. 'If you'll follow me to the kitchen you'll find a buffet meal set out. We thought today would be a good day to wish the Bluebird Girls a happy future in show business. Complimentary tickets have been issued to Alice Wilkes for her choir.' At this news there were cheers from Jo and Maud. 'We have also had good returns from box-office bookings.' This time Jo heard clapping. 'So, good people, help yourselves to food and drink.'

More clapping followed Herbert as he left the room.

Jo didn't go with the first wave of people eager to eat. She took the time to talk to several others she hadn't met before. Wandering, she came upon Bea standing alone, watching birds pecking crumbs off a garden table.

'Not choosing from the buffet, Bea?' Jo hadn't before noticed Bea's pasty face. 'I gather there's a good spread, even chicken!'

'I feel a bit queasy,' Bea said. 'Eddie was treating the roads like a racetrack driving over here. I expect I'll be fine by the time everyone starts on the sweet things.' Bea smiled at her.

Bea looked like a child when she didn't plaster her face with heavy make-up, Jo thought. It was barely four months since she had been involved in that dreadful incident behind the Fox. Jo applauded her for her courage in putting it behind her and for all her hard work in wanting to make a success of her life.

'Are you worried about appearing in front of a theatre audience?'

'Not really,' Bea said. 'We've been over the songs so many times I just want everything to go well. Of course I worry about letting Ivy and Rainey down . . .'

Her voice tailed off.

'I'm sure the Bluebirds are going to be enormously popular.'

'Do you really think so?'

'Good people wouldn't spend money on you if they didn't think you were worth it. Madame knows a sure thing when she sees it.'

Jo saw her eyes were filled with tears. 'I really don't want to let anyone down,' Bea said. 'Honestly.'

Jo couldn't help herself. She put her arms around Bea. 'Don't worry,' she said. 'You'll be fine.'

Chapter Forty-six

Boxing Day and the New Year passed for Jo without incident. The girls returned to work at the factory and no one was more surprised than they were when they requested time off and it was granted.

Jo saw nothing of Blackie. She went out for drinks with Syd. Sometimes she walked round for a chat with Maud. Every morning she rose early and cycled to Alverstoke to take charge of the daily newspapers. Mr and Mrs Harrington were almost as excited as Jo about the revue at the King's Theatre. She'd given them complimentary tickets. One afternoon she and Maud went to visit Solomon. Jo played two games of draughts with him in the Leisure Room; Solomon won both.

The girls practised, not in the David Bogue Hall but upstairs in Bea's bedroom. Although she moaned about the racket, as she called it, secretly Maud was happy they were there. Nineteen forty-one already looked like becoming a year to remember.

On the morning of the matinee, Blackie drove over to Gosport to collect Jo, Rainey, Bea and Ivy. 'In the theatre everyone rehearses in the mornings,' he said.

'Can we watch the other artists?' asked Ivy.

'Of course,' he answered.

'I'm not sure I want to see Little Annette,' said Rainey.

'She may not be a likeable person but she knows her job,' said Blackie. 'Her timing is superb. You could all learn from her.'

Ivy pulled a face at Rainey.

'You're sharing a dressing room with some of the show-girls. I've already dropped off your outfits. Don't forget your make-up. Remember how I showed you how to make the best of yourselves . . ."

'What about their hair? Tied back? French plaits?' Jo inter-rupted. 'Remember they're wearing RAF costumes.'

'I'd prefer each of them to keep it quite natural,' he said. 'Ivy has a distinct long bob, Rainey has her wild auburn locks and Bea's the blonde with curls. They have their own styles and each is an eye-catching beauty.'

Ivy giggled, blushing. 'I wouldn't say that.'

'You won't be seeing yourselves the way the audience will,' he said. 'Trust me.'

When they arrived at the theatre, acts were already in progress.

'Have you ever been backstage before?' Blackie asked.

'I've never seen anything like this,' exclaimed Ivy. 'It's got a special smell, a special feeling – and to think we're going to be part of it.' She waved her arms, encompassing the stage, the seats, the noise.

'Just listen to the orchestra tuning up! It's so exciting!' exclaimed Rainey.

'One day you'll think all this is as natural as breathing,' promised Blackie. 'Later on, nearer lunchtime, I'll have tea and sandwiches brought in. I don't want you starving to death. It's not good to perform on a full stomach, but tonight I'll stand you all a slap-up meal.'

Jo laughed. 'I don't mind if it's pork faggots with onion gravy, corned beef hash or liver casserole – I can eat them at any time.'

'Not all at once, I hope,' said Blackie.

'It even smells different back here,' said Ivy, taking a deep breath.

'It's a special mix of excitement, greasepaint, hope and newly painted scenery,' Blackie said. 'Look, I've brought

you here early so you can get to know what a real theatre looks like and how it works. Each of the people here
has a certain job to do. They're special. You, however, are
only passing through so respect them.' He paused. 'A little
bit about the King's. Noël Coward and Ivor Novello have
played here. Built in 1907, it seats sixteen hundred people,
who, incidentally, at the matinee performance are going
to love you. Local girls made good – Joe Public will take
you to their hearts. Now Jo and I are going to talk about
what happens when this week is over. Trust me, the pair
of us have only your best interests at heart. Later, after a
rehearsal, you'll be free to polish up bits you feel need a
special shine. Jo and I will be here. You need to be ready,
dressed and made up, in the dressing room when I come
to you.'

There was silence. Jo saw the three girls had taken in every
word.

'I need to talk to some people so Jo and I will be sitting
down there for a while.' He moved his arm towards the front
seats. 'Feel free to wander, or to sit and watch the rehearsals.'

Jo watched the three walk away. She could almost feel the
excitement pouring off them.

The rest of the morning passed as if on wings.

*

The patrons were in their seats, the lights went down and the show began. The heavy curtains swung back, the orchestra played and the excitement in the air was almost palpable. Jo took a deep breath and immediately she knew what actors meant when she'd heard talk of magic in the air backstage. The first half of the matinee performance had gone exceedingly well.

A couple of the poodles went on strike, refusing to co-operate with their owner, but the audience understood and loved the act all the more. Little Annette was perfect, though Jo thought her act very similar to the one that had provided her with a certificate at Fareham Festival.

Blackie had told her he'd collect the girls from the dressing room.

Jo now stood in the wings. She'd draped the glittery dresses to her satisfaction to enable her to get the right one on the right girl.

In a short while, the moment they had all worked for so hard would arrive. She saw the girls walking towards her. So grown up, she thought. But wait a moment . . . there were only two.

'Where's Bea?' Jo knew she mustn't appear worried. Surely none of them would jeopardize this wonderful moment.

'She's being sick, Mum.' Rainey's eyes lifted heavenwards

but she had a smile on her face as if she wasn't at all perturbed.

'Last-minute nerves,' said Blackie. 'We've got a full house.' He shrugged. 'I know established stars who heave up before each show.'

Something clicked in Jo's brain. She pushed the thought away, refusing to believe it. Bea's outfits having to be let out, now this sickness?

Quickly she added up the timespan in her head. Bea's terrible experience was how many months ago?

No! No! No!

How she hadn't spoken those three words out loud, Jo didn't know.

And then Bea's voice calling, 'I'm here, Jo!'

The bell had gone, warning the patrons the interval was over.

Jo looked at each of the girls in turn.

Not a sign of nerves. In fact, they looked like the most fantastic thing in the world was about to happen to them, as indeed it was.

The master of ceremonies was introducing the Bluebird Girls – them! Blackie put his finger to his lips. Silence backstage now.

The girls walked confidently onto the stage.

The curtain began to rise.

This was the moment Rainey had waited for all of her life.

She could feel the excitement and longing oozing from her friends either side of her. In the audience she could see familiar faces smiling. Her heart was beating fast. The band started to play. Rainey gave a big smile to Bea, then to Ivy, and once again she was amazed at how wonderful they looked in their blue uniforms. She turned to her audience, opened her mouth and began to sing.

As one song changed to another Rainey felt the meanings of the words sweep over her. She was touched by the sadness in Ivy's voice, then transported by the bubbly quality in Bea's as she began singing 'Tea for Two', practically inviting the whole theatre to believe that tea meant so much more – and the audience loved it!

Rainey took a deep breath. It was time to change outfits. She walked to the side of the stage and, within moments, returned in the glittery costume that was to be their trademark trick for the final song, 'Over the Rainbow'.

Amid cheers for Rainey, Ivy proudly stepped away to the wings.

Yells and claps announced her quick return. Rainey and

Ivy smiled at each other as they continued singing. Bea then left the stage.

Rainey hoped they'd left enough time for Bea to be helped into the beautiful blue dress.

Rainey kept her smile firmly in place as she sang but the end of the song was fast approaching and still there was no sign of Bea. She chanced a look at Ivy and could see she, too, was trying hard to disguise her worry. Panic began to rise . . .

And there she was! Tripping back onstage in her high heels, her voluptuous body stuffed into and practically overflowing the glittery material, Bea came to a stop beside Rainey and Ivy and the audience went wild!

The orchestra paused.

Long enough for the patrons to settle, to wonder, perhaps, what was coming next, and then the beautiful music started up and the three girls began singing. They felt the words, and the audience knew and felt them, too.

Towards the end of the song the first red rose fell upon the stage, followed by others thrown in appreciation.

As the final notes and the girls' voices faded, the theatre was practically shaking with applause.

Rainey, Ivy and Bea held hands, bowed, and tears of joy rolled down their cheeks.

Acknowledgements

Thank you Therese Keating, your input means such a lot to me. Thank you Hazel Orme for doing what I can't. Thank you Juliet Burton, best agent ever. Thank you Quercus for all the people who work so hard to put my books in front of my readers. Thank you, dear readers.

I've taken the liberty of modifying details, facts and events to suit my storyline. My characters bear no resemblance to any living persons.